Second to None

by Felice Stevens

Second to None (The Breakfast Club, Book 3)
February 2016

Edited by Keren Reed
Cover Art by: Reese Dante
www.reesedante.com

Nightclub owner Marcus Feldman never met a man he didn't love, at least for the night. Although his best friends have all found love, Marcus shuns their advice to commit to one man and settle down. His past has taught him monogamy and marriage is for fools, and Marcus is anything but a fool.

Tyler Reiss's dream of dancing professionally is unexpectedly cut short and replaced by a different kind of love. He trades in his ballet slippers for go-go boots, and spends his nights dancing at the hottest gay club in the city. Flirting with the customers for tips is easy, but resisting the dark and sexy Marcus is becoming harder to do with each passing day.

Unforeseen circumstances bring Marcus and Tyler closer, and though they give in to their mutual passion, both still struggle to guard their hearts. When crises threaten, Tyler and Marcus find their strength in each other rather than falling apart. Tyler must choose to either run, or stay and fight for the life he wants, while Marcus must learn that love doesn't mean losing himself and open his heart, making him a better man in the end.

Dedication

To my family, forever first in my heart

Acknowledgments

As always first thanks go to my wonderful editor, Keren Reed for always knowing the right words whenever they fail me. Thank you Hope Vincent for her wonderful editing eagle eyes and Jessica de Ruiter for her mad skills.

Thank you to Hope for being there for me, always. Thank you Jenna for being my friend and for Meredith and Kade for your friendship.

To Felice's Fierce Fans, you guys are amazing. Your support and love of this genre is inspiring. A special shout out to Jennifer Reilly for her fabulous inspiration for Marcus.

Chapter One

"WHAT'S THE MATTER, Boss? No one around to play with anymore?"

The last blessed drops of Glenlivet slid down Marcus Feldman's throat before he answered his chief of security.

"Go away, Darius. Aren't I paying you to stand at the door and be intimidating instead of annoying me like a fly?" He ran an appraising eye over the broad chest of the man, and though he liked what he saw, Darius had made it clear from day one he wasn't available for nighttime fun and games. Marcus set his empty glass on the bar, and the cute, dark-haired bartender he'd hired last week immediately appeared. Without even asking, Marcus was rewarded with a refill and a cheeky grin.

"Thanks, Antonio."

"If you need anything else, let me know." Antonio's dark eyes held his. "I'm completely at your service." With a wink and roll of his hips, Antonio walked to the other side of the bar to help a customer.

Watching Antonio's round ass encased in skintight red leather pants, Marcus could've groaned out loud with frustration. His fingers tightened around the glass of scotch, and he tossed half of it back with a flip of his wrist. He was on the last month of a forced, three-month stretch of celibacy and so horny he could barely see straight. Every morning and night he cursed his two friends for holding him to that stupid bet he'd so carelessly made with Zach.

Running a club and being surrounded by half-naked male bodies he was now forbidden to touch didn't help his strung-out libido at all. He walked around with a perpetual hard-on and aching balls from all the flirting and casual touches he received daily yet couldn't act upon. Knowing his friend Julian, he probably put the staff up to torturing him. Juli always was an evil bastard.

Marcus couldn't get too mad though, since he knew if the roles were reversed he'd enjoy inflicting the same torture on his friend. Besides, it was no secret the bartenders all wanted to sleep with him, bet or no bet. They thought it was their way up the ladder of success at Sparks. Screw the owner they figured, and it would get them the best shifts, and maybe they'd manage to hook him as a steady bed partner and bank account. He sipped his drink and contemplated the writhing bodies on the dance floor. Not a likely scenario. Marcus Feldman was nobody's fool and nobody's boyfriend.

"That Antonio guy is someone you could have in a heartbeat. I'm sure he'll be waiting for you next month."

Marcus shot a venomous glance at the bright, white smile Darius flashed.

"Fuck you."

"Already told you—not interested."

He and Darius leaned against the bar, staring out at the dance floor, and Marcus appraised the male dancers he'd recently hired for the club. They added a bit of flair, and he liked seeing the men in their platform go-go boots and skintight, gold lycra shorts, dancing with the customers, encouraging everyone to have a good time. And of course, spend more money.

Tyler, the newest dancer, caught his attention. Long strands of black, sweat-dampened hair whipped about his shoulders as he shimmied in front of one of the club's biggest spenders, Eduardo Ortiz. Tyler's muscular, lithe body moved with the sinuous grace of someone who didn't dance for fun but used his body as a form of art. It was beautiful to watch, and Marcus stood enthralled, oblivious to everything else around him.

True to form, Ortiz had a fistful of bills and a leer on his heavy-featured face. The man stood around six feet four with a mountainous build; his custom-made Italian suit jacket strained over football-sized shoulders, and his tree-trunk thighs looked capable of crushing a man's head between them like an overripe grape. Marcus's eyes narrowed, watching Ortiz's thick fingers slide below the waistband of Tyler's shorts, only a hairbreadth away from grabbing hold of his crotch.

Pig. "Keep an eye on them, please," said Marcus, gesturing toward the potential problem with a tilt of his chin. "I don't like Ortiz manhandling my guys."

"I'm on it." Darius flashed him an amused smile. "Want to keep the goodies all for yourself, huh?"

"There's still a month left on this stupid bet," said Marcus, distaste twisting his lips. One long, long month of jerking off in the shower, in the bed, or wherever.

Darius smiled into his glass of water.

Marcus shook his head in disgust. "Juli's got you watching me, huh?" He put up his hand. "No, no, I don't expect an answer. I knew that bastard would have spies to make sure I didn't cheat."

"I have to say, I'm pretty impressed. I thought you'd cave right after they left for their honeymoon."

Admittedly, Marcus surprised himself. It was the challenge, he guessed, his gaze returning to Tyler, whose hips never missed a beat of the pounding dubstep. Tyler's arms twined around Ortiz's neck for only a moment, his long graceful fingers ghosting along the man's jowly creases, before he turned and pressed his ass into Ortiz's crotch, grinding and swaying. Idly, Marcus wondered if Tyler would end up in Ortiz's bed tonight. Heat rolled through him at the thought of Tyler's sweat-slicked body under his own. He'd love to wrap his hand around that thick black mane of hair while he pushed inside that tight round ass. Tyler had an exceptionally beautiful ass.

"Damn that man can move," said Darius, the appreciation apparent not only in his voice but in his eyes. "He's way too good to be a simple club dancer."

Silently agreeing, Marcus's eyes narrowed as he continued to watch Tyler's supple body writhe. The effortless motions of his arms and legs coupled with the sensuous motion of his hips all spoke of formal dance training. The muscles in his powerful legs and shoulders bunched and rippled under the flash of lights.

The dance ended, and Marcus watched Ortiz place a heavy hand on Tyler's shoulder, holding him there and whispering something in his ear, an invitation to spend the night in his bed, no doubt. Unfamiliar anger sparked inside Marcus—no patron should be pressuring any of his employees to have sex—and he set his glass down on the bar, curious to see how the scenario would unfold. The thought of Tyler with Ortiz nauseated Marcus. Instead of returning to the front of the club, Darius remained by his side, perhaps feeling the same uneasiness about the situation as he did.

Being that this marked Tyler's first week at Sparks, Marcus couldn't be certain how he'd handle a blatant sexual invitation such as the one Ortiz no doubt made. He held his breath, inexplicably hoping Tyler would...what? Kick Ortiz in the balls? Punch him in the jaw? Marcus rubbed the back of his neck, anxiety tightening a noose around his insides. Why did he care? It wasn't as if he was sleeping with Tyler; hell, he barely knew the guy.

Tyler brushed back some strands of hair sticking to his face and glanced up, meeting Marcus's eyes across the dance floor. It felt like a punch in the gut, and Marcus fought to catch his breath; he'd yet to see such sheer desolation and hopelessness as he saw in Tyler's blue eyes. Then Tyler laughed, and with a shake of his head and a brush of his lips against Ortiz's temple, hurried away into the bowels of the club, leaving Marcus to wonder if he'd been mistaken.

Ortiz adjusted his crotch and leered after Tyler. Marcus shuddered, chilled and disgusted from what he'd witnessed. There was something ugly about Ortiz, and it had nothing to do with his outward appearance—he always dressed in the finest suits and thought nothing of dropping a thousand dollars a night in the club. While Marcus never personally had any unpleasant experiences with him, the rumors of Ortiz's volatile temper followed him.

"What the fuck was that about?" he muttered, tugging down the sleeves of his stark white dress shirt. Ortiz pulled out his phone and spoke into it, gesturing in the air with angry jabs of his fingers and walking away from the spot where Tyler had left him standing.

"Looks like you're gonna find out," said Darius, placing his now-empty glass of water on the bar. "I'm heading back to the front. Holler if you need me." He walked into the morass of dancing people and was swallowed up from sight.

Left somewhat unsettled, Marcus stood uncertain of his next move. As Sparks's owner, he had a responsibility to protect his staff, and he didn't take that lightly. Those who didn't know him well misread his party ways and took him for a fool. They were always surprised by his sharp business acumen. He could never understand a person who thought with his dick and not his head when it came to making money. If there was one thing he learned as a child from watching his father, it was business first. Nothing else mattered.

Tyler was a grown man and could take care of himself. If he wanted to arrange a hook-up with a rich patron, who was Marcus to stop it? Hell, if it weren't for the stupid bet, he'd have Tyler in his bed tonight. And, Tyler should expect to be hit on when he danced barely dressed in front of half-drunk clubbers.

None of his reasoning explained why, after making his rounds of the club, greeting his regulars and sharing several drinks with them, Marcus ended up in the back of Sparks where dressing rooms had been set up for the dancers to change. He didn't bother to stand on formalities and knock before entering—it was his club, and it wasn't as if he hadn't seen naked men before.

The back of a very wet and naked Tyler greeted Marcus when he pushed open the door. He'd obviously taken a shower and seemed to be done for the night, which surprised Marcus, as it was only twelve thirty and the dancers didn't get off-shift until three a.m.

"Hi sweetie, I know it's late and you're asleep but I just got your message." Tyler had his phone to his ear and seemed oblivious to Marcus's presence as he left a voicemail. "I can't wait to spend the day together tomorrow either. I'll see you in the morning."

Marcus held his breath and listened, having no compunction about spying on Tyler's personal phone call. After all, he reasoned, Tyler should be out on the floor working, not talking to his girlfriend.

"I love you. Bye."

Tyler placed the phone on the mirror top of the table and dropped his head in his hands.

"What a fucking mess. I knew this was a mistake."

Marcus closed the door behind him. "But I don't. Tell me why?"

Tyler stilled, then jerked his head up to meet Marcus's gaze. Something strange rose in Marcus's chest that suspiciously felt like sympathy, and once again he fell prey to the desolation in Tyler's eyes.

In his world, business always came before pleasure, and Marcus had no second thoughts about firing people who didn't want to work. Someone skipping out on his shift without a good reason would qualify for immediate firing.

"What are you doing here?" This was a different Tyler than the sexy, confident dancer writhing on the club floor. Marcus had a vague recollection of meeting Tyler a week or so ago and instantly being attracted to him, but had chalked that up to his perpetual hard-on from lack of sex. Plus, it didn't hurt that the man was beautiful to look at and had seemed happy enough to be hired for the dancer position, giving Marcus a wide smile when he was told he had the job.

Tonight though, no welcoming look or smile on Tyler's face beamed back at him. Instead, Marcus sensed an iron gate clanging shut, locking Tyler away well behind unbreachable bars. Marcus knew all about those iron gates. He lived in a fucking compound. But being the nosy bastard he was and, though he'd deny it to the death, he truly gave a shit about everyone who worked for him, he pressed onward, determined to find out what troubled Tyler so much.

"I watched you on the dance floor with Ortiz." Marcus eased into a chair next to where Tyler stood, in front of a mirrored wall. "I know he can be a bit of a pig sometimes. I hope you weren't overwhelmed. Did he say something offensive? Let me know, and I can have him tossed."

An incredulous expression darkened Tyler's silvery blue eyes. "So you're saying you were concerned about me? Is that it?"

"Is that so hard to believe?" Annoyance filtered through Marcus's best intentions. Jesus, the guy was touchy.

Tyler's skeptical expression and raised brow spoke volumes. "Yeah. You don't seem like the type of guy who cares about other people's feelings."

Son of a bitch. Stung, Marcus struck back. "What the fuck do you know about me? You've been here barely a week."

"Two hours is enough time for people to fill me in. I know you've screwed basically every guy who works here, and I'm not planning to be the next flavor of the week."

Marcus couldn't help but admire the man's beautiful, muscled physique, including his dick. He met Tyler's eyes in the mirror.

"Exactly. You can't stop staring at me. All you care about is a guy's dick and getting some."

Marcus folded his arms and sneered back. "If you're going to wave it in my face, I'm going to look. It's only natural."

Tyler reached for a pair of dance shorts and slipped them on, then faced him with his hands fisted on his hips. At least he planned to go back to work, so, Marcus thought, Tyler couldn't be too upset about Ortiz touching him. Personally, Marcus didn't like the thought of Ortiz touching Tyler, but attributed it up to his overall dislike of the man. He wouldn't like Ortiz touching any of his dancers.

"The decent thing would be to look away or even knock first before coming into a dressing room. But you know we're naked here, so you like the free show." Tyler yanked a brush through his damp hair and pulled on his boots.

Incredulous at this unprovoked attack, Marcus tried to reason with Tyler. "What the hell is wrong with you? I came here because you're my employee and I was concerned about your treatment. I'm not interested in your dick or your ass, which seems to have a stick up it at the moment. Don't worry—you're not my type."

"I thought breathing and with a heartbeat was your type." Tyler turned his back and headed toward the door.

Fucking hell. "Don't think you're going to talk bullshit to me and walk away like some fucking drama queen." Marcus strode over to him and grabbed him by the shoulder.

Pain rocketed through his jaw, and Marcus stumbled backward. He landed hard on the floor and looked upward at a red-faced Tyler whose sharp, staccato breaths punctuated the silence of the dressing room. The floor quaked from the muffled pounding of the music. Marcus shook his head to calm the ringing in his ears. Damn. Tyler had a mean right hook.

"You may be my boss and pay me, but that's as far as it goes. I don't have to like you, or put up with your crap like everyone else here does." The door slammed shut behind Tyler, leaving Marcus flat on his ass, dumbfounded.

What the hell just happened here?

Chapter Two

H E RETURNED TO the dance floor to continue his shift, but Tyler could barely concentrate. Lucky for him, he didn't have to worry about that guy Ortiz waiting for him, as the man had already moved on to someone else. Marcus, however, wasn't as easy a man to forget; through sheer will Tyler forced his irritating boss out of his mind.

The pounding beat insinuated itself in Tyler's head, and he instinctively let the music take over; his blood ran hot and smooth through his veins until nothing mattered but moving and coming alive to the rhythm. In a burst of enthusiasm, he jumped up on one of the bars and began to dance in earnest, rolling his hips, flinging his head from side to side, his hair whipping across his face.

Tyler could hear the claps and whistles of the patrons and the calls for more rounds of drinks, but he remained cloistered in his cocoon of music—the place where he'd always felt safest.

"They're going crazy out there, Ty. Every time you wiggle your ass I swear ten guys come in their pants," Shane, the red-headed bartender who'd tried to be friendly with him when he first got hired, called up to him. "Keep it up, and you'll be making more tonight in tips than I've made in a month working here."

Swallowing hard against the bile rising in his throat, Tyler threw his head back and poured his bleeding heart into his dancing. All the training he'd been through in school and afterward hadn't been for this—one step away from a stripper. He was going to be a Broadway star. But someone thought Tyler Reiss had it too good and yanked away his chance at fame and everything that went with it as well.

Water under the bridge, he told himself as he opened his eyes to survey the crowd that had gathered around him. No matter the obstacles thrown in his way, Tyler did the best he could, holding his self-respect tightly to him. It was the only thing he had that was completely his. What he did to make ends meet now had nothing to do with who he was. Staring at the leering faces of the men and women who Tyler knew thought of him only as a piece of ass, he wondered— not for the first time—if taking this job was a mistake. But then, the reality of the bills they tucked in his shorts and threw at his feet made it impossible for him to walk away.

In the dark recesses of the club he spied Marcus standing with his back to the wall, an inscrutable expression on his face and the ubiquitous glass of scotch in his hand. Arrogant and cocky—traits Tyler hated in a person—Marcus Feldman remained a conundrum to him.

From the day he began dancing at Sparks, Tyler had heard stories of Marcus's good will toward his staff and friends, yet he found it hard to reconcile that Marcus with the hedonist he knew resided behind that violet-eyed, handsome facade. As Tyler continued to watch him, Marcus drained his glass and walked away.

From that point, Tyler shut down all thoughts of Marcus and smiled into the slack-jawed faces of a group of men who teetered on the edge of silly drunkenness. He jumped down into their midst and swayed and shimmied his way around them until his shorts couldn't hold any more bills. Hopefully there would be enough from tonight to cover their expenses for the month, which always seemed to be growing. Hands groped his ass, and he allowed a few squeezes, even smiling up at the well-dressed man whose hand rested at his waist.

"Why don't we go in the back?"

The stale scent of beer gusted past Tyler's face, and he forced himself to keep that frozen smile on his lips.

"Sorry, but I'm on shift." Tyler hoped his refusal and apologetic tone would be enough to put the man off, but his grip tightened painfully.

"No problem. How 'bout a kiss?"

Without waiting for him to respond, the man crushed Tyler up against his hard chest and planted wet, beery lips to his while walking them to the back of the club. Tyler tried to respond, knowing this was how the game was played, but he couldn't withhold the shudder of distaste while the man's lips moved over his.

"You like that, huh?" The guy's arm rested like a lead yoke around his back, and Tyler began to struggle in earnest as he found himself backed up against the wall. "All you sluts like it. And I got what you want right here." He thrust his bulge against the thin fabric of Tyler's shorts.

They were hidden by darkness, and Tyler felt alarm trickle through him. He forced himself to accept the man's tongue in his mouth, rationalizing that he was safe. He was in his place of work, and security was there to protect him.

"Get on your knees, and show me what I spent my money on." The man's heavy hands landed on Tyler's shoulders, attempting to force him to the ground, but Tyler stood fast.

"I'm not blowing you. Get off me."

"Fucking cock tease." The man's handsome face twisted in an ugly sneer. "I'll make sure you don't work here or anywhere again if you don't. He reached between their bodies and grabbed Tyler's soft cock and balls in his hand, giving them a vicious squeeze.

"Fuck. Oh my God." Tyler cried out, the pain shocking in its intensity. "Get off me."

"What the hell is going on here?" A furious, disembodied voice echoed from down the hallway.

"Nothin' man. Jus' havin' some fun." The man kept his hands on Tyler's crotch, slurring his words.

"No, wait, please. He's hurting me." Tyler wrenched free, reeling from the shock of pain as once again his private parts were mercilessly jerked by the drunken man.

A man appeared, and Tyler recognized Darius, Sparks's chief of security. Relief flooded through Tyler. "Darius, it's Tyler. Help me, please."

Tyler admired the rate of speed and professionalism with which Darius dealt with the drunken man. After speaking into a walkie-talkie, two other men appeared in less than a minute to lead the protesting man to a side door and out of the club. Darius turned to him, concern etched on his face.

"You okay? Do you need a doctor?"

Tyler shook his head and exhaled. "No, thanks. But I think I need to call it a night. I know it's early but…"

"It's fine. I told Marcus there was a problem, but you'll need to fill him in on exactly what happened. He's waiting in his office for my report. Do you want to come with me now or talk to him tomorrow?"

Exhausted and a bit unsure if Marcus would believe him, Tyler wanted nothing more than to go home and go to sleep, but knew if he wanted to keep his job he had to tell his side of the story. Marcus would understand it wasn't his fault.

"I'll come with you." He managed a tired smile. "I thought this was supposed to be a fun gig, you know?"

"Sometimes you do your job too well and the consequences are unexpected," said Darius with a tight, grim smile.

"Yeah," said Tyler, grateful at least Darius understood. "I hope Marcus knows it wasn't my fault; I only dance like that for the tips."

They halted outside a wood-paneled door Tyler recognized as the entrance to Marcus's office. "You're good, man. Too good for this kind of place." Darius patted him on the shoulder and knocked on the door.

His throat tight with some strange emotion, Tyler followed Darius into Marcus's spacious office. Marcus sat behind a big wooden desk that featured a computer and nothing else. No photographs, no knickknacks or anything personal. If Marcus disappeared, there would be no trace of him left in that room. It rang as odd to Tyler, knowing how social a creature Marcus was.

"Sit down, Tyler. Do you want a drink?" Marcus nodded toward the bar behind him.

He shook his head and dropped into one of the chairs in front of the desk. It was then he became uncomfortably aware of all the money stuffed down his shorts. Shit. The tight lycra left nothing to the imagination. Marcus quirked a brow.

"Go ahead; you can take out the money. I'm sure it doesn't feel good."

Damning his flaming cheeks, Tyler pulled out enough bills so he could sit with ease.

Gesturing to the money, Marcus remarked, "That's quite a haul. You must've done well tonight."

"Marcus, Tyler was assaulted by a drunken guest tonight. That's why he's here. To give you his side, in case the person makes some bogus complaint."

Tyler threw Darius a grateful smile but jumped slightly when Marcus slammed his hand on the desk.

"What the fuck are you talking about? You just said there was an incident; last thing I saw, Ty was dancing on the bar, surrounded by an adoring crowd." Marcus's eyes blazed, and Tyler now understood he was witnessing the other side of Marcus Feldman, Party Boy.

"One of those adoring men had Ty backed up against the wall, squeezing his nuts." Darius stretched out his legs. "I saw it with my own eyes, Boss."

"Shut up with that boss shit." Marcus flicked Darius a glance, then returned that steely gaze to him. "Talk to me, Tyler." His voice softened. "What happened?"

The concern in Marcus's voice startled him. Embarrassed, Tyler shifted in his chair, wanting nothing more than to forget this night in its entirety. But the encouraging sound of Marcus's voice held him to his seat to repeat his story and watch anger descend like a black curtain over Marcus's face.

"Where is that son of a bitch now?"

Tyler had to strain to hear Marcus's low voice. He'd yet to hear the man sound so deadly.

"I had my guys toss him out and told them to add him to the no-fly list." Darius checked his phone. "He'll never be allowed back here again."

"He's fucking crazy to think he can touch one of my guys. Do you know who he is?"

Darius nodded. "Yeah. Some hedge-fund party boy. His friends all left as well." He checked his watch. "I mean, it's almost two a.m.; the club is still full, but by now it's mostly regulars."

"Okay. Thanks for all your help, man. You can go back outside. I want to talk to Tyler alone for a minute."

Darius shot Marcus a troubled look but left the room without speaking.

When the door shut behind Darius, Tyler grew nervous. This was different than his initial job interview where he met with Marcus. Desperation made people act in ways they never thought necessary, and Tyler had buried his normally quiet and introspective nature, forcing himself to flirt with the other bartenders and even Marcus when he met him at the interview.

He didn't know Marcus then, not that he knew him any better from the little interaction they'd had, but the staff loved to gossip, and their sexy and sexually voracious boss was the number one topic of discussion. He learned Marcus loved the pretty boys, and heard the stories of how Marcus went through the staff as if they were a bottle of scotch.

Shane the bartender had clued Tyler in that Marcus was on the tail-end of a three-month stretch of celibacy, and he'd be ready to blow off steam with any man in striking distance. Warily, Tyler eyed Marcus, who continued to study him from beneath ridiculously long dark lashes.

Tyler would rather flirt with the customers who tipped him or the friendly bartenders who made no secret their mission was to get in Marcus's bed. All of them seemed safer than his enigmatic, desirable, but hedonistic boss. He vowed never to fall prey to Marcus's undeniable appeal.

Right now all he wanted to do was go home. Tyler cherished the little downtime he had, where he could relax, kick back in sneakers and jeans and enjoy being himself. Although, after the upheavals in his life these past few years, Tyler couldn't feel quite certain of who he was anymore.

"I'm sorry you had to go through that, especially after the earlier incident with Ortiz. This isn't how I normally run my business." The gentleness in Marcus's voice surprised Tyler but set his internal bullshit meter on high alert. Was Marcus truly concerned about him as a person, or only because his business would be affected?

"Uh, well, thanks. I'm glad you saw my side of it."

"Did you think I wouldn't?" Marcus's dark brows drew together, and he frowned.

Tyler shrugged. "I don't know you well enough to know what to expect from you." Swallowing hard, he put aside his pride and appealed to Marcus. "But I need this job, so I'm thankful you believe me."

"I'll call a car and send you home."

"It's okay." He didn't want to be beholden to Marcus. "I'm fine taking the train."

"No. You're my responsibility, and I take care of my own."

Unblinking, Marcus held his stare. For one crazy moment, Tyler wondered what belonging to Marcus would be like. An unexpected bolt of lust shot through him, licking like a flame through his bloodstream.

It had been forever since Tyler desired anyone sexually. His cluttered, nonstop life precluded relationships or any time for even the most casual hook-ups. Tyler had no business imagining Marcus naked, his thick cock jutting straight up, begging to be sucked. His breathing grew heavier, and his heart slammed in painful beats. He wanted a taste of him. Badly. He shifted in his chair, willing away his sudden craving.

A knowing light glowed in Marcus's eyes, and a faint smile ghosted over his lips. "Don't worry. You're safe with me. I only bite when asked.

Besides." Marcus's stare intensified, sending Tyler's pulse rate into overdrive. "I'm sure we'll get to know each other much better in the coming months."

Bastard. The idea that Marcus had a view inside his head rattled Tyler. If Marcus thought Tyler would end up underneath him at some point, he was sadly mistaken. Tyler had priorities in life that didn't and never would include Marcus Feldman.

He stood so abruptly his chair toppled over and crashed to the floor. Marcus didn't flinch; he merely relaxed in his own chair with the same insufferable smile that only increased Tyler's confusion and anger.

"I don't need your help, and no, we won't get to know each other better. You're my boss, and you pay me to work for you. That doesn't include fucking me."

Marcus raised a dark brow. "I wasn't aware I asked." Tyler's face flamed, but Marcus continued on blithely, as if he was having a polite conversation about the weather. "But I've seen you in action, and I believe in never say never." He smirked at Tyler and lazed back in his chair.

Shaking with repressed anger, Tyler balled his hands into fists. What was it about this man that made him lose control? But his job came first, so he tamped down his antagonism and bit back the stream of curses he longed to hurl.

"Thank you for your help tonight. I appreciate it, and I'll see you tomorrow." He gritted out the words like spitting tacks.

"You most certainly will."

Marcus's mocking voice followed him all the way home.

Chapter Three

"**S**O HOW ARE you two lovebirds doing?"

The familiar pink blush spread over Zach's cheeks even as he gave the waiter his order, and Marcus grinned. He might love Zach and wish him the best in life, but that didn't mean he couldn't enjoy teasing him about his relationship with Sam.

"We're fine and so happy you called to get together." Zach handed the menu back to the waiter, then leaned into Sam. "I said to Sam this morning I missed you and was going to call, right?"

Sam smiled down at Zach. "Yeah."

"Did you see Julian's pictures? He and Nick look like they're enjoying themselves at the Amalfi Coast." Marcus tapped the screen of his phone.

"Yeah, they're having an amazing time. One day I'd like to go to Italy."

"I'll take you." Sam brushed his fingers along the side of Zach's neck. "We can go on our own honeymoon."

Zach's blush deepened, and he tipped his head into Sam's shoulder. For the first time, instead of making a cutting remark, Marcus studied his friends. The two of them were a perfect unit; Marcus couldn't be happier for Zach, knowing how much he craved love and being loved, but the concept of one man and monogamy seemed as far-fetched to him as traveling to the moon. And much less desirable.

Marcus accepted his mimosa from the waiter. "Keep them coming, please." If he had to spend the morning watching Zach and Sam act all dreamy-eyed and moony, he needed to get drunk fast.

"How's the club? Are the dancers working out as well as you hoped?" Zach took a piece of sourdough bread and offered him the basket.

He shook his head. "None for me, thanks. The dancers are great. They're bringing a lot of people into the club during the week on off-nights. Now it's always busy." His gaze roamed the restaurant and stopped short on a couple in the corner. Disbelieving, he blinked a few times and stared hard. It couldn't possibly be, but it was.

Paul Feldman. There, at a small round table sat his fucking father, in all his glory, with a woman, not his mother of course, but that was no surprise to Marcus. His father had never had time for his mother, or him, for that matter. Work and women dominated his life, not his family.

"Marcus, what's wrong?" Zach's voice penetrated the fog in his head.

Above everything, Marcus had always kept a tight lid on his home life. He and Zach had grown up together, spending the majority of time at Zach's house. Marcus's mother was too worried about him creating a mess that might upset his father, who was a stickler for order and precision, and his father and his needs and wishes were her main concern in life.

Not Marcus; never her son.

"Uh, nothing. Something in my eye." He rubbed it for effect and turned his attention back to Zach and Sam and their conversation. "So the dancers, yeah. Last night we had sort of an incident. One of the new guys I hired was hit on twice."

"Is that so unusual?" Sam buttered his bread and took a bite. After chewing and swallowing, he continued, "I figured the guys flirt for tips."

"Yeah, that's true, but this went beyond the norm. The guy was backed up against the wall with his nuts held in a twist." Marcus couldn't help glancing over to where his father sat, finishing his coffee.

It had been several years since Marcus had seen him, but from the way the waiters hovered, that proud, arrogant demeanor of his hadn't changed. The bastard expected and received deference.

"That's horrible," said Zach, clearly distressed at the thought.

"That's assault," said Sam the ex-cop, shooting him a hard, flinty glare. "You're gonna press charges, right?"

Marcus finally jerked his attention back to the conversation. "What? No. I didn't report it."

"Why not? Your employee was assaulted on your property and place of business. He could sue you as well as the guy."

Marcus sipped his mimosa before answering. "I don't see that happening. Tyler doesn't seem like that type."

"Oh yeah?" Zach put his fork down and gave him an amused look. "Who is this Tyler, and how well do you know him?"

"Not at all; don't be stupid." Marcus shot Zach a dark scowl. "He's a flirt on the dance floor and off, so I'm sure he gets hit on all the time. Besides," he said, "when I spoke to him last night after the incident, his main concern was making sure he still had a job, not suing me."

"What do you mean?"

"He wanted to make sure I didn't believe the asshole who groped him instead of his version of events."

"Well of course you wouldn't. And Sam's right."

Marcus finished his mimosa. "About what?" His father's laughter rose above the din of the other diners in the restaurant, and suddenly Marcus's throat turned dry as sand. He held up his empty glass to the waiter for a refill.

"That you should report the guy for assaulting your employee, and either Tyler or you should think about pressing charges. People can't simply touch other people against their will and think they can get away with it."

It wasn't only the tone of Zach's voice that bothered Marcus. Zach's white, anxious face stirred an uneasy feeling in the pit of Marcus's stomach. With rising anger and fear he watched Sam put his arm around Zach to comfort him.

"It's okay, baby. Don't get upset."

"Zach? What's going on? Talk to me." He braced his elbows on the table. "There's something else, isn't there?"

Sam opened his mouth as if to answer, but Zach cut him off. "It's fine. I want to talk about it. It's time." His blue eyes shone with that damn honesty only Zach possessed. Fear gripped Marcus's heart, anticipating what his best friend was about to say.

"Remember Nathan?"

At the mention of Zach's long-ago college boyfriend, whom both he and Julian hated, Marcus's lip curled in a sneer. "Yeah, what about that asshole loser?"

Zach's gaze fell to the tablecloth where he dug a hole with the sharp edge of a knife. "He…he used to hurt me. First verbally; then he moved on to the physical, but before it went too far he broke it off."

The room spun, and Marcus didn't realize he'd stood and knocked over his chair until he found himself staring down at Zach's mournful face. His breath came in pants, and his vision grayed.

"He fucking touched you, and you never told me? Why? You know I would have killed that bastard for you." His shirt clung to his back, damp from the sweat that poured off him.

"Because of this reaction. Back then I was too afraid and thought I didn't matter enough. But now I know I do. With the help of Dr. Landau and Sam, I'm working past it and making progress. I know I'm important. That I matter."

Unreal. Zach had suffered like this, and he hadn't had a clue. What a shit-ass, selfish friend he'd been all these years. The waiter had silently righted his chair, and Marcus sagged into it, unable to take his eyes off Zach.

"You matter more than anything. And I didn't see any of this happening." Marcus blinked against the sudden stinging in his eyes.

"You saw what I allowed you to see. But this isn't about you, Marcus, it's my problem and I—actually Sam and I are dealing with it."

Zach threw Sam a smile. "But that's why what happened to Tyler last night isn't insignificant. I think you should talk to him about it and ask him if he wants to press charges."

Now, finally, Marcus understood how Sam had changed Zach's life, making him stronger and more self-assured. Sam was Zach's anchor, his steadying guide to hold on to while he navigated through the hellish parts of his life, in addition to providing him with the love and support he deserved.

Envy rose within Marcus for the first time, shocking him with the violence of its intensity. What would it feel like to have someone care about his well-being more than their own? To have a loving, equal relationship, like Zach and Sam had, or Julian and Nick?

He squelched those thoughts and drank his mimosa in one tasteless gulp. That type of love wasn't meant for him; he'd never been first in anyone's life. Once again he eyed his father laughing and chatting with his latest "woman of the week," and the ever-present blackness wrapped itself around his heart. His own father cared more for his girlfriends than his son or wife. And as for his mother... Marcus always came a distant second to her husband's pleasure.

"I don't know; I can always talk to him tonight, I guess, but I don't think he'll care, as long as he keeps his job. That's the most important thing to him."

"You two sound the same; the job first and everything else second." Zach picked up his fork and cut into his French toast.

Aside from Tyler being a wonderful dancer with a gorgeous face and body, Marcus knew nothing about him or any of the other people who worked for him; their personal lives meant little to him. Even if they were fucking, he didn't care what their dreams were or where they went once they left his bed.

The one thing Marcus did know was that he'd never been important enough to anyone; even Zach, whom he'd loved more than he'd ever thought himself capable of loving anyone, hadn't believed in their friendship enough to entrust him with his secret. And now, as it should be, Sam took precedence in Zach's heart and was the man with whom Zach shared his trust and his life.

There was a twinge of regret at the inevitable loss of his close friendship with Zach, but he'd spoken the truth at Julian's wedding when he told Zach he loved him as best he could. He didn't know how to love anyone, not like his friends loved their partners. He'd seen Julian give himself to Nick and Zach to Sam so completely, and it scared the shit out of him to lose that control, to put someone else first.

Since he'd discovered the power of sex and his body, Marcus managed life his way, putting his needs before everyone else's. It had been a heady experience, freeing him of the gnawing inferiority of his youth, which, with a winning smile, he hid so deftly from everyone. Growing up in a home where he was nothing but an afterthought, an unwanted child, he'd made certain that as an adult he'd always be his own first priority.

"I don't know why you'd say that; you know nothing about him, and I don't know much more than you. He's a new dancer who seems to have caught the eye of every bartender and party boy on the floor."

Zach's brows drew together in confusion. "You sound like that makes it all right for him to be manhandled."

"That's not true. But maybe he needs to tone down shaking his ass."

Sam, who'd remained silent, tossed his napkin down on the table and spit out his words, his voice reverberating with anger. "Don't ever blame the victim. He's doing his job, the one you hired him for, and it's your duty to protect him while he's at your place of business. Period."

Prickles of shame hit Marcus. "I'm sorry; you're right. I'll talk to him tonight." No longer hungry, he toyed with the remains of his eggs. They finished their meal with small talk about the holiday season coming up and Julian and Nick's return.

After settling the bill, Marcus checked his watch; he had an appointment with his accountant, stock to check, and other endless details before Sparks once again opened for business tonight.

"Why don't you guys stop by the club and have a drink tonight?"

Zach shrugged. "We were only planning to hang out at home, but I'm willing." He nudged Sam. "You're not on a job now, are you?"

Marcus remembered Sam did undercover security work and had an idea. "If you come by, Sam can maybe let me know if my system needs any tweaking."

Sam slipped his leather jacket on and zipped it up. "Not a problem; I'd be happy to. I'm not working on anything at the moment."

"Great. Come whenever. I'll be there."

He hugged Zach. "Thanks for telling me about Nathan. I'm glad you know how much better you are without him."

"I'm sorry I held back, but it had nothing to do with you."

"I know."

They left, and through the front windows of the restaurant, Marcus watched Sam slip his arm around Zach's shoulders and kiss the top of his head. He wondered if having a steady lover would free him of his cynicism about relationships and love but dismissed that immediately. He'd never had the desire to have any one man for any period of time. They grew needy, whiny, and demanding.

"Still hanging around with the gay boys, Marcus?"

Years had passed since he'd heard that condescending voice, but Marcus would recognize it in his sleep.

"Well, if it isn't my dear *old* dad."

With delicious satisfaction, he watched his barb score a hit. His father winced; then his lips narrowed to a thin white line, and he drew back his shoulders as if preparing for battle.

Bring it on, Daddy. I've been waiting for years.

"Oh, are you Paul's son? I didn't know he had children. Nice to meet you; I'm Savannah." The busty, dark-haired young woman flashed her perfect teeth in a white, Miss America smile.

"Of course you are," said Marcus, barely paying her any attention. It wasn't rude of him; she'd be gone in a week or two anyway, so why bother?

"I thought you would've gotten that out of your system." His father brushed back his silver hair, slightly long and curling over his shirt collar, and Marcus made a mental note to never pretend to be younger than he was. It looked desperate and pathetic.

"What, that I like dick?" He grinned at the gasp made by both his father and Savannah alike. "It's not like it's a twenty-four-hour bug. You don't 'get over' being gay; I've known I like guys since the fifth grade. It's not my problem you can't deal with it; it's yours."

Without waiting for a response, he headed out the door and back to Sparks.

Chapter Four

TYLER STRETCHED HIS arms over his head, unknotting the kinks in his back. When he accepted the dancer position at Sparks, he'd worked out with management that he would be able to use one of the back rooms for practice, provided there were no events. So far it hadn't been a problem, and one of the rooms was usually free.

Even though he wouldn't trade his life for anything now, it still hurt to have come so close to his dream, only to have to give it up, through no fault of his own.

The room filled with the melancholy sounds of the violin concerto he had cued up on his phone, and he began to dance. The stretch and pull of his muscles and tendons, coupled with the sound of his feet hitting the floorboard, sent the blood singing through his body. Dancing here at Sparks was going to save their lives, allow him to pay the bills, and put a bit away each month, but dancing on a Broadway stage was all Tyler had ever dreamed about. It *was* his life and giving it up had almost killed him.

But, Tyler reasoned, it wasn't always about him and his dreams. Sometimes reality and life took a big bite out of your ass. That's when it was time to man up and be there for his family. And the $350 in tips he made from just last night was fucking unreal. He put the cash away in a safe place and prayed he could make the same tonight, even though it was Sunday.

Forty-five minutes later, he finished his practice and wiped off the worst of the sweat with a towel. Good thing Sparks had showers for the employees; he could almost feel the beat of hot water on his sore muscles and couldn't wait to get under the spray. He picked up the phone to shut it off.

"That was wonderful."

"Shit." Tyler jumped, and the phone flew out of his hands and crashed to the floor. If it broke, he was in deep shit. His fingers shook when he turned it over, and he could've cried, spying a spider's web of cracks spreading from the center of the screen. God damn it. He didn't have the money to buy a new phone.

"Did it break?" In two long strides Marcus joined him from where he'd stood in the doorway. "Damn. I'm sorry. Look, I'll replace it, don't worry. I'll even buy you a better one."

"No thanks." Of course he would. Like every typical rich guy, all Marcus knew was to throw money at a problem to make it go away. This man hadn't a single clue about the real world and making ends meet. Tyler didn't want to owe him anything.

He grabbed the broken phone from Marcus, shoved it in his gym bag, and zipped it up. Maybe one of the cheapie places in Chinatown could fix the screen for him. Tyler slung the towel over his shoulder and walked toward the door.

Undeterred, Marcus followed him. "Why not?" He placed himself in front of Tyler, effectively barring his way. "It was my fault; I startled you."

The man's refusal to take no for an answer, coupled with his dog-like persistence, frustrated Tyler no end. Marcus failed to understand the basic concept of personal space and stood way too close to Tyler for comfort. So close he could touch Marcus's stubble-rough jaw. Power rolled off Marcus's body, and Tyler inhaled the heady concoction his body heat emanated. Marcus's scent traveled straight through his bloodstream to Tyler's rapidly swelling dick, and Tyler, already suffering from pent-up anger and frustration, wanted no part of this cat-and-mouse game he sensed Marcus played. Especially since Tyler suspected he did it with every man he met.

"Because I don't want you to. I don't need your charity. Now if you'd please move, I need to take a shower."

But Marcus stayed put, crowding even closer to Tyler, their eyes clashing in a test of wills he knew without asking Marcus enjoyed playing. His heart jackhammered watching Marcus's eyes deepen to a violet so dark they looked inky black, that infuriating shadow of a grin curling his sensuous lips up at the corner.

Alarmed at the pulse of desire through his veins, Tyler started forward, expecting Marcus to step to the side and allow him to pass. Instead, Marcus planted his feet wide, all traces of that sensual, teasing smile gone.

"I need to see you in my office afterward."

Tyler's heart, thumping madly only moments before, stuttered to an almost nonexistent beat.

"Wh-why? What's the matter?" Did Marcus change his mind and decide to fire him? Did the guy from last night complain about him? Dread replaced the lust simmering in his bloodstream.

"We'll talk when I see you." Marcus stepped to the side, and Tyler raced past him to the staff bathroom.

Not twenty minutes later, Tyler, still damp from the shower and ignoring the water dripping from his hair down his back, stood outside Marcus's office. He hesitated only a moment before knocking.

"Yeah."

He opened the door and stuck his head inside. "Uh, hey, I'm here." His voice caught, and he hated how unsure and scared he sounded.

"Come in and sit down." Marcus waved to him and pointed to the sofa. "Can I get you a drink?" The deep, assessing look Marcus gave him swept through his bones, rendering him almost sick with anticipation. Tyler doubted he could hold a glass with how his hands trembled.

"No, I'm okay." Cursing his shaky legs, Tyler perched on the edge of the sofa. The uncertainty floating around in his mind made his stomach cramp.

"Really?" Marcus joined him, holding two glasses of amber liquid

Tyler assumed was scotch. "'Cause you look like shit."

"Are you going to fire me?" Tyler blurted out, unable to hold back any longer.

"Take this," said Marcus, holding out one glass.

"I don't—"

"Take the glass, Tyler."

The sharp edge of Marcus's voice shocked Tyler into compliance, and he took the drink, the warmth lingering on the glass from Marcus's hand penetrating his own.

"Now drink."

Tyler's gaze clashed with Marcus's, and his lips tightened. "I said I didn't want a drink."

Marcus leaned back. "And I don't like to drink alone." His voice turned wheedling. "Come on, Ty, just a little sip. Don't make me drink alone and feel all pathetic."

Pathetic was the last adjective Tyler would use to describe Marcus. Annoying, frustrating, and sinful—all sprang to mind when he thought about his boss.

Marcus's foot nudged his. "You've had a rough few days and should unwind a little."

More to shut Marcus up than anything else, Tyler raised his glass and took a deep swallow. Unused to hard liquor, it burned, firing a scorching trail down his throat. Tears sprang to his eyes, and he wheezed, gasping for air.

Marcus took his glass and set them both down on the desk then held him close, patting his back.

"Th-that shit's horrible." His words came out throaty, like an aging cabaret singer who smoked too many cigarettes and drank too much gin.

Marcus, who still held him, vibrated with silent laughter. "You get used to it."

"Ugh. Give me a beer anytime." Tyler sat up, but Marcus kept his arms around him. "Uh, you can let go of me. I'm not choking anymore."

No surprise, Marcus paid his protest little attention. Tyler stiffened when Marcus ran his hands down the length of his back, kneading the muscles. Shit, that felt amazing, but getting laid wasn't going to pay his bills. Annoyed at himself for falling for what was obviously a practiced seduction technique, Tyler pushed away from Marcus.

"You wanted to talk to me?" Tyler wet his lips, and Marcus's gaze dipped to his mouth. Tyler's cock ached, but he ignored it. "Am I in trouble?"

A gleam entered Marcus's eyes. "That depends."

"On what?"

Strong fingers returned to caress his neck, and despite his brain screaming at him to get as far away from Marcus as possible, Tyler's heartbeat accelerated, and the rhythm of his breathing amplified.

This cannot be happening.

Tyler refused to fall prey to Marcus and end up as an easy fuck on the office sofa. He knew too many guys who worked their way up the ladder that way in the performance field, and he vowed never to use his body to get a part or a job. It had been one of the reasons he never landed a job on stage. He wrenched away from Marcus's grip.

"About last night? Isn't that why you wanted to talk to me?"

Before Tyler could react, Marcus kissed his cheek, and with a dark look of regret he stood and walked to his desk. "Yes, before you distracted me."

Anger bubbled to the surface, and Tyler allowed himself to vent.

"I didn't do anything. And for the record, I'm not here to wind up on this sofa, fucking your brains out."

Marcus angled a dark brow. "If it ever came to that, you think you'd be fucking me?"

"Why am I here, Marcus?" Tired of this cat-and-mouse game, Tyler wanted to get something to eat and call home before he started his shift tonight. "I have things to do."

Shooting him a hard glance, Marcus sat on the edge of his desk. "I wanted you to know that I stand behind you after what happened last night, and if you wanted to press charges against the guy, I'm happy to help you and offer you the benefit of my lawyer."

Stunned for a moment, Tyler couldn't speak. To have someone believe in him, no questions asked—a virtual stranger no less—gave him a foothold on the slippery slope his life had taken for the past few days. He was so weary of proving himself day in, day out. Grateful yet hesitant to accept, Tyler struggled for clarification. He didn't want to be beholden to Marcus, knowing the man would probably expect him to repay the favor with his body.

"Why are you being so helpful?"

Marcus's leg swung back and forth from his position on the desk, and Tyler sensed his untapped nervous energy.

"I'm a nice guy."

"You? Nice?" Tyler blurted out, the laughter dying on his lips when he realized Marcus wasn't joining him.

Instead, Marcus looked hurt. And extremely pissed off.

"Yeah. I am. I'm really fucking nice. You don't know me from shit. Here I am, trying to help, and you laugh in my face?"

Defensive, Tyler struck back. "Oh come on, man. You know your reputation. I'm not saying anything everyone isn't already saying."

"You know what, Tyler? That's fucked up, and so are you. Ask anyone who knows me, and they'll tell you I'm no fucking saint and don't claim to be one. But I can look at myself in the mirror ever morning and know I've never fucked anyone over who didn't hurt someone I loved or cared about. So yeah." Marcus got up from the desk and walked over to the door and opened it. "We're done here, so you can get on with your busy life. I offered the help of my lawyer if you're interested. If not, I'll see you on the dance floor when your shift starts."

Ashamed but unable to think of a way to make it better, Tyler hustled out of Marcus's office, wincing when the door slammed shut with a loud bang reverberating down the hallway.

"Damn." Shane blocked his path, his brow furrowed in confusion.

"What's wrong? I've never known him to slam doors."

Miserable and confused, Tyler couldn't answer. Why did he feel like he was the bad guy here? He'd done nothing wrong.

"Aww, honey, don't look so sad. Lemme give you a hug." Shane put his arms around Tyler, and it was good to be held by someone who sought only to give him comfort, wanting nothing in return.

From his first day, he and Shane had been friendly, with little sexual tension or chemistry between them. Tyler hadn't had a real friend in forever, and Shane's sweet personality and giving heart drew him in and broke through the barrier of silence he normally submerged himself under at work.

With a grateful smile, Tyler sank into Shane's arms, laying his head on Shane's narrow shoulders. Tyler had heard numerous stories of the sad state of Shane's love life, and he'd even given Shane advice on how not to get kicked around by men who took advantage of his kindness. For once Tyler needed holding up against the winds.

"Well, this is sweet, but I wasn't aware I paid you two to hug. Or whatever else you planned to do to while away the hours until Sparks opens."

Marcus stood in the doorway to his office, his face dark, eyes devoid of emotion. The man was like a damn jungle cat—quiet, elusive, and dangerous as hell.

"Just giving Tyler a little pick-me-up friendly hug," said Shane, his arm remaining around Tyler, who squirmed under Marcus's stone-cold glare.

"Hug time is over. Shane, you need to get back downstairs and count the stock for tonight, please. We need to make sure we're full up." He hesitated. "If you need the night off, Tyler, you can have it."

"I'm fine," he said. "And I appreciate your offer from before, but I can handle things on my own."

Marcus's empty expression flickered over him. "Sure; whatever you say." He went back inside his office and closed the door behind him, this time with a quiet snick of the lock.

"Wow. Whatever you said really upset him. I don't know if I've ever seen him this angry." Shane kissed his cheek. "I'll see you later, honey."

Tyler barely noticed Shane's departure. His own anger grew exponentially as the minutes flew by. He'd done nothing wrong. If Marcus wanted to be an ass, let him. Tyler Reiss was going to be the biggest moneymaker Sparks had ever seen, starting tonight.

Chapter Five

"REMIND ME AGAIN why we're here?" Zach accepted a beer from the bartender, then stood with his back to the bar. Sam was busy with Darius, checking out the security system like he'd promised.

"Because you love and miss me." Marcus smirked over the rim of his glass of scotch. He searched the club until he found what—or rather who—he was looking for, and his smile faded. A party of regulars, whom Marcus knew had money to burn, surrounded a bare-chested Tyler, whose perfectly sculpted abdomen and powerfully muscled thighs gleamed when the lights hit his exposed, lightly oiled skin.

"Yeah, but I can barely hear you over the music, and I just saw you at breakfast today."

"What?" He couldn't concentrate with Tyler flirting and grinding his ass to whatever tune the DJ cranked out.

Wide-eyed, Zach leaned over to whisper in his ear. "Oh, is that Tyler? The guy you're interested in?"

Deliberately turning his back on Tyler's perfectly shaped ass, Marcus protested. "I'm not interested in him. He's my employee, and it's my duty to make sure he's safe from anyone who may try and hurt him again."

"Tell me, though." Zach nudged him, and from behind his glasses, his blue eyes danced with unrestrained glee. "Who's going to protect him from you?"

"You bastards have made a game of my sex life, and I've been going to bed every night for months now with the worst case of blue balls since I was a teenager and discovered how good sex was." Marcus drained his glass, and once again Antonio, the cute bartender, stood at the ready with a fresh one. Damn, he was very well trained.

"I'm surprised your dick hasn't fallen off from overuse all these years." Zach cracked up laughing, and Marcus peered at him with disgust.

"Go ahead and laugh. Just because you're finally getting it regularly you think you can hold it over me."

With a sympathetic smile, Zach patted Marcus on his cheek. "It's not that. I thought by now maybe you'd have learned to see things differently. That a loving and stable relationship was something you'd want to have instead of run away from."

"Why?" Whistles and clapping sounded from behind him, in the area where he knew Tyler danced. It took considerable fortitude for Marcus not to turn around and instead, continue his conversation with Zach. "Why do you think you and Julian have all the answers to what makes me happy?"

At once serious, Zach placed his beer bottle on the bar and gazed up at him. "Because you're not. Happy I mean. Happiness isn't about endless guys and drinking every night to forget whatever it is that made you so gun-shy of relationships."

"Why is your definition of happy the right one?"

"Because you watch us when you think no one's looking, and I see the sadness in your eyes. Don't forget I know you better than anyone here, maybe even better than you know yourself."

Marcus couldn't dispute that fact, so instead he remained stubbornly silent.

"There's nothing wrong with wanting to be loved, Marcus. Or with loving yourself."

Sam joined them then, and Marcus watched Zach light up in ways he never had in all the years he'd known him. The two of them made each other happy now, but for how long? How long would it take until Sam decided his way was the only way, pressuring Zach to follow or tossing him aside?

A love like they had made a person weak, bending to the will of someone else instead of taking control. Even Julian, who Marcus always believed put business before the personal, had signed over half his company to his assistant Melanie. None of these changes had taken place until his friends fell in love.

Love was the culprit; the enemy of independence and self-reliance. He didn't have to look far—his own mother had spent her life waiting patiently every night for his father to come home, making herself sick to keep the house and everything in it perfect. Marcus was glad he wasn't dependent on such sentiments and enjoyed his own company.

Love, Marcus decided, seeing Tyler pressed between two men as he danced, was for the weak. Lucky for him, he was strong and focused.

The touch of skin damp with sweat, a hot, wet mouth against his— that was his reality. All he required was a willing body, and right now, that was Tyler. The palpable sensuality rolling off Tyler's body called to him, and Marcus, already frustrated by the man's don't-touch-me attitude, couldn't see the need to hold back any longer. He downed half his drink and with purposeful strides pushed his way through the dancing crowd, moving away from the sweaty writhing bodies until he reached the group surrounding Tyler.

"We were wondering if you were ever going to join us." Jerry Connelly pulled him close for a quick bear hug. "Not that the entertainment isn't keeping us busy."

The flash of lights hit Tyler's face, and Marcus lost his concentration. With his eyes closed and a slight smile tipping up the corners of his sensuous mouth, Tyler's face was a study of the raw passion he held so tightly in check when he wasn't on the dance floor.

"He's hot and eager. You hired a winner."

Marcus paid Jerry no attention, deciding if everyone else had a taste of Tyler, he, the boss, should have one too.

"Step aside, gentlemen, and watch the professional at work." Marcus took the place of the man grinding behind Tyler and easily fell into the sway of the music. He rested his hands lightly on Tyler's hips and pressed his rapidly stiffening cock into the cleft of Tyler's ass. He didn't count this as cheating on the bet. He wasn't having sex, although his poor neglected cock was hard and ready to bust loose.

Holding Tyler's pliant body, Marcus drifted; the pounding music and din of the crowded club faded in the background until all he could hear was the beating of his heart. Tyler leaned back and hummed into Marcus's neck, and Marcus couldn't help but slide his arms around Tyler's sweat-slicked body to hold him close.

Tyler arched up against him, thrusting Marcus's cock deeper between the globes of that round, perfect ass of his. "Umm, baby, you smell better than any man I've ever had. Go on and rub yourself up on me."

The fight for self-control was an epic battle Marcus was more than willing to lose at this point. Uncaring that they were on the dance floor and in full public view, Marcus knew he had to kiss Tyler right then.

With one hand grasping Tyler's jaw, Marcus meant his kiss to be hard and devouring, a clash of souls and wills. Instead, at the first touch of Tyler's lips, Marcus hesitated, their softness coming as a complete surprise. Changing tactics, Marcus pressed his mouth against Tyler's in a gentle kiss, sliding his tongue inside the plush warmth of Tyler's mouth; their breaths mingled, and their tongues tangled hard, neither giving the other any leeway or control. Tyler turned in Marcus's arms, and Marcus groaned, his hands playing over all the half-naked muscled body flush up against his. Lips locked together, their kiss deepened while the rest of the world fell away.

Lost in the dark and sensual recesses of Tyler's mouth, the ground swayed beneath Marcus's feet. The mask of self-control he fought so bravely for slipped, and Marcus's heart slammed against his rib cage. Breathing hard, he sucked at the tender flesh under Tyler's ear, inhaling the scent of sweat and hot skin. Tyler intoxicated, and Marcus had to have him.

"God, I want you bad, Ty. I'm ready to say screw this bet and drag you back to my office right now." Fuck, he wanted to mark him, show everyone who he belonged to. He tamped down the inexplicable, needy possessiveness that consumed him and continued to nip and lick along the smooth lines of Tyler's neck. At Marcus's murmured confession, Tyler froze, then twisted out of his arms and stood breathless and shaking before him.

"What the fuck are you doing?"

With his hair disheveled in sweaty ringlets and his lips bruised and swollen, Tyler looked like a debauched angel. An angry angel, but Marcus had every intention of putting that dreamy smile back on Tyler's face. He held out his hand.

"Don't lie. You know you loved it. Now come on."

"I didn't know it was you. I thought it was one of the guys here." He gestured to the five men grouped around them on the edge of the dance floor, all of whom tried hard to pretend they weren't listening in on the conversation and failing.

Unwilling to be the focus of their gossip, Marcus took hold of Tyler's hand and yanked him close. "You kissed me like you wanted to fuck me."

Tyler pushed his damp hair off his face. Even in the dim lighting of the club his eyes blazed, hot and stormy with anger. "I thought you were a customer. If I'd known it was you, I'd never have let you touch me like that or kiss me."

Reeling as if he'd been physically slapped, Marcus remained silent. It was like his childhood all over again; never first for anyone, never good enough.

"You liked it; you can't lie to me."

"I'm here to do my job. First I get harassed by the customers, and now I'm getting harassed by you. Leave me the hell alone. I'm not interested."

Joining him at his side, Zach put a reassuring hand on his arm. Sam, as always stood next to Zach.

"Hey, come get a drink with us. We've hardly had a chance to hang out all night, and Sam wants to talk to you about some ideas he has for the club."

Breathing hard, Marcus's gaze dipped down to his best friend, who stared back at him with sympathetic eyes. Shit. He could accept a lot of bullshit, but people feeling sorry for him wasn't on his menu. Choking back the slashing words he longed to hurl at Tyler, he nodded at Zach, and without acknowledging Tyler's existence turned his back on the man and walked away to the bar at the back of the club.

Zach followed him with Sam trailing behind. "What happened?" Zach shook his head when Marcus took a bottle of beer from the bartender. Sam accepted it instead and gave him a grateful smile.

"Not a fucking clue." Marcus slumped against the bar, watching the crowd pile up. The two bartenders made fast work of the customers and never lost their smiles. "One minute we're dancing and grinding together and the next he's telling me I'm harassing him."

"Did you ever get a chance to talk to him about last night?" Sam twirled the neck of the bottle between his fingers. "You know, to explain how you were willing to help him."

"Yeah I did. And he didn't seem all too thankful. He's such a fucking touchy guy."

"But you like him," Zach stated with a quiet certitude. "I can tell."

"What are you talking about?" Irritated, Marcus drank down half his beer in one long gulp, then scowled back at Zach. "I just told you he's pissing me off, and that's all you have to say?"

"You can't take your eyes off him. Even now, after Tyler brushed you off, you can't stop watching him; don't think I haven't noticed. He's gotten under your skin."

Annoyed at Zach's perception, Marcus mumbled, "You're fucking crazy." Marcus nudged Sam's arm. "Take him home, and get him laid."

Sam laughed and shook his head. "That's your answer for everything." His gaze turned serious. "But I tend to agree with Zach. You seem to be very preoccupied with this Tyler guy, more so than with anyone else since I've known you." Sam smirked. "I trust Zach's instincts."

Time to shut this down. "Since you two have gotten together, all Zach can think of is matchmaking. It's like he's living on Noah's ark and every living thing has to be paired off for survival."

"That's not true," Zach protested, his voice defensive. "I don't believe that for everyone. But with you..." His gaze turned sad. "I love you, and you're my best friend. I don't like seeing you alone and unhappy."

"That's all your fault. If it wasn't for that stupid bet, I'd be with someone right now." His grin failed to elicit the same response from Zach.

"That's lust; it doesn't last. I'm talking about relationships, not one-night hook-ups." Zach moved his chair closer, and his voice grew urgent. "We've been friends forever, and I want you happy. Deep inside I know you want love. Once you find that, you won't need to wander, having empty, meaningless sex."

Being with Zach lately was like watching an afternoon reality talk show. Marcus patted Zach's cheek. "Sex with me is always meaningful; you never have to worry. And once this bet is over, I'll show you how happy I can be, probably starting with my bartender Antonio." Ignoring Zach's eye roll and Sam's groan, said bartender rewarded Marcus with a wide smile, a wink, and a fresh drink.

That's what he needed: someone easy and willing to take the edge off the gnawing hunger eating away at his core. If Marcus found himself aching for what Zach and Julian had with their lovers, that thought got ruthlessly squashed. That hunger within him to prove his desirability swelled and festered, clamoring for its rightful place. It fed his ego and watered his soul. And the more men he had, the greater his need. It became a vicious, never-ending cycle with no escape outlet.

At first Tyler's rejection pricked him. Now, with a clear head, he didn't give a damn. His parents didn't care about him either, and he did fine without them as well. He'd easily find a man who wanted him; there was never a shortage of willing, eager men to warm his bed. But even as he said good night to Zach and Sam, kissing them each goodbye with promises of dinner later in the week, his gaze searched the crowded club for Tyler and found him dancing on a table top, the now familiar salivating crowd of men waving money or tucking the bills into his tight shorts, sometimes giving him a squeeze or a fondle. Marcus's jaw tightened when Tyler failed to push them off or snarl at them the way he had at Marcus earlier.

Why did Tyler push him away?

Chapter Six

TYLER SLEPT BADLY that night; interspersed with his dreams of auditions he didn't get because he failed to give sexual favors, and horrendous injuries he suffered, ruining his ability to dance, was the hurt expression that had flashed across Marcus's face when Tyler pushed him away.

He'd only gotten to sleep at four a.m., yet not two hours later Tyler found himself drinking a cup of coffee, sitting at the counter that doubled as a kitchen table and so much more. New York City one-bedroom apartments rarely had eat-in kitchens, and he knew to be grateful for what he had.

The oversized mug warmed his hands, and he made a note to call the landlord again about the lack of heating, although Tyler knew it wouldn't do much good. The area consisted of a mix of Pakistanis, Russians, and a slow but steady influx of Manhattanites who'd only recently discovered the surrounding neighborhoods of old Victorian homes. His landlord didn't give a shit about the tenants; all he wanted was for them to pay the rent. If Tyler wanted action, he'd have to call 311 and make a complaint.

But the cold apartment wasn't the culprit for his fitful dreams and wakefulness; Tyler had become almost immune to it and had plenty of blankets to stave off the chill. No, Marcus was the catalyst for his sleepless state; that disturbing, erotic kiss they shared was like an earworm: he couldn't get rid of it replaying in his head.

The pure rawness and lust of the kiss scorched him; Tyler had never been quite as owned by a kiss before. Even now, he touched his lips with tentative fingers as if expecting to find them chafed and blistered from the searing heat of Marcus's mouth.

Raw, carnal, and passionate. When he'd been as yet unaware of whom he was kissing, Tyler had wanted nothing more than to drag the man off to a corner, shuck his pants down, and fuck him hard. Whoever this man was, he'd reignited a fire inside him that he'd thought burned out long ago yet now found fuel in that one, amazing kiss.

But when he opened his eyes and Marcus's face loomed before him, Tyler froze and went on the defensive, pushing him far away. And when Marcus made that suggestion to go back to his office, he couldn't know how hard Tyler struggled against the impulse to take his hand and run. His body had positively vibrated with need.

That's when his innate good sense kicked in, grabbing him by the shoulders and shaking him until his teeth rattled. Getting involved with Marcus would be a horrible mistake, and Tyler wasn't foolish enough to take that first step. He had zero time in his life for a man as complicated as Marcus.

Between his personal observations and the gossiping tidbits he picked up from listening to coworkers, Tyler's image of Marcus was that of a spoiled and self-centered man, one whose focus centered on his libido and desires alone. Tyler hadn't lived through personal hell to end up worshipping at the altar of Marcus Feldman. His obligations today far exceeded his need for sex anyway. He'd been doing fine with his right hand for a while now.

A knock at the door startled him; he checked his watch and saw it was only six-fifteen a.m. Who the hell could it be? His rent was paid, and he didn't owe anyone anything. All he knew was that nothing good occurred early in the morning, so with his heart banging and much trepidation, Tyler hurried to open the door before the knocking woke people up.

"Who is—" The words dried up in his throat at the sight of Marcus. With his haunted eyes, unshaven face, and windblown hair, he proved more desirable than Tyler had ever imagined.

"I need to talk to you."

Tyler remained frozen in his doorway, fear, worry, and excitement whizzing through him so fast he felt dizzy from the rush. Reflexively he glanced behind him, making certain they were still alone. His heart slammed in hard painful beats against his rib cage.

The expectant yet hesitant expression on Marcus's face shocked Tyler; he usually seemed so calm and in control. That familiar, hardened look in his eyes coupled with his annoying arrogant grin were nowhere in sight. For the first time, Tyler knew he had a glimpse of the man behind the flashing lights and glossy exterior. Always supremely confident, now that the cracks in his armor showed, it made Marcus more likable and relatable.

And ultimately more dangerous. Tyler didn't want to think of Marcus as vulnerable and emotional; that created a man who Tyler might come to like as a friend.

"Can I please come in and talk to you for a minute?"

Without speaking, Tyler opened the door wider, turned around, and walked to the kitchen area, which was no more than an open space with the small counter, stove, and refrigerator. He needed a moment to gather his thoughts and get away from the disturbing emotions Marcus stirred up.

Tyler's strength had been tested so many different ways these past few years that there were times he was amazed he was still standing upright and undamaged. Priorities had a way of changing in a split second, leaving consequences that lasted a lifetime, and Tyler's priority was no longer himself. From a career change that forced him to give up his childhood dream, to a life-altering decision that he never regretted but sometimes doubted he was capable of handling, Tyler reminded himself exactly what was important to him now. Not random sex, nor the good-looking man in front of him, whose earlier kiss he could still taste in his mouth.

For a brief moment Tyler closed his eyes, imagining what sex with Marcus would be like. Volcanic, fiery, and ultimately, for him, heartbreaking, since Tyler knew how easy it would be to fall for Marcus without having the feelings returned in kind.

He opened the cabinet to take down a mug to offer Marcus a cup of coffee. The brush of cool, early morning air wrapped around him from behind, and Tyler knew Marcus stood close enough to touch. He could smell him, for Christ's sake. Gulping down his nerves, Tyler turned abruptly to face him.

"Why are you here?"

Those violet eyes searched his. "I have no fucking clue, but I have to find out."

"Find out what?" Tyler's voice caught in his throat, and he damned his treacherous body for betraying him. The memory of their hot, needy kiss, drawing the breath from his lungs, had his cock hard and leaking.

"I don't know." Marcus crowded him so his back hit the counter, and there was nowhere for him to run this time. "Why you let other men touch and kiss you, but me you push away." With a sigh of frustration, Marcus brushed the tangle of hair off his brow. "Why it matters to me."

"It's my job, Marcus. Obviously I need the money; I'm not independently wealthy. I have to play the game to get the tips they give me."

Marcus's eyes turned dark. "And when you kissed me?"

Tyler corrected him. "I believe you kissed me."

Marcus made an incoherent noise in his throat. "Fucking hell, who cares?" He braced his hands on either side of Tyler's hips, effectively trapping him. Their bodies touched, and Tyler's cock, loose in his sweats, swelled even further, tenting out the fabric. Marcus groaned at the sight and rubbed himself up against Tyler. "You enjoyed it, didn't you?"

Marcus's lips grazed his jaw, and Tyler bit back a moan. He could hardly think straight – he was so turned on.

"Yeah, so?" Coherent thought was about to leave his brain as Marcus continued to nibble along the side of his neck.

"So why did you stop? We could have fun together. Let me show you."

Marcus dipped his head and kissed him, and Tyler, overtired from lack of sleep and dizzy from repressed desire, gave up all pretense of resistance. Just for once, he gave into temptation and put his needs first, before everyone else's.

Their lips touched again, tentative at first as they learned the shape of each other's mouths and each other's tastes. His fingers ghosted along Marcus's strong jawline, then curved around the nape of his neck. Tyler sucked the swell of Marcus's full lower lip into his mouth, his body surging with pleasure at Marcus's grunt of approval. He molded his body to Marcus's, and they slanted their mouths together, feeding off their mutual rising hunger. All sound abated save for their ragged breaths as they fused their bodies and their mouths together, licking, biting, devouring, as if each was the other's first meal after a prolonged fast.

This was more than a simple kiss; this was possession, fueled by lust. Tyler gasped, sucking in much-needed air, and clung to Marcus's shoulders like a lifeline, his fingers curled around the bunched up fabric of Marcus's shirt as if by letting go he'd drown.

Marcus's eyes were closed, his face soft with desire, in direct opposition to the hard body flush against Tyler's. With supreme reluctance, Tyler let go of Marcus and touched his fingers to his lips briefly, wondering if he'd imagined the perfection of their kiss.

Marcus finally opened his eyes and trailed kisses down Tyler's neck. "I'm glad to see you've decided to give in. Made the trip out to this godforsaken part of Brooklyn worth it."

"So you got what you came for, then?" Tyler hitched up his sweats and tied them tighter on his hips.

"Somewhat." Marcus pounced on him, crushing his mouth over Tyler's before he had a chance to react and move out of reach. And damn his fucking traitorous body—again—he accepted it. More than accepted; he dived into that kiss head first like a kid into a fresh pile of snow. He loved kissing, and he missed sucking in another man's breath and feeling the play of muscles beneath his fingers.

So fucking sexy. The taste of Marcus in his mouth sent his head spinning. It had been so long since he'd been touched and smelled another man's scent. For a last, brief second Tyler allowed himself the pure pleasure of falling into Marcus's kiss; then he pushed Marcus away.

"We need to stop."

Marcus stepped back, his face dark with lust. "What's wrong? I didn't hurt you, did I?" He drew in a deep breath and let out a shaky laugh. "It's been a while for me, so I'm a little out of control."

"Yeah, I know about that bet." Tyler slid out from under Marcus's grasp and escaped to the living room where he sat on the sofa that doubled as his bed. "And you didn't hurt me. I was as into it as you, and that's the problem."

Marcus followed and joined him on the sofa. "You're talking in riddles. As a matter of fact,"—that now-familiar gleam entered Marcus's eyes, and Tyler inched farther away until the wooden arm of the sofa dug into his back and he had nowhere left to go—"you're talking too much." He scooted closer and ran his hand up Tyler's arm, clasping his shoulder in an almost possessive grasp. "Why don't we move this to the bedroom and get better acquainted?" His thumb smoothed the skin under Tyler's chin.

Tyler shook off his hand. "This was a mistake. I told you at the club I don't want to get involved with you."

Nuzzling his neck, Marcus smiled against his skin. "Who said anything about getting involved? I'm talking about some hot and heavy fucking. You and me and a king-size bed that I guarantee will be banging up against the wall in seconds flat once I lay you down."

If he'd been wavering before, the cavalier manner with which Marcus spoke sealed it for Tyler. He couldn't afford to let his cock rule his head right now. He jerked away and froze when, about to speak, he heard the door from the back of the apartment squeak open, then the unmistakable shuffle of footsteps from down the hallway.

"Uncle Ty?"

In her purple footie pajamas, four-year-old Lillie rubbed her eyes and gave him a sleepy smile.

"I had a bad dream."

He hurried over to scoop her up in his arms, and pressed a kiss to her sleep-tousled curls. "It's okay baby-girl. I'll tuck you back into bed."

"Who's that?" She pointed at a stunned Marcus who, for once, seemed incapable of speech.

"That's my boss. His name is Marcus."

She studied him with serious blue eyes, and Tyler couldn't help but laugh at the uncomfortable expression on Marcus's face. He wondered if the man had ever even spoken to a young child before.

"He looks sad." She wriggled out of his arms and before Tyler could stop her padded over to Marcus who studied her with a quizzical expression, as if she were an alien requiring further investigation. "Are you sad? When I'm sad Uncle Ty dances for me; then we have hot cocoa."

Marcus's unreadable gaze met Tyler's when he answered Lillie. "I don't think your uncle will want to dance for me anymore."

At the double entendre in those words, Tyler's heart twisted painfully. Trained as a classical dancer, surprisingly Tyler had come to love his job at Sparks despite the drunken, pushy clients. In the past week he discovered he enjoyed interacting with the people and the freedom the music brought to his body. It poured through him like liquid gold, igniting something visceral inside him. When he danced he felt his soul soar.

And much as he didn't want to admit it, Marcus intrigued him. Lillie was right: Marcus was a sad man, and despite all his internal warnings, Tyler wondered why.

"Were you mean to my uncle?"

Tyler met Marcus's hungry gaze and knew he was thinking of how only moments before their tongues had been down each other's throats, both of them moaning in ecstasy. Tyler had never fallen so hard, so fast. His breathing quickened.

"No, honey, he wasn't mean to me." He choked out those words, heat rising in his cheeks. "But—"

"Your uncle and I had a misunderstanding, but I think it's cleared up now, right?" Marcus cut in smoothly.

"Uh, it was?"

"Yes." Marcus's earlier discomfort seemed to have melted away, leaving in its wake the confident, slightly arrogant man Tyler expected. He longed to contradict Marcus, but Tyler couldn't afford to lose this job. It wasn't only about him now. He had responsibilities he couldn't afford to screw up.

Lillie tugged on his sweats. "Can Marcus stay for breakfast?" She glanced over her shoulder at Marcus, and damn the man if that cocky grin wasn't plastered all over his face.

Lucky for Tyler, he knew Marcus had better things to do with his mornings than hang out in a run-down apartment with Tyler and his family, eating pancakes. Lillie would have to understand.

"I don't think—"

"I'd love to." Marcus gave him a smug smile. "I can make the coffee."

"Don't you have someplace you need to be?" said Tyler, more sharply than usual.

"That's not nice." Lillie stood with her hands planted on her hips. "You always said to be nice to visitors. And he's your friend, isn't he?"

Was he? Marcus quirked a brow in a silent question, a quizzical smile curling his lips.

Knowing defeat when he saw it, Tyler conceded to the only person who ruled his heart. "I guess he is." He held out his hand to Lillie who squealed and took it, pulling him into the kitchen. "Let's make pancakes."

Chapter Seven

"MARCUS." JULIAN RUSHED past the crowd waiting at the front of the restaurant and grabbed him in a hug.

A month had passed since Julian and Nick had returned from their honeymoon, yet this was the first time they'd all had a chance to get together for a late-afternoon brunch. He, Zach, and Sam may have gone to dinner once a week and they'd even come to the club several times, it was never the same when all of them weren't together.

The hostess, Steph, led them to their usual table, and her face lit up with happiness when Julian and Nick gave her a present from their honeymoon.

"Thank you, guys." She opened the box to reveal a beautiful leather handbag. "Oh wow, it's gorgeous."

"It's for putting up with us, especially Marcus hitting on all the waiters and busboys." Julian kissed her cheek, and Nick hugged her; then they slid into their seats.

Marcus surveyed his friends, and the tension he hadn't been aware of melted away. He didn't often speak of it, but he needed these men, probably more than they needed him, especially now that they'd paired up and were creating homes that, knowing Zach, eventually would include children. He wondered how long it would be before these times would be lost forever.

"It's good to have you back, Juli."

"Aww, did you miss me, Marc?" Julian teased. "Don't say you've gone all sentimental on me."

"Oh, fuck off."

"There's the Marcus we know and love." Nick smiled at him and sipped his beer. He nudged Julian. "Are you going to ask him, or will I?"

"It was your idea from the beginning, so you get to do the honors."

"Ask me what?" After choosing a breadstick, Marcus offered the breadbasket to Zach, who took a roll, then handed the basket over to Sam.

"Well," said Nick, bracing his elbows on the table. "How'd you do with the bet? It's been over three months now, so I'm sure you're back on the prowl, but did you hold out?"

He hesitated for only a brief second, but that was long enough for Julian the Jackal to scent blood in the air and pounce.

"Ah." His green eyes gleamed with unholy light. "I knew you couldn't last."

Zach, about to put a piece of roll in his mouth, returned it to the bread plate to stare at him wide-eyed with surprise. "Marcus?"

Since he'd turned up so unexpectedly at Tyler's apartment, the two of them had maintained a wary yet professional relationship. Much to Marcus's inexplicable annoyance, Tyler continued his provocative dancing, raking in the tips while occasionally granting a customer a kiss or a feel. Marcus had seen to it that Darius assigned a special security guard to stand watch whenever Tyler danced, to make sure there would be no further problems with physical attacks from the more insistent customers.

Discovering the man was responsible for his little niece had made Marcus all too leery of pursuing a physical relationship; the last thing Marcus was interested in was a man with a child or any type of responsibilities. When Marcus was with a man, the only person that man needed to concentrate on was Marcus. Tonight he planned on bringing that sexy bartender Antonio home with him. He knew the man was interested, yet something kept interrupting his plans to score.

"What?" He shrugged and sipped his mimosa, refusing to meet his friends' eyes. "I didn't have sex with anyone; I kissed a guy."

Of course Zach couldn't be content and let it go. "Who was it?"

"What does it matter? It's not likely to happen again." Edgy and uncomfortable under the scrutiny, Marcus raised his hand to call the waiter over. Anything to avoid those concerned and sympathetic looks he hated.

"Was it Tyler?" Zach's softly worded question hit him like a fist in the stomach.

"Who's Tyler?" asked Julian and Nick at the same time.

Terrific; now he had nagging in stereo. Maybe he didn't miss his friends as much as he thought. When neither Zach nor Marcus responded, Julian nudged Sam. "Do you know who Tyler is?"

"He's a dancer at Sparks."

"A dancer? Well, you always did like them bendy, Marcus. But why is Zach giving you those big, puppy-dog eyes?" Julian studied him for a moment; then a wide smile broke across his face, and Marcus tensed, ready for the onslaught.

"Holy shit. You actually like this guy. Outside of the bedroom and with his clothes on." He elbowed Nick. "Do you see it?"

Nick, unconcerned, popped the rest of his roll into his mouth, chewed and swallowed it before answering. "So what if he does? It's about time, is all I can say."

"You're fucking crazy. There's nothing going on between us." Thank fuck the food finally came and he could concentrate on that instead of the knowing glint in Julian's eyes.

"I never said there was anything going on between the two of you." Ignoring his meal, Julian the Jackal continued to pick at him, as if he were a roadside carcass. "I said you liked him. And I know I'm right because you're all defensive now."

"Read my lips: nothing's going on. He's a fucking tease who doesn't mind shaking his ass for everyone, but when I kissed him he pushed me away."

The sight of Julian's eyes bugging out of his head would've been funny if it wasn't directed at him.

"He turned you down? The great Marcus Feldman finally met a man who didn't succumb to his beauteous charms." Julian elbowed Nick. "We have to go to Sparks as soon as possible to see the guy who finally has Marc running in circles."

More irritated than ever at Julian, Marcus slammed his hand down on the table, rattling the silverware. "There's nothing going on between us; we haven't even had sex."

"That doesn't mean a thing," Sam chimed in, taking Zach's hand and giving it a brief squeeze. "I knew Zach was it for me from the first time I met him."

Right before his eyes, Zach melted into a big messy pile of goo. "I love you too, Sam."

"Oh for Christ's sake; this is nauseating." Unable to take this crap a minute longer, Marcus stood abruptly and threw a few bills on the table. "I knew this would happen once you all hooked up. You're trying to fit me into your little domestic happy boxes and make me one of you." He pulled on his jacket. "I'm not playing that game. Call me when you come to your senses."

He didn't care where he went as long as it was away from his friends and their once-upon-a-time, fairy tale lives. Glancing briefly at his watch, he figured while he was pissed off and bitter he might as well deal with another distasteful chore he forced himself to perform every few months. He stuck out his hand and hailed a cab. In less than twenty minutes, he found himself on the familiar doorstep in Carroll Gardens, and he rang the bell. There was no need to call ahead.

The door opened.

"Hello, Marcus."

"Mother."

There was no welcome kiss or hug, no genuine smile of hello. There never had been. His mother's smiles were reserved for his father.

He trailed behind her, noting her immaculate dress, the usual shining floors, and the overall sterility of the house. He couldn't call it a home; home was where you felt welcomed and loved. Those two concepts were foreign to him... Zach's mother had given him more affection than either of his parents ever had.

After his mother ushered him into the living room, where the guests were entertained, she sat and gave him a brittle smile. "It's nice to see you."

"Sure it is. How are you?"

Two strangers might have a more honest conversation than he and his mother.

"I'm fine. I'll be going to Europe next week. Your father bought me a trip to Paris for my birthday." Her face glowed with happiness like it always did when she spoke of his father. "He knows I love Paris."

"Will he be joining you?" He already knew the answer, yet he wanted to hear it for himself.

"No; only for the weekend. You know how busy he is; I hardly see him. But he's such a perfectionist with details, he's arranged everything for me, for once he leaves. Isn't he wonderful?" Her beatific smile at the paltry attention his father chose to pay her angered Marcus to no end.

The extent of his mother's naiveté was breathtaking. "Oh yeah, he's wonderful." He made no attempt to hide the sarcasm from his voice.

"I don't understand why you two can't get along. Your father worked like a slave to give you whatever you could possibly want."

"I didn't want trips to places that weren't for children or toys that were too expensive to play with. I wanted parents who wanted me." Marcus's mouth snapped shut. He hadn't meant to speak out loud. "I'd better go."

"Very well. I have a dinner party to get ready for, and I can't be late." She twisted the string of pearls around her neck. "You know your father hates when people are late."

"Everyone except himself."

Ironic that a man who hated other people's foibles would be guilty of the same. The times were too numerous to count when his mother prepared dinners she then had to throw away because his father didn't come home. And when he did come home, he'd apologize with a careless "I'm sorry" and retreat into his study. At some point, Marcus had grown old enough to understand that his father had been seeing other women.

"I can't keep him to a schedule. Things come up."

If it was anyone but his mother, he'd make a lewd joke about the only thing coming up was his father's dick in some other woman. But even he wasn't that cruel. After over thirty years of marriage, if she couldn't see her husband's faults, it wasn't Marcus's job to point them out. Some people preferred to live with their head in the sand, believing that if they were never confronted with a problem, it didn't exist.

The obligatory visit had run its course. He visited her every few months or so, and each time was as painful as the last. There was no pretense of a loving family; neither of them made an effort. She was no different to him than a stranger on the subway.

"Well, I'll see you." Marcus itched to get out of the house and walked back to the front door.

She gave him an odd smile. "Your father told me he saw you about a month ago. You were with a group of men."

He never had come out directly and told his mother he was gay; there was no attempt on his part to deliberately withhold the information—they simply didn't have a personal relationship where he found it necessary to share his sexual identity. He was reminded of Nick's family and how loving they were to Julian, how accepting of their marriage. Zach too had hit the lottery in the parent-prize category.

"Yes. I saw him. I was with my friends." He owed neither of them anything, least of all an explanation of his life and the choices he made. The fault lay with them; their behavior had molded him into the man he was today. "Goodbye." He opened the door and left without waiting for a response.

Marcus checked his texts, and as expected there were several missed calls from Zach and Julian as well as a string of texts, beginning with Zach's: *Please come back, we won't say anything*, and ending with one from Julian, which said, *You're being an asshole. There's nothing wrong with admitting you might have feelings for someone. You don't need to be lonely.*

He shoved the phone back into his pocket and began to walk with no destination in mind. He left Carroll Gardens and walked toward Park Slope, taking in the crowds of people along Smith Street, waiting for lunch and browsing the eclectic, expensive boutiques. The area had flourished in the past decades, changing from a veritable wasteland, full of run-down stores, bodegas, and brownstones cut up into multi-family dwellings, to high-end, fashionable restaurants and multimillion-dollar single family homes. Marcus wasn't so sure life—as he knew it at least—was any better now than when he was young.

After picking up a slice of pizza and wolfing it down as he meandered up President Street to Fifth Avenue, Marcus looked for a coffee house where he could relax for a while and not be hunted down by his well-meaning, nosy best friends. Unused to spending so much time alone, he discovered he enjoyed his solitude instead of surrounding himself with the usual hangers-on and sycophants who only wanted to use him for their own personal gain. He walked up to Eighth Avenue, a block away from Prospect Park.

Eventually Marcus wandered into one of the small, independent coffee houses so fiercely protected in this liberal bastion of Brooklyn. He ordered a large latte and a big chocolate chip cookie and chose a seat by the window, where the warm rays of the late afternoon sun slanted inside.

He sipped the coffee and gathered his jumbled thoughts. He'd never wished for relationships like Julian and Zach had; it was his belief that a person couldn't remain monogamous. And for what purpose? Sex with the same person ultimately became tedious and repetitive. Half of the fun was the thrill of the chase, the ultimate surrender, and a new body to explore. Reminding himself of his plans for later that evening and sexy Antonio, he texted him.

Have any plans for later?

His phone buzzed back almost immediately.

I'm wide open.

That brought a smile to Marcus's face.

Keep that position for later. He didn't wait for a response; he knew Antonio was hot for it. He'd been giving Marcus signals since he'd started. Tonight they'd both get what they wanted.

With his friends paired up now and maddeningly domesticated, he waited for one of them to complain about boredom setting in, but to his surprise, no one had. Instead, they fed off one another and became stronger; Zach especially had come into his own and no longer shied away from expressing his opinion or asserting his wants and desires. And damn it all if Sam didn't act inordinately pleased and happy to give Zach exactly what he asked for. And Nick had smoothed Julian's brittle edges, making him less controlling and rigid.

Were Zach and Julian now weak, having given up their independence by falling in love? He'd never dare say something to Julian's face, but Marcus had carefully watched his friend since his rekindled relationship with Nick to see if he'd be proven right. Surprisingly, Julian remained the same: infuriatingly insightful and honest in his convictions. In all their years together he'd never known Julian to be a prevaricator.

But if he was wrong, that meant the foundation of what he'd built his own life on was faulty, constructed on a base no stronger than the clouds in the sky. He drank his coffee, heedless to its cooled bitter taste. It all began when Tyler expressed disbelief that Marcus could be nice, forcing him to question who he was as a man.

Marcus had always lived by his own code of ethics, and while most people didn't understand, it made sense to him: He didn't believe in cheating, which explained why he never wanted a relationship or a steady lover. He never lied, because he had nothing to hide. Life was too short and meant to be lived in the moment. Planning in advance for the future set a person up for heartbreak because, as he'd discovered at an early age, eventually everyone would let you down.

His phone vibrated and with an exasperated sigh, he pulled it out of his pocket. Of course it was Zach with a long text.

> *We're sorry if you're upset with us, but you know we didn't mean to tease you. Don't hide from us, Marcus. We won't let you shut us out. And don't hide from your heart.*

When had his life become a movie of the week? He grimaced, and without answering, slid the phone back in his pocket, collected his undrinkable coffee and the cookie he'd crumbled into an inedible mountain of crumbs, and tossed them in the trash. That familiar itch returned, and his body warmed, his neglected libido stirring. What he needed now, more than well-meaning friends and a hot-bodied dancer with the face of an angel who kissed like a porn star, was release. Antonio's shift had already started, and Marcus wondered if he'd be up for a quickie to take the edge off.

His phone buzzed again. Maybe the time had come to get an unlisted number.

"Get off my fucking back already."

"Marcus, where are you?"

"Darius?" Dread slid up his spine, chilling him. "What's wrong?"

"It's Tyler. Come to the club now."

"On my way." He hit the door to the coffee house so hard it bounced back on its hinges several times, but he paid no mind and took off running to find a cab.

Chapter Eight

"UNCLE TY, WILL you teach me to dance like you?"

Lillie sat cross-legged on the floor of the living room and watched as he practiced. This had become their daily routine from the beginning, after his sister Amber said one morning she'd be right back and never returned. For weeks afterward, Lillie suffered from nightmares, and bit by bit had told him in her sad little voice of his sister's drug habit and the parade of strange men in their lives.

Tyler shuddered to think of what might have eventually happened to his sweet little niece and vowed that even if his sister came back, he'd fight her in court if she tried to take Lillie and leave. If it ever came to that, he'd be more than happy to march into Marcus's office and accept that offer of a lawyer.

"Sure, honey. Stand up and put your feet together like this." He showed her all the different ballet positions he learned when he was only a little older than her, when he first fell in love with dance. He'd go to the library and look at books on ballet, then memorize how he should stand. He'd practice at home and try to sneak in some time at school as well where none of the other boys would see him. Later on, when Mrs. Henderson noticed him staying late in the gym after school, struggling to do his exercises, she knew enough to keep it secret, but to his delight, she taught him everything she knew from her time as an alternate with the Alvin Ailey dance crew.

And Lillie was better at four than he had been at thirteen. Even on her chubby baby legs, she possessed a natural grace and charm that startled him. He took her hand, and they danced around the apartment until they were both breathless and laughing.

"Enough," he groaned, flopping down on the sofa. "You're too much for me." But he held out his arms and with giggles galore, Lillie crawled on top of him and rested her head on his chest. Little puffs of her sweet breath drifted across his neck, and an overwhelming sense of loss stole through him at all the joy his sister missed by skipping out and leaving her. Before Amber had turned up at his door Tyler hadn't even been aware of Lillie's existence, but now that he'd had her in his life for the past two years, the hounds of hell couldn't pry her away from him.

He'd almost drifted off to sleep when a knock sounded on the door. He jerked awake and winced at the painful dig of Lillie's knees and elbows as she propelled herself off him.

"I'll get it. Let me get it."

He heaved himself off the sofa and raced to the door, knowing with absolute certainty Lillie would open the door without asking who it was, and since he wasn't her official guardian, he always remained on guard and kept her presence a secret.

"Wait a minute, please. Remember what I told you."

She skidded to a stop in front of the door and gazed up at him with reproach in her eyes. "I know. I wasn't gonna open the door. I just wanted to see who it was."

He peeked through the keyhole to see the diminutive figure of their next-door neighbor, Sylvia Kirsch, standing there. Breathing a sigh of relief, he undid the battalion of locks he'd had installed when Lillie came to live with him and threw open the door.

"Hi, Mrs. Kirsch." It never ceased to amaze Tyler how fresh and chipper the elderly lady looked, no matter what time of the day he saw her.

She frowned. "I've told you to call me Sylvia, haven't I?" She peered around him, her eyes blinking owlishly behind her huge, purple-framed glasses. "Where's my little Lillie? Is she going to keep me company while I do my baking today?"

"Yes." Lillie poked her head out from behind him.

"Thanks, Sylvia. You know you're a lifesaver." He stepped to the side for her to enter and watched as Lillie hugged their neighbor.

It had taken a week for it to sink in before he realized Amber had left for good and Lillie was his responsibility. He'd been lugging the stroller up the front steps to the apartment building when Mrs. Kirsch, the self-appointed mayor of their block and knower of all goings-on, had stopped him and offered to look after Lillie. When he was working days as a waiter, Sylvia would stay in their apartment. Once he started working late nights, Lillie would stay in Sylvia's second bedroom, and Tyler would bring her home around four a.m. and put her to bed back in their apartment. It was far from an ideal situation, but it was all he could afford right now, until he made enough money to hire someone to watch her in his apartment all night.

Sylvia's kindness had proved to be a godsend to him. Lillie adored her, and Sylvia got a surrogate granddaughter to spoil. The two of them spent hours together, and Sylvia, a former schoolteacher, had begun teaching Lillie to read. That eased his worry because he didn't have money for a private preschool, nor did he have the papers to prove he was Lillie's legal guardian. Plus, he didn't want her natural curiosity and inquisitive nature to be stifled because he couldn't properly provide for her.

"How about some hot cocoa?" Tyler shut the door and went to the kitchen. "Or I could make some coffee before I leave for work."

"You don't have to do anything. We have everything under control, don't we, Lillie?"

"Yes, Uncle Ty. We're gonna bake brownies, and Grandma Sylvia said we can make princess crowns 'cause we're reading princess stories."

He chuckled, happy to disappear and not get covered in the inevitable glitter extravaganza. "Okay. I'll see you tomorrow morning. I have to get ready."

Tyler quickly showered, dressed, and packed up his bag with his outfit for the evening and toiletries for his post-work routine. After a dutiful peck on the cheek from Lillie and a brief discussion with Sylvia about making sure Lillie didn't take advantage of her—which he knew would be promptly ignored as soon as he walked out the door—he left.

The air flowed clean and fresh through his slightly damp hair, rustling the last of the late autumn leaves on the trees. Twilight had already descended upon the city, bathing the sky in its murky darkness. Porch lights snapped on, and lamps glowed behind curtains as he passed the well-kept single-family homes lining the street on his way to the train. He liked to play a mental game, imagining the people living in these beautiful houses, secretly wishing he could one day afford something nicer for Lillie than the slightly run-down one-bedroom they lived in now, especially since the small, dingy bedroom she slept in faced a brick wall.

He ran to catch the train, hearing its squeal of brakes as it slowed to pull into the station. Breathing hard, he found a seat on the surprisingly empty subway car, stuck in his headphones, and turned on his music. He used this downtime to plan his dances for the evening. Contrary to what most people thought, he didn't simply go out on the dance floor, shake his ass, and display his crotch.

When he got to the club, he'd meet with the DJ, and he'd discuss the choice of music he wanted for the night. In the month and a half that he'd been working at Sparks, he'd become enough of an attraction that Marcus agreed to give him a headliner status for part of the evening. The other dancers complained at first, but Marcus, in his usual, flippant attitude, told them to either step it up or shut up.

Marcus.

They'd been cordial but nothing more to each other since the morning Marcus had shown up at Tyler's apartment and kissed him into such a state of oblivion Tyler swore his toes remained permanently curled. Perhaps finding out he was the sole provider for a four-year-old child had finally dampened the strange attraction that always seemed to spark whenever they were together. Marcus was the furthest thing from a father figure Tyler could imagine.

He reached his stop and exited the train, then hurried up the stairs. The sky had darkened from the lavender of twilight to inky blue and not many people were about. It was an in-between time of the early evening when many people were either at home, making dinner plans, or finishing up their shopping before heading home.

Tyler turned the corner on Varick St. and headed toward the back entrance of Sparks when he heard footsteps rushing toward him. With no chance to react, he found himself thrown up against the wall beside the door used as the employee entrance for the club. His head connected with the rough concrete and stars exploded in his eyes, rendering him incapable of movement.

Taking advantage of his momentary incompetence, the men grabbed him under his arms and propelled him down an alley, heedless to his flailing legs and moaning. His head felt as though it had split apart.

"Shut up, faggot or you'll end up with no teeth."

Chilled by the flat deadliness of the assailant's voice, Tyler remained quiet. If they killed him, what would happen to Lillie? He had no time to think of anything else as punches began to rain down on his body. Instinctively Tyler attempted to protect himself by curling into a ball, but the men continued to beat him until he sagged between them. At that point they dropped him, and after aiming a few swift kicks at his kidneys, took his phone and smashed it to the ground, then took off running.

He had no idea how long he lay there, blinded by pain and unable to take a deep breath. The metallic taste of blood filled his mouth, and he moaned. Several minutes passed before he felt safe enough to check how badly he was hurt. His arms and legs moved without difficulty, but when he tried to sit up the pain flashed through his side so piercingly white hot he cried out loud. Tyler suspected he had at least one broken rib if not more, considering the beating he took.

Taking in short breaths that didn't force him to inhale too deeply,

Tyler began the long, arduous task of crawling out from the alley to the street in an attempt to get help. After what seemed like hours, he'd just made it back to the opening of the alleyway when he heard heavy footsteps. Cringing, fearful that the men had returned to finish him off, Tyler held his breath.

"What the hell?" A familiar voice rang out in the dark. "Are you hurt, man?"

"Darius...help me." Tyler could barely formulate the words; the excruciating pain that seared through his chest wiped out the last ounce of his strength.

"Tyler?" Darius's voice rose with anxiety. "Holy shit, man, what happened? Hold on; I'm getting help."

"No, no ambulance. Just some broken ribs."

"You need to go to the hospital."

He licked his impossibly dry lips. "No insurance. Help me up, please."

With a gentleness that belied his size, Darius assisted him to his feet. For a moment he swayed and his vision blurred, turning gray at the edges. Nausea threatened, then receded. He breathed, increasing his inhalations until he could determine how far he could push himself. After several moments he managed a weak smile.

"Thanks. I think I'll be all right."

"The fuck you will." Darius yelled, holding him steady. "You need medical attention."

"I think it's just a few broken ribs. I can get it taped up, and it'll be fine." His face itched from the blood that had dripped down from his hairline to his jaw.

"I'm calling Marcus."

Tyler opened his mouth to protest, but at Darius's harsh glare, he wisely kept this mouth shut as Darius pulled out his phone and made the call.

"Marcus, where are you?"

The phone was too far away for him to hear Marcus on the other end.

"It's Tyler. Come to the club now." Darius shoved his phone into his pocket and with Tyler leaning heavily on his shoulder walked with him back down the alleyway and into the side entrance of the club. Once inside, Darius guided him to Marcus's office and helped him find a comfortable position on the sofa.

"Do you want a glass of water?" Darius hovered, his dark gaze searching Tyler's. "How do you feel?"

Tyler winced through his smile. "Like I got jumped in an alley." He tipped his head back and stared at the ceiling; his body ached, and he wondered how long he'd be out of commission and unable to dance now that he was injured. If Marcus fired him now, he had enough saved away for only three months' rent. After that he'd have to make the choice of unemployment and food stamps, which he loathed, or moving from the city, which tore at his heart. Succumbing to the sudden weakness that swept through his aching body, Tyler closed his eyes.

He dozed off, only to be suddenly awakened when the door to the office banged open and a wild-eyed Marcus rushed in. Nervous anticipation curled at the base of Tyler's spine, but he remained silent, too hurt and exhausted to speak.

"What the fuck happened? Where's Tyler?"

Darius gestured toward the sofa. Marcus, catching a glimpse of him, rushed to his side but stopped short of touching him. Instead, to Tyler's shock, Marcus knelt before him and placed a hand lightly on his knee.

"Ty?"

His nickname on Marcus's lips broke Tyler's composure. A bossy, arrogant Marcus he could deal with. But a concerned and caring Marcus didn't place on his radar. Inexplicable tears filled his eyes, and he blinked furiously, willing himself to regain some measure of composure.

"I'm all right."

"Don't fucking lie to me. You look like shit. Talk to me." His voice didn't rise above its usual quiet tone, but Tyler knew Marcus well enough now to sense the anger bubbling below the surface.

"I got jumped. It happens all the time in the city. Unfortunately, tonight was my turn. I think I may have cracked some ribs, 'cause it hurts to breathe." He pressed his hand to his side and winced. The skin felt tender and hot beneath his shirt.

"Then why are you here and not in the hospital? You need an X-ray." Marcus pulled out his phone. "I'll call an ambulance right now. And you should call the cops and make a report."

"No." He shifted on the sofa and a white-hot bolt of pain sliced through him. "Shit, that hurts."

"You're in no position to tell me no."

"I can because I have no insurance to pay for the hospital bills."

Marcus's jaw tightened, and Tyler could see the muscle jumping beneath his skin. "I'll pay for it. This is your health, and you got hurt coming to work at my club."

"No. I can't accept that."

"You're being a fucking asshole." Marcus stood and fumed as he paced the room, his phone in his hand. He stopped short and stared hard at Tyler for a second before touching his screen, obviously dialing someone.

"I said I'm not—"

"Shut up for a second. Hello, Micah? It's Marcus. Yeah, listen. A friend of mine has been hurt really bad and needs X-rays but has no insurance. Who do you know that can help?"

Tyler gaped at him. "You can't do that."

"Yeah, I can hold." Marcus quirked his brow and covered the phone with his hand. "I can do whatever I want, and that includes having my friends help you." They waited for several minutes before he turned his attention back to his phone call. "Yeah? She'll do it for him tonight? Great, thanks. Tell her we'll be there in fifteen minutes tops." Marcus ended the call and his cocky-bastard grin resurfaced. "You're in luck. My doctor friend Micah called an orthopedist, and she's agreed to see you at the hospital."

Despite his throbbing side, Tyler continued to argue with Marcus. "I told you no. I can't pay, especially now that I'm going to be out of a job."

"Who says you're out of a job?"

As if he was explaining a difficult lesson to a child, Tyler held his patience in check. "It's obvious I can't dance anymore, and I'll be out of commission for who knows how long. You're going to have to replace me."

"Is that what you think? That I'm going to toss you out because you're hurt and can't dance?"

To Tyler's surprise, Marcus joined him on the sofa, close enough that he could sense his body heat and smell his subtle cologne, but not touching.

"Do you remember when I hired you I said we're like a big family here?"

Tyler did and thought nothing of it at the time. It sounded like one of those clichés any business owner would make up to convince a prospective employee to work for them.

"Yeah."

"Well, I take care of my family. I'm going to take care of you now, Tyler. You have nothing to worry about except recuperating, so shut up and let's get to the hospital."

Marcus slid a bracing arm around his shoulder to help him stand and for the first time in forever, Tyler understood what it felt like to be protected and safe.

Chapter Nine

MARCUS COULDN'T RECALL a more hellish night. Even with the "in" of knowing the orthopedist, it took more than five hours before Tyler was seen and taken in for X-rays. Frustrated at being left behind in the waiting area, he knew he annoyed the nurses with his constant questions about Tyler's condition, but the vision of the man's bloodied and beaten face remained imprinted in his mind, vividly there every time he closed his eyes.

The clock moved past midnight and with his barely restrained patience already thinned to the snapping point, Marcus attempted to slip into the Emergency Room, but the nurses impeded his progress.

"Sir. Where are you going? Only family members are allowed."

He'd already decided no one would stop him from seeing Tyler. Thinking fast, Marcus turned on his most charming smile. "I am family. We're engaged to be married. He just said yes, and now he's hurt, and I can't bear to be apart from him." He blinked and rubbed the corner of his eye.

The nurse's stern face softened. "Oh, that's so sad. I hope your boyfriend checks out okay." After consulting a sheet of paper, she pointed at the swinging doors with her pencil. "He's in Room 7. Through the doors, down the hall, and to your left."

Marcus flashed her a grin and took off, entering the chaotic world of the ER. Nurses and doctors rushed past him; patients lay on gurneys, presumably waiting for an open room; police officers and EMS workers congregated around the central station, filling out forms and talking.

There were small, curtained-off areas running along each wall. Marcus counted off the numbers until he reached 7 and pulled aside the curtain.

Tyler lay on a hospital bed with his eyes closed. His chest barely rose from his shallow breaths, and he looked worse than he did when Marcus first saw him at Sparks, as the bruising had settled in, mottling his face and neck in purple and brown splotches. Lucky for Tyler, they hadn't broken his nose or an eye socket.

A savage need to hurt the person who did this to Tyler choked Marcus. "Oh, Ty, what did they do to you?" Making sure he didn't put pressure on the damaged skin, Marcus stroked Tyler's cheek with his fingertips. "Don't worry. I'll take care of everything."

A woman in her late thirties came in. "Are you Micah's friend?" At his nod, she introduced herself. "I'm Dr. Lerner, the orthopedist. Your friend here has a few cracked ribs. Due to the extensive bruising from the beating he received, I had them check out his spleen and his kidneys but luckily they're clean. I'm having him stay the night for observation to make sure he doesn't have a concussion."

"That's good." Marcus approved of this doctor and her no-nonsense attitude.

"He may not even get to a room. We're very backed up with real emergencies." She checked Tyler's chart. "Are you going home tonight?"

There was no reason for him to stay any longer. Tyler's condition seemed stable, and Marcus had a club to run. He thought of Antonio and his planned hook-up for tonight. And technically, Marcus could do nothing for Tyler by remaining at the hospital. He'd be watched, and they'd let him know if there was any change in his condition.

"I'll be staying. Thank you for your help, and please make sure you forward any bills for his care to me." Tyler didn't know it yet, but he'd be coming back home with Marcus instead of returning to that wretched little apartment in the bowels of Brooklyn.

Dr. Lerner was halfway out of the curtained-off area when she answered. "Fill out the paperwork when you go back outside. We gave him a shot, so he should sleep for a few more hours."

Then she was gone, leaving him alone with a sleeping Tyler and his own confused thoughts. He sat in one of the hard, uncomfortable chairs next to the bed and stretched out his legs, dropping his head in his hands. What the fuck was he really doing here? With the bet over, he could be in bed with the hot and willing Antonio instead of sitting in a grungy, smelly emergency room with a man who never expressed anything but lukewarm approval for him.

Marcus knew most of the men he took to bed only did so because they thought they'd get something out of him. He made no promises of a future or even a second night. There hadn't been a time in recent memory he hadn't gotten a man into bed with little effort, except for Tyler.

That hot kiss they'd shared had only juiced him up for more; he wanted more of Tyler. He wanted all of him.

The raw sexuality of Tyler's dancing coupled with his complete immersion in the music mesmerized Marcus. Seeing him move on the dance floor, Marcus knew he'd be a wildcat in bed and wanted to be the one to uncage Tyler's beast. The unexpected hands-off attitude and prickly behavior were a change for him—a challenge. That must be it, Marcus mused as he closed his eyes. He only desired Tyler because he had to work to get him.

A CURIOUS BEEPING noise infiltrated his brain. Why did he have an alarm set? He didn't need to get up in the morning.

"Marcus?"

His eyelids fluttered open to the sight of a hospital room instead of his bedroom. His neck hurt and his legs were contorted in a pretzel-like position. He untangled himself from the chair he'd fallen asleep in after they moved Tyler to a room last night around three a.m., and walked over to the hospital bed where Tyler lay wide-awake.

Tyler stared up at him, confusion apparent in his furrowed brow, but Marcus noticed his bright, pain-free eyes.

"Hey, how're you feeling?"

"Like someone punched my guts in." He licked his lips. "Is there any water? I'm really thirsty."

Marcus took the plastic cup from the swing table next to the bed and poured Tyler a small glass. "Let me raise the bed for you so you don't spill it." Tyler nodded and Marcus pressed the button and watched the head of the bed raise up a few inches before stopping. "Here. Drink it slow."

Tyler gave him a searching look but said nothing and drank his water. His head fell back on the pillow, and he closed his eyes.

"What are you doing here?"

"That's not very nice. How about: 'Thanks Marcus for staying the night. I appreciate it.'"

He grinned at Tyler who rolled his eyes. "Thanks Marcus for staying the night. I appreciate it." He sighed. "But why are you here? And what time is it anyway?"

Marcus consulted his watch. "It's seven a.m. The doctor said last night when they brought you into the room here that if you didn't show any signs of a concussion, they'd spring you out sometime this morning."

"Okay. But that doesn't answer my question about what you're doing here."

"I stayed to make sure you were okay, plus I'm taking you home when you're discharged."

"I can call a cab." Tyler winced as he sat up. "I'm fine, and it doesn't hurt nearly as bad as it did yesterday." His fingers touched his side. "They have me taped up pretty well."

"Let me see." Before Tyler responded, Marcus placed his hand over Tyler's rib cage and felt the bulky bandage through the thin fabric of the hospital gown. He slid his hand around Tyler's waist.

"Marcus, stop," Tyler warned.

"Stop what?" He might be far from innocent, but he could play the part.

"Oh, am I interrupting?" A nurse walked in with a tray and a thermometer. "I'm sorry, but I have to give him his meds and take his BP and temperature."

"I hope you're taking it rectally. I was always told it gave the most accurate reading. Is that true?" He stepped away from the bed and winked at the nurse, who broke out in laughter.

"Marcus, shut up," said Tyler, not even trying to hide the exasperation in his voice.

"Oh Marcus, you're silly." She bit her lips to stop her amusement. "Don't worry, Mr. Reiss. Your boyfriend is right, but we take it by the eardrum method. It's very accurate as well." She busied herself, unaware of Tyler's glare. "Just relax now."

After finishing, she pulled away the blood pressure machine and smiled. "Very good. All your vitals are excellent. How's your head?"

"Hard as a rock," Marcus spoke before Tyler could answer.

"Oh, you're a kidder." She patted him on his arm. "I think it's sweet the way you stayed here all night to make sure everything was okay. And now you get to take him home and baby him."

Watching Tyler grow angrier by the minute was a better show than anything he'd ever watched on television. "I'm looking forward to it. I may have to borrow a nurse outfit."

The nurse's laughter followed her out the door, but Tyler was having none of it. Seeing the hostility in his blue-gray eyes, Marcus girded himself.

"What the hell are you talking about? I'm not going home with you."

"Yes, you are." Marcus scrubbed his face with his hands. "I wonder if they'll give me a toothbrush. My breath must stink."

Watching Tyler struggle to sit up, Marcus rushed over to his bedside to help him up, which only earned him more glowering, but as usual, he ignored Tyler's bad temper.

"Take it slow. You seem to forget you were beaten up pretty badly; lucky for you, the only result is a few cracked ribs."

"Stop it." Tyler shook him off. "I don't understand why you're still here this morning. Shit." A terrified expression clouded his face. "Lillie. Oh my God. What's happening? Where is she?" Hissing in pain, he slid off the bed and grabbed Marcus by the arms. "Who's with her?" Tyler's grip tightened.

Wild-eyed and without waiting for Marcus to respond, Tyler limped over to where Marcus had laid his clothes out. Even with the pain medication, trying to reach behind himself to untie his hospital gown proved too much.

"Can you help me please? I need to get dressed and get out of here."

"Tyler, relax. I took care of Lillie." Marcus gestured to the bed. "Get back into bed."

If it wasn't such a serious situation, Marcus might've laughed at the expression of shock and fear on Tyler's face.

"What do you mean, you took care of her? Where is she?" A horrified expression crossed his face. "You didn't bring her to the club, did you?"

"Don't be an asshole; of course not." Injured or not, Marcus had no problem snapping back at Tyler's ludicrous suggestion. "I called your house and that lady, Mrs. Kirsch, was happy to stay with her the whole day."

Tyler nodded with relief but didn't get into bed. "Okay, yeah, thanks, but I have to get home."

"No." Marcus planted himself in front of Tyler. "You can't go home and live by yourself and take care of a little girl. That apartment is up six flights of stairs. You don't even have a bed to sleep on."

A muscle jumped in Tyler's jaw, and Marcus wanted to cover it with his mouth and lick it. "I'll be fine."

"I know you will be, because I already arranged for Mrs. Kirsch to bring Lillie to my house, and you and she can stay there while you recover."

"You're out of your fucking mind. I'm going home, and if I need anything, Sylvia—Mrs. Kirsch—will help me."

This was more like it. He enjoyed sparring with Tyler, and watching him get all self-righteous was a big turn-on for him.

He folded his arms and looked into Tyler's angry eyes. "Too late."

To his shock, Tyler shoved him backward. "You can't take over my life, Marcus; you don't own me."

Careful of Tyler's injuries, Marcus slid his hands around Tyler's neck and pulled him close. His skin felt soft and warm, and the silky curls at the nape of his neck slid through his fingers. Despite the heat in the room, Tyler shivered, and Marcus suppressed a smile with the knowledge that his touch affected Tyler.

"Trust me, when I do own you, you're going to know it."

Chapter Ten

LIFE WAS PROVING to be one series of disasters after another for him. Tyler fumed, but during the night when he'd been knocked out cold by the medication, Marcus had charmed and befriended everyone in the hospital, so not only did everyone agree he should go home with Marcus, they all believed they were a couple.

The doctor had come by to give him medical clearance to leave, and Marcus, sensing he would bolt at the first likelihood, stood sentry by the door, talking to his doctor friend, Micah, who had arranged for his care. After finishing in the bathroom, Tyler approached the two men.

"Thank you for all your help last night. I really appreciate it." He held out his hand. The doctor took his hand.

Micah Steinberg, as his name tag identified him, reminded Tyler of Marcus. Not only in the physical appearance – they both had a similar self-confidence in their mannerisms.

"Not a problem. I'm glad Dr. Lerner could help."

He ran an assessing eye over Tyler, but unlike Marcus, whose frank gaze sent a multitude of confusing, sexual responses through his body, Micah Steinberg's look was purely professional. Tyler caught a glimpse of a wedding band on the man's hand. Micah noticed his stare and gave him a surprisingly sweet smile.

"Sorry," said Tyler, his face growing hot. "I didn't mean to stare."

"Not a problem. My husband is a lawyer, and Marcus was telling me you have your niece living with you. If you ever need any legal help, give us a call."

His heart stuttered to almost a full stop, and furious, he rounded on Marcus. "Why would you tell a complete stranger about my life? You have no right."

Micah took him by the arm and walked him back inside the room. "I may be a stranger to you, but I'm Marcus's friend, and I have two young children of my own. If you ever need anything, my husband, Josh, and I are happy to help."

"It's not you I'm upset with; it's him." Tyler indicated Marcus, who'd remained at the door. "He swooped in and thinks he's in control of my life."

Micah chuckled. "Yeah, he's like that with everything. His way is the only way."

"Right?" Tyler nodded in agreement. "He's impossible. I don't need someone like him to run my life. I'm fine as is."

"Are you, really?" Micah's silvery eyes bore into him. "Marcus told me a little about you, so understand that I'm not passing judgment. But this isn't only about you; there's a child involved."

Tyler opened his mouth to argue, but Micah held up a hand.

"Hear me out before you jump to conclusions about Marcus. I'm guessing by the extent of your anger you don't know Marcus very well. What you call interfering, he considers helping."

"I didn't ask to be helped. I'm not a charity case," Tyler interjected, frustrated that his opinion was shunted off to the side.

"I don't think helping a friend temporarily makes you a charity case. You're thinking about yourself again, while I'm looking at it from the point of view of what's best for the child. Isn't it better for her to be in a safe place where she wouldn't have to worry about you?"

Begrudgingly, Tyler acquiesced Micah was right, even though he hated to give Marcus the satisfaction. "I don't understand why he's doing this for me, though. We aren't friends, or even that close."

Micah's phone buzzed, and Tyler had a chance to see his screensaver, which showed Micah with his arm around another man, presumably Micah's husband, two young children, and a shepherd dog. Nice to know some people found happiness.

"Hey, babe. Yeah. Just finishing up with Marcus's friend, and then I'll be home to have lunch with the kids." He listened for a moment. "Okay. Love you too."

Without missing a step, Micah continued the conversation. "I can't speak for him, but what I do know is that Marcus doesn't do this for just anyone. Perhaps there's more between you than either one of you realize or are willing to admit."

With those puzzling words, Micah said goodbye and walked out with Marcus to the elevators. That gave Tyler a chance to collect his belongings and ponder Micah's words. Was it possible that Marcus was doing this because he was, in fact, a nice person, or, as Tyler initially suspected, did he have an ulterior motive, such as getting Tyler into bed?

He'd lived so long on his wits and instinct that, unfortunately, it made him leery of most people offering him any type of support. But Micah was right—this was about what was best for Lillie, not him. The thought of climbing all those stairs everyday made him cringe; but even worse, he knew he'd be trapped in his apartment for several weeks while he healed, and that would be unfair to Lillie. And Sylvia wasn't going to be able to watch her as of next week; she was heading down to Florida to be with her own grandchildren.

With all the extra money he'd been making from the tips he'd earned, he'd planned to enroll her in a regular preschool so she could benefit from being around other children, but now that possibility had vanished in a puff of smoke.

Marcus returned and leaned in the doorway, more serious than Tyler recalled seeing before. Not for the first time in his life, Tyler wished for a crystal ball to be able to see into the future and know exactly what would happen between the two of them. Wishful thinking on his part; he knew that a man like Marcus, who lived in and for the moment, wouldn't understand that Tyler's first priority would always be to provide a safe and stable environment for Lillie.

But a few weeks of recuperation at Marcus's apartment would be doable, and, he justified to himself, Lillie would be able to go outside. He could even take short walks with her.

"I'll come but only on the condition that when I'm able to work again you let me pay off what I owe you."

Marcus scowled. "That's stupid. You're my guest. I don't charge guests rent." He left the doorway to place himself in front of Tyler as if to barricade his way. "Why are you being so pigheaded?" His expression turned stormier.

Taunting Marcus enabled him to forget the pain in his side and the fact that he'd be broke within a month, and Tyler grinned inwardly seeing the man standing before him glowering. He knew now he had the upper hand. "Fine. Then we don't come." He looked for his phone, then remembered he no longer had one; it had gotten smashed to pieces in the alley. Another expense he'd have to come up with somehow.

"Once I'm checked out, I'll get a cab and go home. You can send Lillie and Sylvia back this afternoon." He limped past Marcus who put a staying hand on his shoulder.

"Please, Tyler. I don't know why you're being so stubborn, but can't you see this is the best solution for everyone involved? You'll have a place to stay, and your niece will be taken care of."

Marcus turned him around and held him closer, and Tyler couldn't help but sink into his strength. His body ached from the assault, yet for some bizarre reason Tyler wanted Marcus's hands on him. That odd sense of security flowed through him, settling his heartbeat to a steady rhythm.

"Okay, but I'm not sleeping with you. That isn't part of the arrangement."

A devilish light entered Marcus's eyes. "Once again, I don't recall asking you. And you know what they say."

Before Tyler could answer, Marcus brushed their lips together, then nuzzled into the space where Tyler's neck met his shoulder.

"Never say never."

NOTHING PREPARED HIM for the luxury of Marcus's apartment building in Tribeca; certainly not for a doorman who opened his cab door, tipped his hat, and held the door for them, or the concierge waiting behind the highly polished wood-and-marble front desk. Tyler smiled faintly at the doorman as he eased out of the cab.

"Thank you very much."

"Raymond." Marcus shook the concierge's hand. "This is Tyler Reiss. He and his little niece will be staying with me."

Raymond's eyes lit up in his round face. "Ahh, little Miss Lillie? She's a sweetheart for sure."

For the first time today, Tyler's smile didn't feel forced. "Thank you."

"My pleasure, sir."

With a gentle touch to his shoulder, Marcus pointed him to a bank of elevators down the hallway. "Let's go upstairs and see her."

Tyler smiled farewell at Raymond and, leaning more heavily on Marcus's arm than he thought he'd have to, walked slowly. His side and back hurt, his jaw ached, and he wanted nothing more than to lie down. Despair swept over him like a sandstorm, encompassing him head to toe.

Marcus spoke into his ear. "Don't worry. It's going to be all right. I promised you a place to stay, and you and Lillie have it, as long as you need."

Overcome by a tangled set of emotions Tyler couldn't identify, he merely nodded and let Marcus lead him.

Tyler didn't know what to expect, but what he didn't envisage was an elegantly furnished, contemporary apartment in shades of gray, black, and cream, with splashes of random colors like flowers blooming. Tall windows overlooked the water, and Tyler could see boats chugging down the Hudson River.

He dropped his small backpack on the floor near the entrance and saw Lillie running to him. She skidded to a stop in front of him, her round eyes filling with tears that spilled down her cheeks. Sylvia stood behind her, a distressed look on her face.

"Uncle Ty. Your face is full of boo-boos. Doesn't it hurt?"

"I'll be fine after a few days' rest." Forcing a smile, Tyler hoped his words reassured her. He took a few shuffling steps toward the most comfortable-looking sofa he'd ever seen, knowing that if he didn't sit down soon, he'd collapse in a heap on the floor. Panicky at the thought of this happening in front of an already upset Lillie, he gazed at Marcus in mute appeal as his legs trembled.

As if he could read his mind, Marcus put a strong arm across his back and helped him, not to that long, buttery-soft leather sofa, but to a hallway and, as Tyler saw when they halted in a doorway, a spacious bedroom with a king-size bed in the center.

A wave of exhaustion rolled over him, drowning him, and to his mortification, he sagged against Marcus. "Why am I so tired?"

"Your meds make you sleepy, and you're still in recovery."

Without Tyler even realizing it, Marcus led him to the bed and helped him lie down.

"Try to get some sleep."

He thought Marcus's lips brushed his own before he fell asleep.

Chapter Eleven

AFTER SENDING MRS. KIRSCH home with the promise that Tyler would call her and let her know more about his condition, Marcus found himself staring at Lillie, who sat on the floor, playing with a doll. A gnawing sense of panic rose in his chest.

He checked on Tyler, who continued to sleep. For the first time, Marcus was nervous in his own home. As he paced in the living room, he thought about what he could do and realized he had nothing in the house to eat. Kids liked snacks and food. Halle-fucking-lujah, in New York City you can get everything online. Marcus sat down at his desk and opened the computer.

He must've been crazy to bring Tyler and his niece here to stay with him. As usual, he was thinking with his dick not his head.

"Asshole," he muttered to himself.

"Uncle Ty says it's bad to say bad words."

He jumped, not expecting to have this miniature person standing at his elbow. He examined her and decided as children go, she was pretty cute.

"Your uncle is right. I'm sorry."

"What're you doing?" She peered at the computer screen. "Oh, I love that." Lillie pointed to some sugary pastries. "They're yummy."

"Should we get some?" He clicked on the picture, and ten different flavors popped up. "What's your favorite?"

Her answer came out prompt. "Strawberry."

He clicked and ordered two boxes. "Done."

Lillie's eyes shone. "Ooh, can I do it?"

Considering that he never ate a meal at home and only had water and wine in the refrigerator for the overnight guests he might have, this might prove to be a fun activity. "Let's get some other stuff."

"Candy?" she asked hopefully.

Even he knew that wasn't what he should be ordering. He quirked a brow at the little girl. "How about some fruit?"

Forty-five minutes later, Marcus had ordered enough food to feed a family of four for a month. He closed the laptop and to his surprise, Lillie remained at his side looking at him with those big eyes that reminded him of Tyler. Nervous again, he stood and went into the kitchen, but she followed him.

"I'm thirsty."

"I can give you some water." He opened the refrigerator and found a container of orange juice and milk he knew wasn't there the last time he was home. "Or milk or orange juice."

"Juice, please."

Marcus poured her a glass and handed it to her. He could do this, he decided. "Why don't you go sit down at the table." It wasn't a real table, but a wide countertop with three high chairs lined up. He pulled out a chair, and she stood next to it with her glass.

"I can't climb up there myself."

Marcus took her glass, and after placing it on the counter, gingerly lifted her up on the seat. He decided he needed a strong cup of coffee and left Lillie sitting to go make a pot.

Crash.

The sound of breaking glass and a gasp sent him running back to her. The glass of juice lay broken on the floor and tears streaked down her crumpled little face.

"I'm sorry; I didn't mean it."

"It's okay." He didn't give a shit about the broken glass and spilled juice. He thought something happened to her and knew Tyler would kill him. "I'll clean it up, and it'll be fine."

He picked up the biggest pieces of glass and threw them in the trash, then, having no idea if he even had a broom, took the roll of paper towels and began to wipe up the spill. Careful of the shards of broken glass, Marcus squatted and finished wiping up the floor.

"See? It's all gone; like it never happened."

"I didn't mean it. I'm sorry. Are you going to send me and Uncle Ty home?" Her lip quivered.

"No. Everyone makes mistakes. And later, we can go on the computer and order you some plastic cups."

"Princess ones?" She sniffled.

He didn't give a shit what kind, as long as she stopped crying.

"What happened?"

From his position on the floor, Marcus glanced up to see a sleepy Tyler leaning against the open doorway.

"I broked a glass." Holding on to the counter so she wouldn't fall, Lillie slid off the stool and ran over to Tyler who gave her a hug.

"Broke," corrected Tyler.

"I said I was sorry. And Marcus and me ordered stuff to eat for later."

Marcus stood and washed his hands. "It was no big deal. I'm sure kids do it all the time. Do you want a drink? Orange juice, milk or water is all I have that is non-alcoholic."

"I'm fine, thanks." A funny smile quirked Tyler's lips. "You don't have to stay and babysit us. I'll be fine. I know you need to get to the club, especially since you missed last night." With slow steps, Tyler walked over to the sofa and settled himself down.

"How are you feeling?" Marcus joined him on the opposite end, while Lillie climbed up and sat next to Tyler.

"Better, actually. I needed the sleep, and I can breathe a bit easier." Lillie wiggled closer to Tyler and laid her head against his arm.

"Good." This was all very domestic and cute and made him antsy as hell. "Um, so I was thinking that since Micah and his husband have twins who are around her age, Lillie might want to go to the same preschool they go to."

A look of confusion crossed Tyler's face. "I can't afford that."

Bracing himself for the inevitable argument, Marcus began to speak. "Hear me out. I know you can't, but I can. And you need to rest and heal so you can come back to work. So I'm willing to gift you the cost of her preschool tuition, which isn't really that much and won't be for long."

"I don't need your charity."

The stubbornness of the man irritated Marcus to no end. "It isn't charity. I'm helping you as a friend and as your employer. I need you to get better so you can come back to the club." He grinned. "Think of it as me protecting my investment."

"I bet you arranged all this at the hospital with Micah, didn't you?"

Busted. When he didn't reply, Tyler gave an exasperated grunt.

"Uncle Ty?"

Startled as if he'd forgotten she was in the room, Tyler glanced down at her. "What is it, honey?"

"It kinda sounds like fun." She bit her lip and looked at him, and Marcus gave her a wink and a little nod. "I wanna go."

"I don't believe this." The irritation in Tyler's voice would have been comical if he wasn't so angry. But Marcus didn't care. Even he knew it would be much better for Lillie to be around other young children than hang around the apartment all day.

"Come on, Ty; you know it'll be good for her. Micah's kids are nice, I'm sure. And I'll make sure she'd get picked up every day and brought home."

"Maybe I can have a playdate sometime." Lillie gave Tyler one of those big-eyed, hopeful looks, and Marcus knew from his own experience she'd get whatever she wanted.

Sticking him with an evil-eyed glower, Tyler kissed the top of Lillie's head. "If that's what you want, okay. It won't be for too long; only until I'm on my feet again and we go home."

Marcus slapped his thighs. "Sounds good. She can start tomorrow."

He checked his watch. "I've got to get to the club now."

"You're leaving?" Lillie frowned. "I thought you were gonna stay with us."

"Marcus has to go to work, honey," said Tyler gently, rubbing her shoulder. "You'll see him tomorrow. Why don't we watch some television?"

Luckily that settled Lillie down and soon she was happily ensconced, watching something pink on the screen. Tyler lay stretched out and relaxed next to her. Shocked at how this picture of domesticated bliss didn't disturb him, Marcus hurried into his bedroom, took a shower, and got dressed.

"I'll call you later to see how it's going. Take it easy, and order whatever you want for dinner. My delivery account has the credit card hooked up." Shoving keys and wallet into his pants, Marcus couldn't wait to leave and get to the club, where he could ignore the uncomfortable sensation bubbling in his stomach. He caught a glimpse of Tyler's puzzled face before he shut the door.

In the cab on the way over, Marcus stared out the window but saw nothing. Nothing in his life seemed to be going as planned. With that stupid bet over, he'd anticipated working his way through the new bartenders in the club and getting back to having a different man every night. Instead, he had a little girl in his home—to whom he'd promised to order "princess cups"—and a crazy, sexy dancer who put up more roadblocks than a construction site.

It was a short ride from his apartment to Sparks and before he noticed, they'd pulled up in front of the club. It was early evening and preparations should be underway. He hoped that without Tyler there the dancers he still had would be enough to draw in a crowd.

"Marcus, how's Tyler?" Darius rushed over, concern etched on his face. "You never called to let me know."

Damn. "Sorry, man. By the time we got into the ER and then all the X-rays and shit, it was like three in the morning. But he looks good, much better than I expected."

"Oh, great." The relief was evident in his voice. "I'll stop by on my way home and check on him."

"Uhh, no need to. I have everything covered." Marcus ran a hand through his hair and, having no desire to stand there and be interrogated, began to walk as he talked. "How'd it go last night? Big crowd?"

Giving him a curious look, Darius followed him. "Yeah. It was pretty packed. People asked for Tyler, but we said he was on vacation for a few weeks."

Marcus nodded with approval. "Good thinking." They reached his office. "Okay, I'm going to go over some figures, then check the stock before we open."

"See you later. Oh, I put in a few of the suggestions Sam made when we walked through the club together."

"Sounds good." He trusted Sam implicitly. "Whatever he suggested could only help us."

After several hours spent running the club's figures, Marcus was interrupted by a knock on the door.

"Enter."

At the sound of a throat clearing, Marcus glanced up to see Antonio standing before him. With his muscled chest gleaming and the club's signature sparkling lycra shorts that left little to the imagination, Antonio was a wet dream come to life.

"Antonio, what can I help you with?" Two hours sitting in a chair made for a stiff back, and he groaned and stretched. "Damn, I'm stiff."

"That's what I'm hoping for," said Antonio as he turned around and locked the door. Amused, Marcus watched him walk behind the chair. His smile broadened and his head tipped back when Antonio's strong hands began to massage his shoulders.

"I've been getting signals from you for weeks, and now that I've got you alone, I figured I'd help you relieve some of that stress." Antonio bent over and kissed the side of Marcus's jaw, then licked down his neck. "But keep the stiff part. I plan on using that in a while." He reached down and gave Marcus's cock a squeeze.

Marcus moaned and bucked into Antonio's touch. It'd been so long since he'd been touched. He reached back with a hand and grabbed Antonio, bringing their lips together, even as he writhed under Antonio's expert handling.

Their mouths clashed in a hard and brutal kiss. Antonio ate at his mouth; his tongue plunged hard and thick and normally he liked it fast and dirty. But now it seemed…practiced. Like a plan with steps to be checked off one by one. And Marcus expected softer lips and kisses that were sweeter and more searching. Confused, he broke away and wiped his mouth on his sleeve.

Unheeding of Marcus's internal warfare, Antonio spun his chair around. "Oh man, lemme me suck you off real quick." He sank to his knees in front of Marcus, fondling himself as he spoke.

Typically Marcus would simply spread his legs and have the man go at it. He couldn't remember how many times this scenario had played out in this office with too many men to name. From the moment Antonio had been hired, all Marcus had thought about was getting a piece of his ass.

But plans change, sending everything you thought you knew about yourself spinning out of control. Marcus knew if he fucked Antonio right now, any chance he'd have with Tyler would be lost. From that brief time in Tyler's kitchen that had rocked Marcus's world, when Tyler had entered his mind and never left, Marcus had been intrigued and entrapped; he wanted all of Tyler, everything he had to give.

Cupping Antonio's jaw in his hand, Marcus kissed him slowly and not without some regret. "I may be the biggest asshole on the face of the earth, but I have to say no. At least for now."

Antonio sat back on his heels. "You're kidding right? I thought we were gonna get together."

"Things changed, and I can't."

His cell phone rang, and seeing it was his home number, his heart began to bang against his ribs. "Ty? Are you all right?"

"Hey, um, Marcus? Sorry to bother you."

"It's no bother. Is everything okay?"

"Yes, I'm sorry, but Lillie made me call you. She said you told her she could buy something, but I'm not sure she's telling the truth."

Curious now, Marcus heard Tyler shush Lillie and her protesting. He couldn't help grinning when Lillie came on the phone.

"Marcus?"

"Yes, who's this?" He bit his lip to keep from laughing out loud. She really was a cute kid.

"It's me, Lillie. Remember you promised me that I could order pink princess cups? Uncle Ty doesn't believe me, so I made him call you."

He chuckled. "Yes I did. Tell your uncle I said you could order as many princess cups as you want."

The squeal of approval nearly broke his eardrum, but he couldn't contain his laughter, even after he hung up the phone.

"It's Ty, ain't it?"

Marcus had completely forgotten about the sexy bartender he once couldn't wait to get his hands on.

A light dawned in Antonio's eyes. "I had a feeling." He stood and adjusted his cock in the tight confines of his shorts. "I didn't think you were into relationships and stuff. Everyone told me you were always up for some good times." He walked to the door and unlocked it. "Lemme know when you're back in the game, and we can hook up." Then he was gone.

Marcus stared at the door for a long time afterward, wondering what the hell was happening to him.

Chapter Twelve

TWO WEEKS INTO recuperation and Tyler was about to lose his mind. The walk up and down the six flights of stairs would've been brutal, and being stuck inside with Lillie, much as he loved her, for however many weeks until he healed, probably would have driven him mad. Yet even with that reasoning, living here with Marcus had him uneasy as to what the ultimate payback might be. Despite Marcus's reassurances that he didn't expect Tyler to sleep with him, doubt remained etched in Tyler's mind.

Tyler shifted to find a more comfortable place on the sofa and reached for the remote; if another episode of *Maury* came on again he might blow his brains out. Doesn't anyone in the country know who their baby's daddy is anymore? Christ, and they call gays promiscuous. Everyone he knew always used a condom.

Food Network won out again, as usual.

No, none of that was the reason for his sleep-tossed nights and days filled with introspection. It was Marcus. God damn him. What he feared most about coming to live here was that he'd find out the man behind the smirk and glitter was so much more than he assumed, and he was being proven correct.

Like the time he mentioned his back bothered him, and Marcus had ordered a special, very expensive pillow to keep him propped up in a more comfortable position. Or, having revealed how much he enjoyed listening to classical music, the entire Royal Ballet Theatre's productions from the past five years somehow found their way into his music account.

The little things. Those meant the most to Tyler, and it ate away at him because he was coming to like Marcus as a person. It wasn't supposed to be that way. He'd accepted the invitation to stay because he was too tired and broken to fight. What scared him more was he wasn't sure he'd continue to fight Marcus once he was well again.

Luckily there was still enough of a kernel of doubt in Tyler's jaded soul to keep his weakened defenses up.

"Good morning."

Marcus stood in the hallway, freshly showered and shaved but still in his hanging-out clothes—sweats and a tee shirt. The sweats hung just low enough for Tyler to see a bit of skin glowing pale against the black of the fabric. He looked away.

"Hi. I didn't think you'd be up early. You came home late last night." Tyler had wondered half the night if Marcus had found someone and was screwing their brains out. As far as he knew, there hadn't been anyone in this apartment, so if Marcus was with anyone, it would have to be at Sparks, or at the other guy's place.

Not that he was thinking about it.

"Yeah, well, I found you lying dead-asleep on the sofa when I came home at four, and went to the bedroom, but I couldn't sleep. I thought I might go for a run."

Tyler quirked a disbelieving brow. "You? I didn't think you were into exercise or shit like that."

White teeth flashed. "There's much you don't know about me. I'm a man of hidden talents." He slid his feet into the sneakers sitting on the mat by the front door and tied the laces, giving Tyler a perfect view of his strong back and ass. Tyler swallowed hard; his long-neglected libido roared back to life like a kerosene-fed flame. His cock swelled and thickened.

"I'll be back in about an hour. Do you want me to pick up anything?" Marcus looked around. "Lillie left for school, right?"

Tyler nodded. "Yeah, I took her down to meet the bus. It felt good to be able to do it myself instead of asking the neighbor if she could wait with her."

"So, do you want anything? I'm hoping to be able to get in a run before the rain starts."

"No, thanks; I'm good."

Leave already, so I can get off thinking about you. His hand crept under the blanket to massage his dick which seemed to have acquired a mind of its own and insisted now would be the perfect time to come out and play.

"I'll leave the door unlocked so if you're asleep again, I won't have to ring the bell."

"Sure, yeah, whatever." He squeezed the head of his dick, not caring that he leaked all over his boxers. "Better get going."

Marcus looked at him strangely, then left. Tyler waited a minute or two, then threw the blanket off and shoved his boxers down, kicking them to the side. With his legs spread wide he reached for the bottle of lube he discovered Marcus had in the side table drawer and drizzled some over his dick.

At the first downward stroke, Tyler knew he wouldn't last long, so he tried to slow down his breathing and concentrate. He didn't want this to be a fast and messy jack-off. He wanted time to think about Marcus's ass and his cock, which Tyler knew, having seen glimpses of the latter in the bathroom and tucked away in Marcus's pants, was cut and beautiful. Marcus wasn't hung like a horse, but he was long and thick enough to give any man a good, hard ride.

Tyler moaned and worked his erection harder, ignoring the surge of pain from his healing ribs. It only added to the pleasure. The sound of the television faded, leaving him with only the slick, wet noise of his hand flashing up and down his cock. Shit, he wanted to come, but in a savage burst of self torture he squeezed the root of his dick, staving off the first flutterings of his orgasm, to prolong the exquisite pleasure of release.

Tyler palmed his dick slowly, tracing the vein, then reached down to roll and squeeze his balls. He ached for more, and though he never was a fan of sex toys, wanted one now to fill the emptiness inside him. He wished he could trust Marcus, because it was him Tyler wanted but couldn't have.

Fuck it. He began to jerk himself off in earnest, his mind's eye turned inward, imagining Marcus's round ass. How good it would feel to pound him; how glove-tight he'd hold Tyler's dick inside his body. He tightened his hand and slid it up and down, faster, harder, until he could hear his own raspy voice echoing, "Fuck, Marcus, yeah."

Electric-hot ribbons of pleasure raced through his veins, his mind melting and his body feeling too tight for his skin. A deep trembling began, worked its way up his legs, and wove around his spine, clutching it in a death grip. His balls tightened, and he thrust harder into his hand.

"Marcus," he said, sighing into the stillness of the apartment. The fantasy of fucking Marcus proved too much for Tyler, who hadn't had sex in what seemed like forever, and he exploded all over his hand, shooting endless streams of hot come. He kept squeezing his dick, working himself through the orgasm, hissing from the pleasure-pain of his hypersensitive skin, but he welcomed it. It had been years since he'd come hard enough to see stars.

Lying limp and boneless with his eyes still closed, Tyler smiled to himself. "Damn that felt good."

"It was even better to watch."

Fuck. My. Life. Tyler waited a second before opening his eyes to find Marcus, dripping wet and holding a paper bag, standing by the archway to the living room.

More nonchalant than his frantically beating heart should allow, Tyler asked in a hard, clipped voice, "How long have you been standing there watching me?"

Marcus went into the kitchen and set the wet bag on the counter-top. "Long enough to hear you call my name." He pulled out two bagels with lox and cream cheese and put them on a plate, then came into the living room and sat down on the sofa with Tyler. "Don't be embarrassed. It's not like we all don't jerk off. Why don't you go wash up, and we can have breakfast? It started to rain, so I had to cut my run short."

Either Marcus had no shame, or he really didn't care. Cheeks flaming, Tyler stood, naked from the waist down, and went into the bathroom to clean himself up and change.

When he returned to the living room he smelled fresh coffee.

"I already poured you a cup. Come sit and eat."

Tyler scowled but sat down. Pride warred with shame; it was as if his greatest secret had been exposed, an ugly white underbelly he'd wanted never to see the light of day. Yes, he wanted Marcus, but he never intended for Marcus to know. It worried him that Marcus might press him now for sex in exchange for keeping his job, whenever he was capable of returning to work.

"Ty." Marcus slanted a look at him through half-lidded eyes. "I'm not planning on jumping you, so chill the fuck out. You can choose to act all defensive and angry or decide it means nothing more than letting off steam, which I'm sure is what it was."

Still careful of his healing ribs, Tyler braced himself to sit and accepted the plate from Marcus. He chewed and swallowed several bites before deciding to speak. It took him that long to figure out what to say.

"Yeah, it's embarrassing. I didn't want you to think—"

"Think what? That you want to fuck me? It's no big deal. I'll make you feel better—I've jerked off thinking of you too, so now I know you feel the same. It's whether we choose to act on it that takes it to the next level." Marcus wiped his hands on a napkin and tossed it on the table.

When put in such cold terms it sounded worse than it had in Tyler's mind. But he knew Marcus well enough now to know he didn't lie; and Tyler respected the truth and no bullshit attitude.

"I don't want you to fire me if I won't have sex with you."

"That's fucked up, and let me tell you why." Marcus's lips thinned to a pale, white line, and his eyes flashed. "From the first I've held back with you. I may have teased and even kissed you but never once did I cross the line, at least in my mind. I offered you and your niece a place to stay and recuperate because I felt responsible. Sure I want you; what man wouldn't?" He crossed his arms and leaned back on the sofa. "I'm not going to force myself on you, or make it a condition of your employment. That's disgusting and illegal last time I checked."

Help from a virtual stranger didn't sit right with Tyler. He believed all things came with an expectation of payback in some form or another. He set his plate down on the coffee table.

"You don't understand. Every job I wanted to get in the theater came with a price tag attached. There was always a producer, a director, someone who wanted a blowjob or a quick fuck to get my foot in the door or to keep the job. I never wanted to play that game, so I got shut out."

"That sucks, but it doesn't mean it's like that everywhere."

"When people have used you your whole life, it's hard to learn to trust who's real."

The anger on Marcus's face melted away, replaced by a surprising expression of wistfulness. "You can choose to believe me or not, but I understand what you mean."

Tyler sat impassive, wondering if he'd fucked up the best thing that ever happened to him because of his stupid pride.

"I'm sorry. I let my embarrassment get the better of me. I've never lived with another guy, so I'm not used to this."

"I haven't either, so we'll learn together, all right?"

He already respected Marcus as a businessman; now he began to understand why the people closest to him liked him as a person.

"Yeah, sure we can."

"So let me ask you something." He grinned and handed Tyler his plate back. "Was I naked in your fantasy?"

"Asshole." He threw a napkin at Marcus, for the first time thinking things might work out for him.

Chapter Thirteen

MARCUS BALANCED THE empty pizza box in his hands, and Tyler had his hands full with dirty paper plates and napkins. It was Sunday night, and Lillie had designated it pizza night, so for the past three weeks since they'd moved in, they'd had pizza. They'd finished their slices, and she had decided that it was time for her dolls to eat pizza, so she was happily ensconced in her bedroom, playing house.

Marcus couldn't believe he thought of his former spare room as a four-year-old's bedroom now, but then again, so many things about his life had changed since Tyler and Lillie moved in that his head spun.

For the first time he had a male friend whom he wanted sexually but didn't attempt to get into his bed. Partly it was because Tyler was still recuperating from his injuries, but Marcus knew the real reason.

Despite Tyler's prickly attitude and pride and all his attempts to put a wall up between them, Marcus liked him and not as a piece of ass for the night. They were comfortable together in a way he'd never been with any man he'd been attracted to. He recalled something Julian said months ago, and its insightfulness chilled him.

"One day you'll meet someone who'll set your world spinning, and you won't know how to stop it."

At the time he thought it was bullshit and had told Juli exactly that, but now Marcus wasn't so sure. The fact that he was sitting here in his apartment on a Sunday night with a child and a man who'd already made it clear to Marcus to keep his hands off, instead of at his club where every color, shape, and size of man would be his for the taking, was a sign he might have taken that first step off the precipice.

Yet still Tyler fascinated him. His story, which Marcus wormed out of him after a night of tacos and margaritas, made his skittish behavior and hands-off attitude more understandable. Marcus had to respect a man who wouldn't use sex to get ahead and who stood by his core values.

When he discovered Tyler had to give up his dream of pursuing a career on the stage to care for his niece, Marcus admitted he first thought Tyler a fool. New York was a jungle, and it was survival of the fittest; to take care of the weak meant to sacrifice yourself. And Marcus didn't believe in sacrifices.

But then he heard Tyler's story and grudgingly admired what Tyler had accomplished. Marcus wasn't certain he'd ever be able to be as selfless. Yet these past weeks had Marcus reevaluating his priorities about how he lived his life and where his future might lead.

"You can leave it; I'll take it out to the compacter in a little while." Tyler rinsed out the recycling and placed it in a clear bag. "Aren't you going to get ready to go to Sparks?"

He'd planned on it; Marcus hadn't ever spent so much time away from the club, but he found himself missing the scene less and less; when he was at Sparks he'd caught himself on more than one occasion wondering what Tyler was doing instead of mingling with the crowd. He wondered if Tyler jerked off to thoughts of him again; God knows, Marcus had spent many a morning shower with his hand wrapped around his dick, imagining what Tyler's mouth would feel like, taking him deep.

"Uh, I thought I'd hang out here tonight. You know Sunday is pretty slow, especially now that you're not dancing."

Tyler gave him a measured look. "I'm hoping to be back soon."

"Don't rush it. Take all the time you need." Before Tyler moved in, the apartment had been nothing more than a shell, a place for him to hang his clothes and bring random guys. Now, when he stepped through the front door, Marcus never knew what he'd find scattered on the floor. It could be an array of stuffed animals, a jacket, hat, and mittens in frighteningly small proportions, or some pink furry things he couldn't identify. The smell of something delicious and home-cooked often greeted him as well.

A tiny bit of him enjoyed it.

"I'm going a bit crazy not working or being able to practice or exercise. I do stretches, but it still hurts like a bitch." Tyler placed the garbage by the door and rubbed his hands on his sweats.

"What did the doctor say?"

"I go back next week for the check-up. Want a beer?" He returned to the refrigerator at Marcus's nod and took out two cold bottles and handed him one. Marcus took it and went into the living room to relax on the sofa.

"Thanks. So, yeah, I'm staying home since I can do some work on year-end stuff. Get things ready for the accountant, and go through the promotions I want to do for next year."

Tyler settled on the sofa next to him. "Do you do a lot of promotions?"

"Yeah. I do a big Pride event and a few to help the LGBTQ youth organizations here in the city. I've added one to help burn victims, and we sponsor other FDNY and NYPD charities, especially now around the holidays." Marcus noticed the surprise on Tyler's face. "What?" He took a sip of beer.

"I didn't realize you were so charitable." Then, as if understanding what he'd said, Tyler blushed a deep red and stuttered. "Oh shit, that didn't come out right. I meant I never knew you did so much to help—"

Marcus cut him off. "Maybe you should quit while you're ahead. That doesn't sound as if it's going to be much better." He reached over and patted Tyler's knee. "For the record, I know what you meant. And yes, I do a lot of charitable events. It's one of the few ways to give back to the community."

"I think that's great. I hope you'll let me participate in some way when the time comes." Tyler seemed to have forgotten his embarrassment and instead grew pensive. "I'd always hoped that by this time in my life I'd be settled enough to be able to do charity work, instead of being a charity case myself."

There was a weary kind of innocence about Tyler that spoke of lost dreams and fragile hopes; but always underneath the surface, his immutable pride shone through. That quality made him irresistible to Marcus, and he wanted to know more.

"What happened really? Couldn't you keep up the dancing even after your sister came to live with you?"

Perhaps his question was too personal, but Tyler had gotten under his skin, and where normally Marcus didn't care enough about his employees' personal lives to question them, Tyler was no longer an ordinary employee to him.

"For a while." Tyler rubbed the back of his neck and stretched. "I needed the extra money once they came, and the only job I could get that would accommodate my crazy hours was waiting tables. Then I auditioned for a big show I thought I had a great shot at; finally a director was impressed with my merits as a dancer, not with giving him sex."

"And?" Marcus didn't understand. "You didn't get it after all?"

"No, I did, as a matter of fact. But that was right before Amber disappeared, leaving Lillie with me." That haunted, desolate expression Marcus remembered all too well entered Tyler's eyes. "Once I had responsibility for her, I couldn't be in the show, you know? It would require travel, which I couldn't do, and ultimately the pay would have been less than I was making waiting tables." He blinked, returning back to the present. "So I turned it down, and when I saw your ad for dancers and found out how much I could make, I figured I'd try it for a while, make some money to bank, and then hopefully find Amber and start over again."

His heart went out to Tyler. To have come so close to accomplishing your dream only to have it snatched away from you must have been devastating.

"I have every faith you will. Think of this as a momentary blip in your road, Ty. One that occurred through no fault of your own."

Tyler set the beer bottle down and hugged his legs to his chest, hissing slightly at the obvious discomfort from his injured ribs.

"I wish I had your confidence, but I'm more of a pessimist, a glass-half-empty kind of guy. And so far, I've yet to see a reason to change my mind."

Who could blame the guy? Marcus didn't subscribe to his negative outlook, but then again, he hadn't faced adversity like Tyler had. Material things had never been his problem; he'd had more than enough shit thrown at him to keep him busy and out from underfoot his entire life. But not once had he ever been the recipient of the love and attention Tyler showed his niece.

Staring at Tyler now, watching him pick at the threads of his worn sweatshirt, sympathy he was unaccustomed to feeling rolled through Marcus, making him a bit antsy and, for the first time, unsure of himself. His usual modus operandi was to throw money at a problem and make it go away. Tyler's pride made that an impossible fix, so Marcus had done the next best thing: offered up a luxury Tyler couldn't afford, and made it about the child, and therefore impossible to turn down.

Yet that didn't explain why he'd shunned his club as of late, preferring cute pizza dinners to scotch on the rocks with a blowjob at the end of the night, or why he turned down offers to go home with men he'd previously lusted after, with a laugh and a brush-off. He hadn't jerked off this much since discovering gay porn on the internet.

Some evenings after he'd come home late from the club, he'd stand at the doorway of his bedroom and watch Tyler sleep, wishing nothing more than to be able to slide under the covers with him and hold him close. He wondered what his skin tasted like, if his body radiated heat or was cool and smooth to the touch. He imagined burying his face in Tyler's silky hair.

And yet much as he desired Tyler, Marcus waited. He wanted Tyler to make the first move, proving this unintended attraction was mutual. Since he'd caught Tyler jerking off and calling out his name, Marcus had seen Tyler's side-eyed glances and confused expressions. He'd been around enough men to know Tyler wanted him but fought against the obvious pull between them.

Marcus could wait for Tyler to figure out all the shit floating around in his head. Once Tyler allowed himself the freedom to give in to desire, Marcus intended to welcome him with open arms.

Chapter Fourteen

"**Y**OU'RE ALL CLEAR, Tyler. It's healed perfectly."

Dr. Lerner ran her hands with a clinical touch over his ribs. It had been over five weeks since his attack; Tyler's ribs no longer hurt, and all the bruising on his face and back had disappeared as well.

"Thanks. I feel great. I can start dancing again, right?" He slipped his sweatshirt on. That was the most important thing. If the doctor said he couldn't dance again, he didn't know what he would do.

"Absolutely. You'll need to take it slow at first and get those muscles back in shape, but you've made a full recovery." Her friendly smile freed all his bottled-up tension about his future. Now that he'd been cleared, he and Lillie would move back home, and he'd begin dancing again.

"Thank you so much. You have no idea how happy that makes me."

"Have you ever danced professionally, Tyler? Not at the club where you work now, but with a company or on stage somewhere? Not that there's anything wrong with dancing at Sparks," she added hurriedly with an apologetic smile, so he wouldn't take offense.

"That was my plan at first, but I had to put that on the back burner. Things came up and…" He shrugged. "Well, you know how it goes. Best-laid plans and all that."

"Well, if you ever want to make a little money teaching, my seven-year-old has been bugging me for dance lessons."

"I hadn't ever thought about it." Not exactly true. He'd love to have a studio to teach little kids, but he didn't have the money, so that, like other dreams, got shunted off to the side.

"Well," she said as she tapped her folder, "from what Marcus told me, you're the best."

He thought about that on the subway ride back downtown to Marcus's apartment. Lucky for him the train wasn't crowded and he got a seat. He needed to plan how to tell Lillie that their time at Marcus's apartment was coming to a close and they'd soon have to return to their home in Brooklyn.

Begrudgingly, he had to admit Marcus was correct about the preschool; Lillie loved it and thrived around the other children. And as Marcus had also predicted, she'd become fast friends with Micah and Josh's kids and she'd had many a weekend sleepover with her new friends. In fact, he remembered, she was spending the weekend with them again. That meant for the first time he and Marcus would be alone when he was healthy. Thrills of both dread and anticipation raced through him.

As far as Tyler knew, Marcus hadn't sneaked a man into the apartment since they'd moved in, and from the gossip he heard from the other guys working at Sparks, no one had seen him with anyone there either. Plus, Marcus came home every single night and joined Tyler and Lillie at breakfast every morning. Which meant that for months now, Marcus hadn't had sex.

He reached his stop and got off the train, heading upstairs to the street. Turning up his collar against the chill of the wind, Tyler beat a quick path to Marcus's apartment. Raymond, the concierge, greeted him.

"Hello, Tyler. How was the doctor's appointment?"

He stopped to talk to the gregarious man, who, Lillie told him, always gave her a lollipop when she came home from preschool.

"Got the all-clear. I can go back to dancing and move back home." He leaned against the wide marble desk.

A smile flickered across Raymond's face, then faded. "Oh. I thought maybe you'd be staying. I know Marcus has enjoyed having you both here, especially little Lillie."

"I think he did a good job putting up with us, but I'm sure he'll be glad to get back to his normal routine and get us out of his hair."

"You'd be surprised," said Raymond with a shrug. "He looks happier than I've ever seen him since he moved in."

Tyler said goodbye and took the elevator up to the apartment. As always, he marveled at the beautiful view and interior decoration, which he suspected Marcus had left to a professional. Tyler laughed to himself. He'd expected it to be more hedonistic, with mirrors on the ceiling and shit like that.

He stripped and changed into a pair of dance leggings with no shirt and went into the guest room, which now doubled as Lillie's bedroom.

He pushed the twin bed against the wall and bent to stretch. To his joy there was no lingering pain, only a bit of stiffness. Even lying flat on the floor, elongating his muscles brought him nothing more than the standard inflexibility of unused tendons and joints.

He turned on the music on his new phone that Marcus, who insisted he needed it to keep track of Lillie, had bought him when they first moved in. Strains of classical music filled the air, and Tyler's heart beat quicker in his chest, his blood surged in his veins, and he began to dance.

In the background he heard the front door open, but he didn't stop; he couldn't. The music wouldn't let him. For the first time in over a month Tyler felt alive, and he didn't ever want it to end. Awareness prickled as if he'd scented a predator; Tyler knew Marcus watched him from the doorway. It didn't bother him but rather, spurred him on to push himself to the limits of where his body could take him.

He felt like he could fly.

As the music drew to a close, a great crescendo of chords surged, and he went *en pointe* and spun around, laughing aloud with the sheer joy of being alive. He stopped to catch his breath, bracing his hands on his thighs. Marcus said nothing but stared at him with an almost feral, hungry expression. Tyler's blood beat hot and fast and desire pulsed through him.

Advancing on Marcus, he first snagged the towel on the dresser and wiped himself off of the worst of his sweat. Tyler cupped his hand around the nape of Marcus's neck and pulled him in for a kiss. At the first touch of their lips Marcus stiffened, then slid his arms around Tyler and pulled him close.

"What did the doctor say?" His mouth played hot and humid against the ultrasensitive skin of Tyler's throat. "Tell me you're all better." He licked his Adam's apple and the curve of his neck.

"I'm all better," Tyler said, sighing from the play of Marcus's hands over his back, his hips, and finally, blissfully, his ass. "I'm better than better."

"Fucking right you are." Marcus growled in his ear. He pulled back for a moment and grasped Tyler by the jaw. "I want you now—right fucking now. I need to feel your tight ass suck my cock deep inside you. I've dreamed of it, and it won't be pretty because I'm six seconds away from ripping those pants off, bending you over, and fucking you without any lube."

Those insanely dirty words sent an electric current straight to Tyler's cock. He couldn't remember being this turned on, this quickly. "I need a shower." He gasped as Marcus bit down on his neck, then licked the throbbing skin. "I'm all wet and sweaty."

"I like wet and sweaty. I want to make you wet and sweaty." But Marcus took his hand and dragged him toward the bathroom, stripping his own clothes off as they went. He reached inside the shower and turned on the taps. "Take off those pants."

He pulled off his leggings yet couldn't tear his gaze from Marcus's lean-muscled torso. His shoulders weren't overly broad but his chest was well-muscled, the skin smooth and taut. A smattering of black hair led a trail down his flat abdomen to his heavy cock bobbing between them.

"Get in." Marcus pushed open the door.

"I—" Tyler began, but Marcus wouldn't let him finish and pulled him under the spray, holding him in his arms.

"Do you know how hard it's been for me this past month having you here and not touching you? Knowing you lay sleeping in my bed but I couldn't join you?" Heedless to the water pouring over both their heads, Marcus kissed him; lightly at first as if testing Tyler's reaction, then with increasing fervor.

But Tyler had decided to push away any misgivings and indecisions, and go with what his heart and his body were telling him. He wanted Marcus; had wanted him for months in fact, and the reasons Tyler had before for pushing him away—his own inability to trust, doubts that Marcus would use him once and toss him aside and perhaps most of all, that Marcus was a shallow, self-centered person—none of that had been proven true. Under the heated spill of the water, with Marcus naked and wet before him, desire won out.

Tyler opened his mouth beneath the press of Marcus's lips, accepting the slide of Marcus's silky tongue, meeting it with his own. Their kiss deepened until Tyler's breath merged with Marcus's; his head spun from the mingled heat and pleasure. He twined his arms around Marcus's neck, sinking into his chest, the sound of Marcus's rapidly pounding heart beating against his own both comforting and terrifying as their kiss intensified.

Marcus held him close, his breath hot along Tyler's jaw. "You taste fucking fantastic; I knew you would. It's all I've thought about." Marcus sucked at his lips before his agile tongue licked along Tyler's jaw, and then nipped his way down Tyler's neck. Helpless under the onslaught of Marcus's mouth, Tyler moaned, the sound amplified in the glass-enclosed shower.

Their naked bodies rubbed together, wet flesh sliding and slapping. Marcus kneaded the muscles of his back, his fingers brushing the dip below his spine, flirting with the top of his ass. Tyler's breath came in short, hard pants and his cock ached, precome leaking from the slit.

"I'm going to come if you keep that up." He kissed Marcus's wet shoulder, sucking at the warm flesh. It felt so good to taste his skin he wanted to lick him from head to toe. Marcus was like a drug that once taken would become impossible to ever eradicate from his system.

"Good. Easy clean-up."

The smile in his voice brought an answering one to Tyler's face. "Always thinking ahead."

"Mmm." Humming in his ear, Marcus grasped Tyler's cock and began to stroke him, slow at first, his thumb playing havoc with the crown. His fingers twisted around the shaft, while the rough pad of his thumb kept a continuous back and forth liquidy swipe along the wide head.

"Oh, shit." A deep, rolling ache pulsed through Tyler, beginning at the balls of his feet, sweeping through him like a wave, pulling him under. His orgasm flashed through him then and he thrust his hips hard, shooting hot and heavy into Marcus's hand.

"Better now?" Marcus washed them both clean, then turned the water off. He took Tyler's face between his hands. "How do you feel?"

Tyler slid his nose down Marcus's cheek, then pressed small kisses along his jaw. Marcus's erection lay heavy between them, like a promise.

"Fantastic, but it's time for payback."

A wicked smile crossed Marcus's lips. "I expect payment in full. With interest." They dried off and, leaving the towels on the floor, walked back to the bedroom. Marcus pushed him down on the bed, straddling him, his erect cock hot against Tyler's stomach.

"This has nothing to do with you staying here. If you think you have to fuck me for payback, you're wrong. You know I want you, right?"

Confused for a moment, Tyler gazed into Marcus's face, surprised by the hesitancy and vulnerability he'd never noticed before in his eyes. Marcus, for all his ego and arrogance, was as uncertain as the rest of them. It was all a front, a cover, to hide the man Marcus truly was inside. A man who, from everything Tyler had come to know, was kind and generous to a fault to people he cared about, sweetly gentle to a motherless child.

Why create the image of a self-centered arrogant ass whose only mission in life was pleasure?

Tyler slipped his hand around the nape of Marcus's neck and pulled him close so his lips rested against his rough-stubbled chin. "I want you. For you. Not because of what you've given me this past month. I wanted you before that." He kissed the side of his mouth and let his fingertips trail a path from Marcus's strong neck up to his face. "I think I always wanted you."

Marcus's eyes widened, but he didn't answer; instead he began kissing Tyler, running his nose down his cheek, his lips soft and gentle. Little licks of fire flickered inside Tyler's bloodstream and even though he'd come already, his cock stirred with renewed interest.

Marcus continued his trail of kisses, licking down his neck, stopping only to suckle at Tyler's nipples, which Tyler, never having paid much attention to them, had no idea were so sensitive.

"Ahhh, shit." His hips rocked up to Marcus's, and his half-hard cock twitched and swelled. Desperate for friction, he reached down to grab his cock and touch himself.

Marcus stopped his sucking and watched him for a moment. "Yeah, keep doing that. I like to watch your face as you get off."

No longer embarrassed, Tyler moaned and thrust into his fist, his hand becoming coated with his own slick, sticky fluid. His hips rolled, but it wasn't enough, dammit, he needed more. He needed Marcus. Inside him.

"Marcus, fuck, come on."

"Come on what?" The damn annoying man grinned, but reached over and grabbed a tube of lubricant along with a condom from the drawer.

His fingers met Marcus's as both of them now worked his cock. Slick with cool lube, Marcus knew just the right amount of pressure to get him off a second time, although it was now a gentle, sweetly aching release.

Marcus didn't stop at that. With his hand still wet from the mingled fluid and lube, Marcus brushed his fingers over Tyler's hole. Still absurdly sensitive, Tyler flinched and his ass clenched.

"Relax, baby."

Tyler bit down on his lip, willing his hypersensitive body down from its high. Cool fingers brushed against him again, and though he shivered, he didn't pull away. Marcus slid one finger inside, then a second, curling them deep. The burn only added to the flood of crazy sensations bombarding his body.

"If I don't fuck you now, I'm going to lose it all over the sheet, and that'll be the biggest waste of a hard-on."

"Do it." The restrained pleading in his own voice didn't bother Tyler. He was beyond caring; all he wanted was Marcus inside him. "Please."

Tyler heard the ripping of the condom wrapper, and then Marcus was there; the thick crown of his cock pushed in past the initial tight little opening, only to move and sink in deeper. Tyler loved it; Marcus's cock filled him perfectly, beautifully. He swore he could feel every bump and vein as his cock slid inside. Tyler took it all, and when Marcus was seated fully, Tyler gazed into his eyes and smiled.

"Now move." He rolled his hips, and Marcus groaned.

"Fuck, you feel amazing; better than anything. I knew you would." Shifting his knees to get better penetration, Marcus began to plunge in earnest, until that promised banging of the headboard became a reality and their grunts and groans filled the room. Strong hands held his hips as Marcus thrust into him, penetrating him, ruining him for anyone else ever again.

Tyler cried out when the head of Marcus's cock brushed his prostate. Too good, too much. His head thrashed on the pillow, and his body shook, creeping toward overload; his balls ached, his head spun, and the pounding of Marcus's cock inside shattered him to pieces. Tyler's vision blurred and grayed at the edges.

"Ty, *oh fuck*." From a distance he heard Marcus cry out as he came, shaking above him, his dick pulsing and filling the condom to overflowing.

All sound spun away, and everything went black.

Chapter Fifteen

MARCUS AWOKE IN a pitch-black room, unable for a moment to figure out where he was. As his night vision improved, he registered the familiar shapes of his bedroom furniture. For the past month, with Lillie sleeping in the guest room and Tyler recuperating in his bed, Marcus had either slept on the sofa or caught naps at the club.

Tyler. Marcus rolled onto his side and with only a whisper of sound, pulled the sheet off the naked man lying next to him. His beautiful body was a work of art in repose—all tight, well-defined muscles and long, smooth-skinned limbs. And he tasted as good as he looked; Marcus couldn't recall ever enjoying kissing anyone as much.

His cock stirred and swelled, and Marcus reached over and grabbed the lube and another condom. The sex between them had been wildly hot and intense; Tyler fell asleep as if drugged, and after Marcus had cleaned him up, he'd crawled into bed next to him and for the first time in many months, slept without dreaming.

Waking up and finding himself sharing a bed was never part of his life plan; normally he'd send his nightly pick-up home with a half-forgotten kiss and nothing more. He never sent mixed signals about what he expected; he was responsible for himself and owed no one an explanation for the way he lived his life. Right now, he wanted Tyler again, and if that was unusual, he didn't care.

He slicked his fingers with lube, then began kissing Tyler down the long lines of his back, while at the same time inserting his finger in between the globes of his ass to push past the hole. Tyler sighed and shifted, unconsciously spreading his legs wider, assisting Marcus in his cause.

Hopefully he'd be giving Tyler one hell of a dream or a wake-up. Marcus slid his finger all the way inside, then added another, loving the unique velvety wet warmth of Tyler's body.

"Mmmm. Best wake-up I've had in forever." Tyler moaned and pushed his ass farther onto Marcus's fingers, making hot little noises of pleasure that drove Marcus crazy. He began to plug away in earnest, and Tyler writhed beneath him, working himself on Marcus's hand. Unable to stand it any longer, Marcus withdrew his hand, rolled a condom down his aching cock and pushed himself inside Tyler, burying himself in to the hilt. That place of perfection, the absolute rightness of being inside Tyler settled over him. Instead of running scared, Marcus rocked his hips and kissed the side of Tyler's neck. Tyler keened a high-pitched whine of need and scrabbled at the sheets.

Unable to hold back his own satisfied sounds from the inconceivable pleasure of Tyler's body, Marcus slid an arm around Tyler's waist, grasped his now rigid cock and began to stroke him off. Almost immediately Tyler began to come, pumping hot streams through his fingers.

"So fucking hot," said Marcus, then bit down on Tyler's shoulder as he thrust inside and came so hard he saw stars.

Together they shuddered to completion and lay pressed together, watching the early morning light filter into the room through the curtains. Loathe to move and break their connection, Marcus held on to Tyler's waist, pressing tiny kisses along his jawline.

Tyler sighed, then pushed away, and Marcus slid out of his warm body. He rid himself of the condom, then returned to bed where Tyler lay on his side, facing him. Marcus stood and stared at him, waiting for the usual anxiety to rise up and suffocate him at the presence of someone who thought because they fucked, there was ownership and therefore a right to make demands.

But Tyler made no such demands; he remained silent in the dark, the glint of his eyes and the flash of his smile catching the glow of early-morning light in the room. Marcus climbed back into the bed, and Tyler curled around him, nestling his soft cock in the cleft of Marcus's ass. It was warm, comforting, and peaceful. Marcus drifted off to sleep.

SEVERAL HOURS LATER, Marcus had showered and gotten dressed, while Tyler remained in bed. Saturday morning was Marcus's lazy time; a rest from his usual wild Friday-night exploits. Marcus had been particularly looking forward to it all week, since he'd be seeing Julian and Zach for the first time since his angry outburst of last month. He'd called both of them and apologized, and though they each brushed it off, it weighed on his mind.

He poured himself a cup of coffee and sat at the kitchen counter. Nothing had been the same since they'd each met someone and paired up. It might be childish, but a tiny part of him resented Nick and Sam and how they usurped his place in his friends' lives.

Glad that he wasn't falling prey to the love bug, he finished his coffee and, hearing the shower stop, poured one for Tyler. He knew how he took his coffee now and made sure to have on hand the hazelnut creamer he liked. It wasn't a big deal.

It seemed strange not to have Lillie prancing around, making a mess with her crayons, or having the television turned to some God-awful show about unicorns and princesses. But she'd begged to spend the weekend with Micah and Josh's kids and Tyler conceded to her, as Marcus had no doubt he would. Tyler would pick her up tomorrow, and Marcus thought she'd probably like some of her favorite chocolate chip ice cream, so he made a note on his phone to pick some up later.

Emerging from the bathroom damp and smelling like his coconut soap, Tyler's eyes lit up at the sight of the coffee pot on the breakfast bar.

"Oh, thank God. I'm dying for a cup." He reached for the cup, and Marcus pushed over the bottle of creamer.

"Here, I got you another bottle. You finished the last up a few days ago."

"Oh, thanks; that was nice of you." He poured the creamer in and took a sip. "Damn, that's good."

He tipped his head back and drank it down, while Marcus stared at the strong lines of his throat, remembering the warm taste of his skin, and wondered if it was too late to go back to bed. He blinked back to awareness.

"Shit," he mumbled, scrubbing his face with his hands.

"What's the matter?"

Tyler's question threw him. He didn't know exactly, but something was off-kilter and he couldn't figure out what. Meeting the guys would help set him straight; it always had in the past.

"Nothing. I don't know. Maybe I'm coming down with something."

Tyler raised a dark brow. "You seemed perfectly fine to me earlier. Better than fine, in fact." His slow smile over the rim of his coffee mug unfurled a hot and needy response in the pit of Marcus's stomach while a ridiculous flare of happiness settled in his heart.

"So what are your plans today?" He carried his mug to the sink to spill out the cold dregs and place it in the dishwasher.

"Uh, I hadn't thought about it." Tyler gazed into his mug. "I'm so used to having Lillie around I'm kind of at a loss as to what to do for myself."

"Come to brunch with me," said Marcus, then stopped short. What the fuck did he just do? Moving from the kitchen to the living room, he checked his phone, then put it back in his pocket. He suddenly didn't know what to do with his hands.

The panic inside him must've shown on his face, because Tyler gave him a wry smile and shook his head.

"That's okay. You don't have to entertain me. I can hang out here. Plus, I need to start getting our things together."

A chill ran through him. "What are you talking about? Getting what things together?"

Tyler bent to touch his toes, and Marcus watched as his tee shirt slipped up his back, revealing a pale expanse of smooth skin. Marcus had to restrain himself from pouncing.

"Damn, I'm out of shape." Tyler tucked a curl behind his ear. "I meant mine and Lillie's stuff. Now that I'm recovered, it's time for us to move back home."

Marcus nodded slowly, his mind working at warp speed. "I understand why you think you need to go back, but have you thought about how it's going to impact Lillie? She's in school now and has friends. If you move back to Brooklyn, she'll have to stop."

"This wasn't a permanent arrangement; you knew that." Tyler leaned against the wall. "I can't impose on you any longer. I'm sure you want your bedroom and your life back."

"I didn't mind it last night." He walked over to Tyler and placed a hand on his neck, stroking him. This he could do. He had no qualms about seducing Tyler to stay with him. The troubling reason why he wanted him there so badly, Marcus pushed to the side for now. Instead, he pulled Tyler close, settling their hips in line, and his cock thickened in his pants. "I'd tell you if I did. Please, come with me to brunch, and we can talk."

Doubt clouded Tyler's eyes. "I don't belong there. Those are your friends, the people you're closest with."

"I had my dick inside you twice last night, Tyler. How much closer could we get?"

It took Marcus many minutes of deep, persuasive kisses to rid Tyler of his confusion. When he pulled away though, the ground under his feet reeled, and Marcus needed a moment to compose himself.

They remained standing close; Tyler's hands rested on his shoulders while he clasped Tyler around his hips. He nuzzled Tyler's ear, then pleaded with him.

"Come on; you have to help me out here. They're all coupled up, and the last thing I want is to listen to them be all disgustingly loving and happy."

An amused glint lit Tyler's eyes. "And you hate that, huh?"

"Bet that sweet ass of yours I do." He gave Tyler's ass a squeeze for effect, and the light in Tyler's eyes smoldered.

"If you want me to come, you'd better get your hands off my ass."

Marcus's lips curved up in a grin as he popped open the button of Tyler's jeans and drew them down.

"I definitely want you to come; in every way possible," he said, and sank to his knees, uncaring of how late he might be to meet Zach and Julian.

THE ARGUMENT OVER Tyler's living conditions resurfaced on the way to the restaurant and started with the doorman hailing them a cab.

Tyler nudged Marcus. "Tell him we don't need a cab. We can take the train."

Hopefully Tyler was kidding; Marcus couldn't remember the last time he'd been on the subway. "Hell no. I don't take the train. That's what cabs are for."

But Tyler wouldn't back down, and by his narrowed eyes and the mutinous set of his jaw, Marcus could tell the argument meant more than a ride on a train.

"I don't need to travel by cabs everywhere. I'm used to taking the train. Plus,"—Tyler took a deep breath then exhaled—"you can't keep paying for me for everything. I'm not your charity case."

"It's what I'm used to. I'm not forcing it down your throat."

"But you are. You're so used to it that you don't even notice any-more." Becoming red-faced, Tyler gestured with his hands. "But I'm not into being dominated or bullied by anyone, no matter how large their checkbook."

Normally so calm and unruffled, Tyler's blowup surprised Marcus. Remaining silent, he studied Tyler's angry face. There'd never been anyone Marcus had ever been with who cared how much money he spent. If he took them to dinner, he'd always pay, and inevitably his date would order the most expensive item on the menu. Perhaps they thought it was their payment for having sex; in truth, Marcus never cared enough to find out.

Tyler's sense of self-worth and fierce independence were a welcome change from the men he knew used him as much as he used them. And Tyler's viewpoint wasn't coming from a selfish place. Marcus enjoyed their battle of wills. Tyler's reluctance to accept his help forced Marcus to change his outlook on certain aspects of his own life and, strangely, didn't send him running in the opposite direction as it usually did if the men he took to his bed tried to bend him to their desires.

"So," he said mildly after Tyler had stopped talking. "You want to start taking the subway. I can do that, I suppose."

He didn't know whether to laugh or be offended at Tyler's skeptical gaze, but he waved off the doorman's assistance and began walking.

"Let's go. We're already late."

Tyler laughed and pulled his arm. "First of all, if we're late, it's all your fault." His eyes sparkled in the sunlight, and Marcus's breath caught at the wave of desire sweeping through him. How wrong he'd been to think one-time sex with Tyler would end his lust. Even with his body heavy and sated from the sex they'd had right before leaving the apartment, Marcus wanted him again. He'd never had the urge to kiss someone as he did Tyler right now. And since he never held back on what he wanted, he took Tyler's face between his hands and kissed him hard, imprinting Tyler's laughter on his lips.

"Second," said Tyler after they'd stopped kissing, "you're going the wrong way. The subway station is behind us."

Lighter than he'd been in years, Marcus took off running down the block. "What are you waiting for?"

Tyler caught up easily, and they raced down the steps to the sound of the oncoming train. Since Marcus didn't have a train pass, he borrowed Tyler's, and they slipped in right before the doors closed.

It had been years since he'd been on the subway, but it wasn't the dirty, overheated mess from years past. Then again, it was only three stops to where they got off.

"See? That wasn't so bad," said Tyler.

"It wasn't horrible."

They entered the restaurant, and Marcus spotted Steph, who waved to him and pointed to the table, already occupied by his friends who were on their first round of mimosas.

"Can you bring an extra setting? This is Tyler, and he'll be joining us today. Tyler, this is Steph. Best hostess in New York."

She arched a brow. "Marcus, you dog. How long have you two been dating?" She assessed Tyler, who'd turned red under her scrutiny. "I'm not surprised though. You're gorgeous, Tyler. Make sure you keep this one on his toes, and don't let him give you any shit."

Marcus made a face. "Very funny. We're not dating; we're friends." He turned to Tyler. "Let's go. By my estimate we're only one round behind."

They threaded their way through the tables, and Marcus reached his friends and placed his hands on Zach's shoulders, who sat with his back to him. "Hey, don't drink up all the champagne without us."

The conversation halted mid-sentence, and if Marcus was hoping to make an entrance, he'd gotten his wish. Everyone at the table stared not at him, but at Tyler, who stood fidgeting and uncomfortable at his side. Zach peered over his shoulder to see what people were looking at, and when he spotted Tyler, a huge smile broke out over his face.

"Julian said you probably weren't showing up, but I told him to give you a few more minutes. I knew you had a reason to be late."

Marcus scowled at Julian who hadn't taken his eyes off Tyler. "Why the hell would you say that? I said I'd be here."

Julian quirked a brow, finally making eye contact with him. "You've said a lot of things lately, much of which made no sense to me. Until now." He focused his gaze back on Tyler. "Hi, I'm Julian, Marc's voice of reason. This is my husband, Nick."

Nick choked on his beer and laughed. "Nice to meet you, Tyler.

Welcome to the show."

"You're a fucking pain in the ass." Marcus sat down in the empty seat next to Zach, pointing to Tyler to take the seat next to him.

"So you've said. Yet you love me anyway."

When he didn't answer, Zach cleared his throat. "Um, hi Tyler, I'm Zach. I've seen you at the club. This is Sam, my boyfriend."

Sam leaned back and waved, then patted Marcus on his shoulder. "How's it going?"

"Zach is Marcus's conscience," said Julian, with an evil cackle.

"Nick, can't you hose him down or slap a mask on him? Anything to shut him up." Marcus leaned over to whisper in Tyler's ear. "Nick's a fireman."

Tyler said nothing, only nodded and sipped his water.

"Tell us about yourself, Tyler." Julian hadn't taken his eyes off Tyler since they sat down. "You're one of Marcus's dancers at the club, right?"

The waiter brought him and Tyler their drinks, and they ordered. Marcus noticed Tyler only ordered a toasted bagel and knew it was due to the high cost of the food. It shouldn't have bothered him that it bothered Tyler, but it did.

Tyler played with his silverware a bit before answering. "Yeah. I was until I got injured, but I've been cleared by the doctor, so I'd like to start again as soon as possible." He glanced over at Marcus.

"Tonight?"

"Yeah. I need to start making money ASAP."

Marcus took a deep drink of his mimosa, then waved his hand. "I've told you not to worry about it. It's no big deal."

The moment the words left his lips, Marcus realized he made a huge mistake. Between Tyler's pride and the sensitive subject of him accepting help from Marcus, Marcus should've chosen his words with more care. Especially in front of his friends.

Tyler's eyes shot angry sparks, and he slapped his hand on the table. "It's a big deal to me. I'm not taking any more of your charity. As a matter of fact,"—he stood and fumbled in his wallet, then finally pulled out a twenty-dollar bill and tossed it on the table; it might even have been his last; Marcus knew how little money Tyler had—"I don't even understand why I'm here. I'm going back home, I mean to your apartment, packing our stuff, and moving back to my apartment. Sorry to ruin your breakfast everyone. Bye." He stormed off, out of the restaurant.

Reeling as if he'd been physically slapped, Marcus couldn't believe Tyler had left him. When he'd recovered somewhat, he drained the rest of his drink in one gulp, studiously avoiding meeting anyone's eyes. It came as no surprise to him though, that Julian spoke first.

"Aside from everything else, did I hear right? Did Tyler say he was living with you?"

"Julian," said Zach in a stronger voice than Marcus ever heard before. "I don't think this is the time to start questioning Marcus." Zach leaned over and whispered in his ear. "I think you should go after him and talk things out."

Refusing to let anyone, even his best friends, know he hurt inside, Marcus lifted his empty glass to the passing waiter. "Can I get another one, please?" To Zach, who gazed back at him, puzzled and disappointed, he laughed. "Don't look so sad. I gave him and his little niece a place to stay because I felt sorry for them after Tyler was beaten up and injured on his way to work at my club. He was my responsibility. That's all it was."

"It didn't seem—"

"Drop it, Zach," he said, snapping at his friend harsher than he'd intended. "I'm fine."

And he would be, as soon as the ache in his chest disappeared.

Chapter Sixteen

IT TOOK TYLER less than fifteen minutes to pack his clothes, which entailed throwing the few pairs of jeans, tees, and sweatshirts he owned in a bag. Lillie's clothes would prove more of a challenge, since she'd mysteriously accumulated more outfits and toys in these past few weeks than she had in the whole year, including her birthday and Christmas.

After surveying the explosion of stuffed animals and dolls in her room, Tyler picked out the toys she loved best and packed up only the clothing she came with, leaving behind all the pretty clothes she loved wearing. It tore at his heart to disappoint her, but he refused to accept charity and owe Marcus anything in the end.

Passing by Marcus's bedroom, Tyler stopped for a moment and leaned in the doorway, surveying the unmade bed; memories of them making love under the warmth of the covers last night and this morning threatened to derail his anger. His heart thudded, and his body ached with a longing to return to this morning and erase everything that happened once they left the safe cocoon of the apartment.

He'd never been kissed until he thought his heart might explode or touched with such tenderness and passion; his skin still felt the imprint of Marcus's hands. How stupid to imagine a future where he might give up Sparks to run his own studio, or train for Broadway, or that he and Marcus could put aside their differences and make a relationship work. It had been a thread of an idea he'd hoped to work on and had hugged to himself.

In the end, Marcus wanted things his way and thought to keep Tyler like his little pet. Angry at himself for both wasting his time and giving his body to a man who proved to be less than what he hoped but exactly what he feared, Tyler marched into the bathroom, swept up his toiletries, and dumped them in a plastic bag, then dragged the two duffel bags full of clothing out of the apartment and down the elevator. He didn't want to keep the new cell phone Marcus had given him, but since it was the only number Micah and Josh had to call him on, he had to keep it. For now.

Lugging the two big bags on the subway might prove a daunting task, but it couldn't be helped. He wouldn't waste his money on a cab, especially now when he was back to dancing for tips. And when he showed up at Sparks tonight, he suspected he might be out of a job, although he hoped for Lillie's sake that Marcus wouldn't be so cruel to toss him out with no notice.

Lucky for him the trains were relatively empty, and he stood the bags on their end so as not to take up precious standing room. Still, he received the evil eye from some people, which he chose to ignore. With the usual, inexplicable delays, it took him an hour to reach his stop in Brooklyn, and it was late afternoon and already turning dark by the time he hauled the two bags up the station stairway and down the block. The side where his ribs had cracked twinged in protest at the all-but-forgotten climb up six flights of stairs to his apartment. By the time he reached the top floor, his shirt stuck to his back, wet from a chilled sweat.

The atmosphere in the apartment had an alien quality, as if he no longer belonged within its walls. A fine shimmer of dust lay over everything, and Tyler sighed at the amount of cleaning he needed to do for when Lillie returned home tomorrow.

His heart clenched at the inevitable upset this would cause Lillie, but it had to happen. The strange attraction he and Marcus acted upon may have lit up the sheets, but that type of all-encompassing lust and desire to possess eventually burns out, leaving little behind of the original inferno but smoldering ruins. He shivered, remembering how high he flew, how intense and brightly hot their hunger for each other had been.

Dragging a bag behind him, Tyler walked to Lillie's bedroom, determined to put Marcus out of his mind for good.

IT HAD TAKEN him the better part of the evening to clean the apartment, unpack Lillie's things (his clothes were merely tossed in a chest that doubled as their coffee table), and fill the refrigerator with some essential food and milk for when she came home. Remembering how Marcus thought nothing of spending hundreds of dollars on food and drinks to satisfy Lillie, Tyler was more determined than ever to make sure she understood they couldn't afford Marcus's lifestyle.

By seven o'clock Tyler had showered and prepared himself, and with a final look around the tiny apartment, he locked the door and headed back to the city, to Sparks.

All the bartenders greeted him with a hug and a kiss, even Antonio, who Tyler thought didn't like him, believing him a rival for Marcus's affection. Now would be the time to tell Antonio to go for the gusto. Tyler hesitated a second, then waved at the man.

"Hey."

Antonio, who stood with Shane chatting about the new signature drink Sparks planned to serve tonight, pointed to himself.

"Me? What's up?"

With a tilt of his head, Tyler indicated they should move to the end of the bar, away from the others.

"So I just wanted you to know that if you're interested in Marcus, there's nothing going on between us. You're free to take a shot, and I'm sure Marcus will be thrilled."

Antonio's lips curved upward in a grin. "You're kidding me, right?"

"No, why?"

Fascinated, Tyler watched as Antonio popped a maraschino cherry in his mouth and with practiced skill, produced it on his tongue with the stem tied in a knot.

His teeth flashed as he crushed the piece of red fruit. "'Cause about a month ago I hit on him, knew I had it in the bag."

All news to Tyler. He must've still been recuperating from the cracked ribs. It made sense though; Marcus used sex like addicts used their drugs.

"Oh yeah?" Tyler attempted to keep his voice diffident, like the thought of Antonio and Marcus didn't matter and the pain in his chest wasn't his heart shattering to bits. "Hope it was good." The words tasted like chalk on his tongue, bitter and dry.

Antonio glanced around like he had a secret no one else should hear. "That's just it, man. He turned me down. Me." He ran his hands down his chiseled abs. "I offered to blow him, but then you called, and it's like he forgot I was even there."

The obvious disbelief in Antonio's voice should have made Tyler laugh, not jump-start his heart. What he and Marcus had was sex for convenience's sake; it wasn't the beginning of a relationship.

"Well, take your shot again if you want; there's nothing going on with us."

"Man, you stupid or something?" Antonio planted himself in front of Tyler, his brows twisted with confusion. "Marcus has it bad for you. No guy turns down a blowjob unless he's really into someone else. Besides," he said, popping another cherry in his mouth, "I seen the way he looks at you when you dance. That ain't the sign of a guy who just wants to fuck you. I swear anytime another guy even looks at you he wants to rip his face off." Brushing his hands, Antonio turned to go, then stopped. "Do this tonight. Dance all dirty for the crowd in front of Marcus, and watch his reaction. That'll tell you everything you need to know about who he really wants." He walked behind the bar and began to polish and stack the glasses.

Lost in thought, Tyler jumped almost a foot when someone tapped him on the shoulder. A familiar chuckle brought a smile to his face.

"Darius." He hugged the big man, and it hit Tyler then how much he missed the people here. Having never had much of a family or home life himself, it took this absence for him to understand what he stood to lose if Marcus fired him.

"You look great, man. Are you back to dance tonight or just to hang out?"

Tyler picked up his gym bag that had his tiny dance shorts and the oil he rubbed on himself to catch the lights.

"Walk with me to the back? I need to warm up for later."

"So you *are* dancing." They reached the locker room, and Darius pushed open the door, allowing him to pass by. He set his bag down on the bench and began to untie his sneakers while Darius leaned against the row of lockers the employees used to hang their clothes in, and continued to chat. "I didn't think Marcus would want you to."

When Tyler finished, he straightened up and frowned, pushing the hair off his face.

"What does that mean?" He frowned, toed off his sneakers, and placed them in the locker. "Why would he have a say in what I do?"

Darius looked supremely uncomfortable. "Um, well, you two are together, so—"

Exasperated, Tyler lost his patience. "We're not together. Damn, first Antonio, now you…" He shook his head and sat heavily on the bench. "I never intended to get involved with him."

Darius slanted a glance at him. "But you did, didn't you?"

"There's a reason people call their private lives private," said Tyler grumbling under his breath, unwilling to reveal too much even to himself. If he admitted what he suspected, there'd be no turning back, no recourse for the havoc coursing through his body every time he saw Marcus. Better that he keep it all at arm's length and let this strange attraction between them wane, until Marcus, as he suspected, would grow tired and move on to a different man.

"It doesn't matter anymore. We were thrown together by circumstance and convenience, nothing more nor less. Marcus can go back to his party boys, and I have my life to lead; I don't see the two mixing. Besides, I moved out today."

Darius joined him on the bench. "Why?" He handed him a bottle of water. "I thought you had everything taken care of living there."

Tyler took the bottle only to have something to do with his hands. "Because I got tired of him treating me like a kept man. I don't take handouts from people."

"I doubt Marcus thought he was giving you a handout. He did it because…" Darius stopped a moment. "Honestly I'm not quite sure, because he's never behaved like this. Marcus has always been a generous man, but with his money, not himself or his time."

Tyler spun the dial of his lock around and around. "You know him better than I do."

Darius snorted. "I doubt that." He pierced Tyler with a dark, knowing gaze. "No one really knows Marcus; I'm not certain his best friends even do. But since you've been here he's different, less restless. Like he's found something."

"Yeah," said Tyler grimly. "Someone he thought he could keep like a toy. Soon he'd begin telling me what to do, how to act. He's very persuasive; all his life all he's had to do is smile and *bam!*—he gets what he wants." Tyler pulled his sweatshirt over his head. "But I don't need that bullshit; I don't have time for it. Other people depend on me. My first priority is Lillie."

"You know he hasn't been with anyone else since you began working here. And it's not for lack of others trying."

"I don't need to hear this."

"If you're asking me, I think you're afraid because you see something happening and Marcus is the opposite of everything you thought you'd want. Life isn't so black or white. Things aren't always as they seem, and neither are people. Maybe you have to ask yourself why you're so afraid of finding out the truth about your feelings for Marcus. What's the worst that can happen if you give it a chance?" With a shake of his head, Darius pushed open the door and left.

Contemplating Darius's words, Tyler remained on the bench in the locker room for a long time. When he left to begin practicing, he knew what he had to do.

Chapter Seventeen

DUMBFOUNDED AT TYLER'S outburst, Marcus endeavored to save face with his friends by pretending none of it mattered. Through the rest of their brunch he joked with Nick, ignoring Julian's pointed glances. He knew his friend wanted to talk about Tyler, but Marcus couldn't deal with Julian's well-meaning prying into his personal life.

Although he'd never admit it out loud, this past month had been somewhat of a revelation to him. Having Tyler and Lillie living with him brought a sense of peace and comfort to his life he hadn't known was missing. He no longer needed to brush away the darkness with strangers; he finally had a home.

Tyler's anger shocked him into introspection. Controlling the world around him, fitting it to his specifications was how he lived his life. Growing up, his wishes had never been considered, so the adult Marcus made certain never to let anyone rule him. He never thought he treated Tyler like a plaything.

"I'm sorry, Marcus. I didn't mean to push."

Zach's soft, apologetic voice squeezed at Marcus's already bruised heart. How many more people was he destined to hurt today? At least he could still repair his friendship with Zach. Knowing how sensitive Zach was, he couldn't have it on his conscience to hurt the sweetest person he'd ever known.

"No. Don't apologize. I'm the one who's sorry. I shouldn't have snapped at you like that."

"I know. And I know why you did it too."

"Oh yeah. I didn't want Sam to punch me again."

"You can't fool me. You're dodging the issue."

Zach's sharp scrutiny unnerved Marcus, and though he tried to foist Zach off with a laugh, it died in his throat.

"Come on, Zach; don't make a big deal out of it. I helped the guy out 'cause he was in trouble. Now he's all better, and I can get back to normal."

"Normal meaning what, Marc? Screwing every stranger you see? When are you going to wake up already and see you're too good for that?"

Obviously waiting for the right moment to jump in, Julian let loose. "You're worth more than a quickie fuck from some random who cares nothing about you except where you can take him to see and be seen."

Those words rang in his head all the way home and as he dressed for the club that night. He wasn't sure if Julian was correct. If Marcus was worth it, wouldn't his mother have cared and put her child's needs first, before his father's? He was her flesh and blood. If his own family didn't care, why should a stranger?

Angry at himself for doubting who he was, and even angrier at Tyler for leaving him, Marcus pocketed his wallet and keys. Out of habit now, he glanced over to the living room where Ty used to lie stretched out on the sofa with Lillie snuggled on his lap, watching some God-awful schlocky kiddie movie. Now it sat bare and dark; the silence suffocated him until he couldn't bear to be there any longer, and he left for Sparks.

When he arrived at the club he was shocked to see not only Julian and Nick, but Zach and Sam hanging out at the bar. He approached them warily.

"What is this, an ambush?" He gestured to Antonio who presented him with his glass of scotch. He'd need the whole bottle to spend the evening fending off his friends sniffing around his private life. Then the lights flashed, and the noise in the club died down until nothing could be heard save for the pounding beat of the music.

Marcus froze as Tyler, chest gleaming and golden shorts molded to his ass and cock, outlining every fucking perfect inch of him, stood in the center of the now cleared dance floor, his hips swaying to the beat of the Nine Inch Nails song "Closer."

"Shit," he heard Julian exclaim behind him. "What the hell is this about?"

Ignoring his friends and striding past his employees who all stood staring in shock, Marcus walked toward the center of the club, the crowd of people giving way before him like he was Moses parting the waters of the Dead Sea. Swaying in place, his eyes shut and a dreamy smile on his face, Tyler was everything Marcus never knew he wanted until that moment.

Marcus stood admiring his face. And though the music filled up every corner of the club with its pulsating, erotic beat, Marcus suspected Tyler listened for his footsteps and knew he was there.

He refrained from speaking, preferring to remain gazing at the beautiful symmetry of Tyler's form. Muscles flexed beneath the surface of his smooth naked skin, and beads of sweat formed on his temple and the hollow of his neck between his collarbones, glittering where the strobe lights hit.

Marcus discarded his jacket, tossing it with careless abandon to a familiar face in the crowd, and continued to watch Tyler dance. That mysterious smile continued to rest on the corners of Tyler's lips, as if he hugged a secret only he could unlock. Tyler opened his eyes, lifted his arms, and twined them over Marcus's shoulders, his fingers sliding through Marcus's hair until they twisted in the waves resting at the nape of his neck.

"Marcus." His quiet voice caressed Marcus's ear, and he shivered at the soft touch of Tyler's lips to his skin. The music faded in the background, leaving behind only the achingly sensuous beat thrumming through his veins. Passion bloomed through his bloodstream, warming him from within, as if having lain dormant for so long, it now sought to take root in what was once the wasteland of his soul.

The music pounded on, and Tyler danced, twining his body around Marcus's torso like a boa. His nimble fingers unbuttoned the top button of Marcus's shirt, and at the touch of Tyler's hands, his body lit on fire.

Marcus sought to grasp Tyler around the waist but Tyler eluded him, slipping through his hands. With a wicked smile curving his lips, Tyler slowly rolled his hips in a sensuous striptease, then reached over and finished unbuttoning his shirt, his fingers teasing against Marcus's chest. He pulled the shirt off, then danced away again, waving it like a victory flag above his head, before tossing it to the cheering crowd. This must be a joke, Marcus thought, until Tyler pressed himself up flush against Marcus's naked back and bit him on the shoulder, then licked away the sting.

The crowd went wild, but Marcus was too far gone in a haze of lust so heavy, he could barely keep his eyes open. He turned and managed to grab Tyler and kiss him, heedless of the catcalls from the crowd which faded to nothing as he fell into the perfection of Tyler's tongue owning his mouth. Velvet stroked velvet; their mouths fused together as his hips thrust into Tyler's groin and for a moment Tyler relented, holding him close. He cupped Marcus's ass, their erections nestling together, giving him that friction and pressure he craved, and he bucked into Tyler's hips.

Then Tyler spun away, curling himself around Marcus, burrowing into the curve between his neck and shoulder, while his hands continued to play havoc with Marcus's nipples. This couldn't continue, or he'd end up taking Tyler on the floor in front of everyone.

"Ty, what're you up to?" he murmured directly into Tyler's ear, seeking to pull him closer. Elusive and teasing, Tyler twisted around and slipped out of his grasp.

"Come with me."

He opened his eyes then, and the raw hunger blazing in Tyler's gaze ignited a corresponding flash within Marcus. As if in a somnambulant state, Marcus allowed himself to be led to the back, oblivious to the whistles and raunchy outbursts from the crowd.

The ache of suppressed desire curled low and deep in his belly; the need to touch and be touched by Tyler rose hot and thick, like warm honey sliding over his bones. It drenched Marcus in its sticky sweetness and for one brief moment panic seized him, as if his body and mind had finally awakened and realized what had happened.

He stopped short; Tyler turned to him with a questioning glance, and Marcus remained rooted to the spot, simply staring at this man who'd upended his life without him even knowing it had happened. Marcus struggled with the fear of giving in to the complete and utter safety of Tyler's arms around him. Then, at Tyler's smile, a terrifying kind of happiness rolled through him, and all thought of protecting his heart vanished. Tyler tugged him close and kissed him until his mind spun, their breaths merged, and nothing mattered anymore but Tyler's tongue in his mouth and his hands moving with purpose and strength over his body.

"Ty," Marcus groaned, the sound of his voice reverberating gritty and pained in the narrow confines of the hallway, but he didn't give a fuck who heard him. "Want you."

"I know."

They fell inside his office, kissing and groping each other. A button popped off, skittering and pinging on the floor, but he didn't care as he ripped at the flap of his pants. Watching Tyler shimmy out of those golden lycra shorts, revealing his reddened, thick cock, already wet and standing straight and proud between them, Marcus could've gotten off without even touching himself. Tyler was beautiful.

Marcus raised one foot then the other, ridding himself of his pants, and stood naked, save for his boxers, never taking his eyes off Tyler, who, with a decidedly wicked grin, peeled down the zippers of his shiny boots and kicked them off, leaving himself completely naked. "I'm going to make certain that when you leave here tonight, there will be no doubt in anyone's mind who you belong with from now on." He gestured to the sofa. "Go sit down."

Impatient, Marcus reached out to grab Tyler, but the infuriating man stepped out of reach. "I'm calling the shots; now go sit down." He began to stroke himself, and Marcus's breath caught at the erotic sight of Tyler fondling his cock, the raspy sound of hands sliding over naked flesh stimulating a primal urge to touch himself as well.

Marcus slid his hand over the head of his dick and squeezed, the sticky fluid seeping giving him just enough friction, and he sighed; the ache in his balls intensified to a pleasurable pain. "I'm gonna blow if I don't get inside you now," said Marcus with a warning growl.

With one last tug of his own cock, Tyler came near and placed his hand over Marcus's, both of them jerking his cock so fast and hard that spots blurred before his eyes and he came, shooting streams of hot ejaculate over their hands.

"Fuck me." Marcus leaned heavily on Tyler's shoulder and on shaky legs walked with him to the sofa where he collapsed in a boneless heap. He hadn't come so explosively from a hand job in years. But then he'd never wanted anyone like he wanted Tyler.

"I intend to." Tyler joined him, kissing his shoulder, licking at his collarbone, and sucking on his neck. His lips rested in the curve of Marcus's neck, and Marcus sensed his smile. "I'm going to fuck you so hard you'll always feel me inside you, no matter where you are."

Marcus choked, the laughter dying in his throat when Tyler didn't accompany him. "You're not serious. I've never bottomed."

"Are you willing to let me in?"

The obvious double meaning in that question caught him up short. When he looked down at Tyler's dark head resting on his shoulder, Marcus sensed this might be the turning point for the fragile skeleton of a foundation they were building.

Without waiting for him to answer, Tyler resumed kissing his neck, and Marcus shifted to give him greater access. Using his silence as acquiescence, Tyler grew bolder and pinned Marcus's shoulders to the couch while he straddled him, sucking his nipples to tight, reddened points until Marcus writhed in abandoned, unaccustomed ecstasy.

"Say yes," said Tyler, pressing kisses to Marcus's lips. "I won't hurt you; I never would; you know that." Tyler ghosted his fingers along Marcus's cheeks, his touch sweetly gentle, and their eyes met. An unfamiliar calm settled over him, and for the first time ever, Marcus gave a piece of himself away.

"Yes." He swallowed down the thrill of fear shooting through him even as he broke out in a cold sweat. "I want you. Inside me."

Tyler laughed and kissed him hard. "Where's your lube and condoms?"

With his hair in tangled waves and his face shadowed by rough stubble, Tyler looked like a rakish pirate you might see in an old-fashioned Hollywood movie.

"Top drawer of the desk."

"Why am I not surprised?" said Tyler. But there was no condemnation and Marcus made no apologies. He'd never pretended to be a saint.

"I may never have been a Boy Scout, but I've followed their motto of always being prepared."

Tyler pulled out a big box of condoms and a bottle of lube. "There's a difference between being prepared and devaluing yourself." He drew out a long strip from the box, leaving the box on the desk, and walked back to Marcus, standing over him. "Once you're with me, you don't get to fuck around with anyone else. Ever. I know you've never been exclusive, but that's my condition. Is that going to be a problem?"

Marcus could barely fathom it; the idea of being with only one man was something he teased his friends about and never sought for himself. He always looked for the next someone and something better, believing a life unexplored was a life half-lived.

But strangely enough, Tyler's ultimatum didn't faze him or scare him off. His entire world had flipped around, and Marcus had no qualms about committing himself to Tyler, where before, the thought of one man—the same man—would have sent him running in the opposite direction. Tyler's warm body blanketed him, the push of his hard cock insistent on his thigh.

"No," Marcus said with conviction. "I don't want anyone else. I want you."

A smile of pure delight lit Tyler's eyes, and he began to kiss his way down Marcus's body. Unbelievably, though he'd come only a few minutes ago, his cock twitched with renewed vigor. Tyler swiped his tongue across the broad head but kept moving, swirling his tongue around and in Marcus's belly button, grazing the slant of Marcus's hip with his teeth, and lapping at his balls.

"Your mouth is extremely talented," said Marcus, threading his fingers through Tyler's wavy hair. The shock of a fingertip brushing against his hole shot off fireworks through his brain. "Fucking hell." As it was, his cock had hardened once again.

Tyler continued with those maddeningly featherlight touches that soon had Marcus pushing against his finger, searching for something, anything to fill the emptiness inside him. His hands dug into the sofa as he bucked his hips against Tyler's finger, trying to push it inside.

"Fuck," he panted. "Do it already."

Tyler sat back on his heels, an amused smile curving his lips. "Do you think it's going to be wham-bam?" With firm deliberation, Tyler slid one finger up to the knuckle, then added a second into Marcus's hole, not resting until they were buried halfway inside his ass. "I'm going to make it so that you'll wonder why you never did this before. I want to hear you begging for it, crying for my dick." He curled his fingers, brushing against the walls of Marcus's passage and slid halfway out, then plunged in deep again, touching his gland.

"God damn you." If Tyler thought to make him suffer, he'd wait an awfully long time. Marcus had never had to beg for anything in his life, especially sex. "Go to hell." He barely recognized his strangled voice.

"Oh yeah?" Tyler leaned over him and softly kissed the corner of his mouth, at the same time sinking his fingers in as far as they'd go, rubbing them mercilessly over his prostate.

A silent scream built in Marcus's throat as every nerve ending in his body imploded, racking his body with uncontrollable shivers. Everything outside this room ceased to exist, save for the touch of Tyler's hands. He closed his eyes tight, feeling the dampness of his lashes brush against his cheeks.

Shit, he never cried. Embarrassed, he kept his eyes closed, hoping Tyler wouldn't notice.

"It's okay." Tyler slid his fingers from his body, kissing his shoulder.

Marcus didn't answer—he couldn't. Nothing he could say would make sense or do justice to what Tyler had just given him. And it seemed Tyler didn't need his words; he didn't press him for an answer but rather continued to kiss down Marcus's body until he reached his hips, then turned him so he lay prone on the sofa.

Marcus tensed as Tyler separated the globes of his ass, licked down the cleft, then ran the tip of his tongue inside his hole. His sigh of pleasure brought an answering chuckle from Tyler.

"I gather you like this?"

"I'll like anything you do to me with that mouth of yours."

Tyler kissed each ass cheek, then proceeded to sweep his tongue back and forth in the crease. Still spent from the orgasmic bliss that had shattered him earlier, little frissons of excitement buzzed through him at every stab of Tyler's warm, wet tongue.

He heard the rip of the condom packet; how many times had he done that with no regard for anyone's pleasure except his own? Having now been on the receiving end of Tyler's lovemaking, Marcus recognized the difference. He felt valued and wanted, not like a trick for the night. And he felt shame, for all the years of reckless living, treating men as disposable.

"If you breathe out and push back, it will make it a bit easier. I promise to go slow." Tyler wouldn't hurt him, still, at the first push, Marcus tensed at the invasion.

"Remember," said Tyler, little puffs of his warm breath drifting past the shell of Marcus's ear. "Relax and push back."

Marcus gritted his teeth against the pain as Tyler moved past his ring of muscle. He must've been out of his mind to let someone put their dick in him. And then the pain ceased, and all that existed was a fullness inside him so all-consuming and enveloping that once again he struggled to accept it. What possessed him to give up the control, the power?

"It's going to be okay." Tyler kissed his shoulder. "I have to move now. Are you all right?"

"Yeah." He bit his lip, feeling surprisingly emotional. "Go ahead."

Tyler began to rock, withdrawing slowly to plunge back in again. The curve of his cock fit so snug, Marcus could feel the thick veins and ridges as his passage held on tight. Wondering if he could grasp him closer, Marcus tightened his muscles and was rewarded with a moan of absolute pleasure he'd never heard from Tyler's lips before, not even when Marcus made love to him earlier.

"Marcus." Tyler shouted; his thrusting grew stronger, and his hands gripped Marcus's hips tight, pulling him onto his knees. At that angle Tyler's cock hit his prostate again, and Marcus rocked into Tyler's hips, which were pressing into him fast, then slow, then fast again. This was a different kind of power, the control from within his body to give Tyler the lovemaking he so richly deserved. All his focus was on the man above him, inside him—the man who'd changed him forever.

Marcus found his rhythm, intent on giving Tyler the maximum amount of pleasure he could. The faster Tyler moved, the tighter Marcus clasped him inside, until with a shout he swore the crowd must've heard back out on the dance floor, Tyler came, flooding him with heat. Tyler collapsed on top of him, their bodies slicked with sweat.

Thoroughly impaled on Tyler's cock, Marcus's ass hurt yet he remained still, craving the connection between the two of them, wanting to make it last. A few minutes passed, and he shifted, and Tyler, as if he'd come to his senses, moved, sliding gently out of him.

After disposing of the condom in the wastebasket, Tyler returned to the wide sofa but didn't sit down. Puzzled, Marcus turned his cheek against the soft fabric and gave him a sleepy smile. "What's wrong? You look too serious for someone who only a moment ago was screaming the walls down."

A brief smile flickered across Tyler's face, but his eyes remained serious. "You seem okay. I didn't hurt you, right?"

Marcus flopped over on his back. "I'm good." He winced. "Well, I will be in while. Why?" A sudden urge arose to touch Tyler, and Marcus reached out his hand and drew his finger up Tyler's arm, tracing the pale blue veins lying right below the surface of his skin.

"Shift over." Marcus moved, and Tyler slid in next to him on the sofa, and as if they'd been together for years, Marcus draped his arm over Tyler's shoulders. "Is this for real? I'm not talking about the sex; I mean the whole situation between us."

It was on the tip of Marcus's tongue to make a flippant remark and suggest a purely physical relationship. The mechanics would be easy enough; they could be together at the club every night and go their separate ways each day. Easy, simple, and uncluttered with the ups and downs of everyday life.

Tyler's warm body fit in that perfect curve under his arm, and he tightened his hold. Marcus didn't want Tyler to move. Or to leave. Waking up with Tyler this morning, making love with him, broke a cycle of indiscriminate, anonymous sex that never went beyond the pure physical release he sought to find.

"It is for me. I know you're thinking I'm lying or that I'm clueless, and maybe I am." Marcus stroked Tyler's shoulders. "But I don't want you to leave. Thinking of you with someone else makes me want to hurt someone. And I've never felt like that before."

Instead of answering, Tyler sat up. "And there's something else we have to talk about as well."

For a brief moment, Marcus wanted to say "fuck it" and give up. Sex was supposed to be free and easy, not bogged down with complications and issues. This was why he'd kept away from relationships. Then he thought back to leaving his apartment earlier, the vast emptiness on his rooms, and the swirling gray solitude that awaited him, and it dawned on him that he didn't want to be alone anymore.

"Tell me. But if we're going to have a heart-to-heart, maybe we should get dressed." He grinned lazily and splayed his hand on Tyler's thigh. The strong muscle jumped beneath his fingers and a flush of heat arose in Marcus, recalling Tyler powering himself into his body. "You're too distracting naked for serious conversation."

They collected their clothes, and Marcus shook his head when Tyler bent to slip on his shorts.

"Those can't be comfortable. I'll give you a pair of jeans. I keep a second wardrobe here in case something comes up." He went to the closet and found a favorite pair of well-worn jeans and tossed them to Tyler who frowned as he slipped them on.

Knowing Tyler was naked inside his jeans, his cock resting soft and warm behind the buttons, was a huge turn-on for Marcus. He swallowed hard, buttoned his own pants as best he could, and slipped on a solid black V-neck sweater, while Tyler remained shirtless.

After grabbing each a bottle of water from the bar, Marcus returned to the sofa, Tyler following him. He accepted the bottle and sat, tucking his legs underneath him.

"I know you've never been in a relationship. And I'm not the type for one-night stands. So right away we're at opposite ends of the spectrum. But the most important thing in my life right now is making sure Lillie is safe and protected."

"I wouldn't hurt her." Marcus frowned. "You can't possibly think I would."

"Not intentionally, no. But she likes you, and I think you tolerate her because of me. Which is perfectly fine. But what I can't have you do is throw money at her and buy her toys and clothes or anything else she wants."

"It's not intentional. If I'm on the computer, she likes to watch. I can't help it if she shows me stuff. It's not a big deal." He sulked, picking at the label of his water bottle. "I wasn't doing anything wrong."

To his surprise, Tyler laughed, then scooted over and gave him a hug. "No, and it's incredibly sweet. But I don't want her spoiled and thinking all she has to do is ask you and you'll give it to her."

That was exactly the truth, though. Secretly Marcus liked it when Lillie sat with him at the computer. She was a lively, bright little person, smarter than many adults he knew.

"I can try, but she's a very convincing child. Does that mean you'll come back to the apartment? What about preschool—you know she loves it there, and she's made friends."

Tyler rubbed his hands on his thighs. "I don't know. Maybe for now, until after the holidays, we can keep her there. But if we stay," said Tyler shooting him a hard look, "I'm paying you rent and doing the cooking."

"Naked cooking sounds good." Marcus tugged Tyler close. "You can bring me breakfast in bed."

"Naked cooking sounds terrible," said Tyler, laughing. "Things could catch on fire or get stuck or burned. But I'm all for breakfast in bed."

Marcus dipped his head down to meet Tyler in a kiss. His thoughts turned to getting naked on the sofa again when there was a sudden, loud banging on the door that sent them springing apart.

"Who the hell is that?"

The door opened, and Julian's blond head appeared, with his hand shielding his eyes.

"Are you decent? Or should I say is Tyler decent, since you're beyond hope, Marcus."

"Oh for fuck's sake," said Marcus groaning as he watched all his friends traipse into his office. "What do you all want?"

"We had to check and make sure you were all right." The wide smile on Julian's face tipped Marcus off his friend was up to no good. Juli had always had an evil streak, the bastard.

"The only problem I have is you. Do I look like I'm not all right?" Facing Tyler, he pointed at his friends. "Do you see what I have to put up with?"

"Oh come on. The noises coming from inside here were loud enough to hear down the hallway, probably in the next building." Julian circled around his desk and picked up the open box of condoms, putting them back in the drawer. "Might want to hide the evidence."

"You know, Juli, you're one step away from getting that pretty face of yours punched." Marcus half rose, but Tyler pulled him back.

"You realize he's baiting you and you're falling for it." Tyler murmured in his ear. "I'd expect nothing less from your friends."

Letting go of his not-giving-a-shit attitude would be the hardest thing about a relationship. He'd never had to care about someone else's feelings or concerns.

"You're normally the one who gets a fist to the jaw, not me," said Julian, returning to Nick's side. "How could you forget Nick's first time meeting you?"

"Or Sam's," said Zach, piping up from his place by the door. "Don't forget Sam laid Marcus out right by the bar."

Tyler shook with laughter next to him. "You mean," he gasped, "each one of you punched Marcus the first time you met him?" At their nods he fell back on the sofa, howling with laughter.

"It's not that funny," said Marcus sulkily. "And aren't you supposed to be on my side?"

Finished with the hysteria, Tyler wiped his eyes and kissed him on the cheek. "I'll always be on your side. But you have to know how funny that is."

Marcus slipped his arm around Tyler and shot a glance at his friends. Each of them stood with big stupid grins on their faces, except for Julian.

"Well, well. What do we have here?" He raised a brow. "Something you want to share with us?"

"It's a wonder we've remained friends all these years, Juli," said Marcus, biting back a grin. "I can't for the life of me figure out why."

"Because you love me," said Julian promptly. "So, if I'm right, you two are together now?"

"Yes to that and maybe to the first," he said, granting the smile threatening his lips full access. "Go ahead; give me your best shot. I'm waiting." To think he was in a committed relationship with a man who had a young child. What the fuck was he doing? Then Tyler took his hand and laced their fingers together, and Marcus remembered why.

To his surprise, Julian merely shook his head and slid his arm around Nick's waist. "I'm happy for you, Marc."

Those simple words, with no sarcasm or joke behind them tore Marcus up enough that he couldn't speak. And from the small nod and warmth shining in his eyes, Julian understood.

Julian was never one to let a question remain unanswered or a topic slide. "Aside from obvious reasons, Tyler, why is the fact that both Nick and Sam punched your boyfriend so funny?" He paused and shook his head. "Marcus and boyfriend in the same sentence. The Earth may have stopped on its axis."

Having regained his ability to speak, Marcus squeezed Tyler's hand. "You don't have to answer him, you know." Marcus nudged Tyler. "He's having entirely too much fun with this conversation at my expense."

"As he should." Tyler kissed his cheek again, then addressed Julian. "And it's funny because I decked him also. Put him right on his ass in my dressing room."

"It wasn't that funny," Marcus grumbled, though even he found it hard to contain his grin.

The room exploded with laughter; several minutes passed before the hilarity quieted down and they could speak.

"Priceless. We might need tee shirts for you all." Julian wiped his eyes and picked up his coat from the coat rack in the corner. "Well, we're heading home. Thanks for this momentous occasion, Tyler." He gave him a hug, and Zach waited right behind him.

"Welcome to the family."

Watching his friends accept Tyler with such ease, Marcus beat back the doubts circling his mind. Could he be the man they believed him to be—faithful to one person, taking someone else's needs into consideration. He hadn't prepared for Tyler walking into his life; a life he'd planned on sailing through alone, easy and unencumbered.

Julian once said one never plans for something like this to happen, and he had to admit his friend was correct. Lately he'd been more dissatisfied, helpless and angry, watching his world change and unable to control his friends creating lives apart from him. Lives he'd no longer had a place in.

Tyler made him happy, and he hadn't been happy for a while. He wanted to make him happy as well, and protect Lillie from all the evil in the world. The one thing he didn't want was to be the man his father was. He'd do anything and everything to prevent that from happening.

Chapter Eighteen

"L IVE HERE FOR keeps? With Marcus?"

Lillie sat on the sofa next to him while Marcus chose to sit on the overstuffed club chair. She'd never know what happened that weekend, how they'd almost split apart, then came back together, and he and Marcus decided when she came home from school on Monday, they would have The Talk with her.

He and Marcus had planned what they were going to tell Lillie. Marcus had thought to keep it from her, but Tyler refused to sneak around and insisted they tell her the truth and let her ask as many questions as she wanted.

"Would you like that?"

Serious round blue eyes met his own, and she sat still, her face screwed up in thought. Every few seconds her gaze would flicker to Marcus, then skitter back to him.

Tyler had no doubt Lillie would love living in Marcus's apartment; who wouldn't want to live in a luxury building? His concern ran deeper than that; if Lillie didn't feel comfortable with Marcus and him together, they'd have to figure something else out.

"Are you gonna get married like Jacob and Rebecca's daddies?"

Marcus's brows rose high. "Uhh, sweetheart, your uncle Ty and I don't know each other well enough to get married."

At the panicky, deer-in-the-headlights look in Marcus's eyes, Tyler choked back the bubble of laughter threatening to escape. "We aren't getting married, but we will be more than friends."

"I saw Micah kissing Josh; have you kissed Marcus?"

He nodded and waited for her response. She surprised him by sliding off the sofa and going over to Marcus, who watched her with a mixture of amusement, fascination, and a touch of fear. It was a dichotomy Tyler had never thought to see: Marcus holding a conversation with a child. He only hoped Marcus would learn to tolerate Lillie. In the month they'd lived here, he and Lillie had only minimal contact, since his hours at Sparks prevented him from spending time at home in the evenings.

"Are you Uncle Ty's boyfriend?"

To his credit, Marcus didn't treat Lillie like a walking doll. He gave her question great consideration. Tyler understood her need to assign a label to their relationship; it was the way children saw the world. They needed order and structure and giving him and Marcus an official title made it easier for her to picture their relationship.

"I guess you could call us that." His response was guarded and measured and surprisingly, Marcus didn't seek validation from him for his answer. His concentration was on Lillie. "Is that okay with you?"

"Okay." She patted Marcus's knee, and Tyler didn't know whether to laugh or give in to the tears that threatened. "But no fighting. Mommy used to fight with her boyfriends, and sometimes they'd be mean and she'd cry."

The laughter fled from Marcus's eyes. Tyler had heard the stories before from his sister when she first came to stay with them. How she never knew who Lillie's father was, and the string of boyfriends she had afterward didn't like it when Lillie made noise or bothered them. She'd never said, however Marcus suspected she'd been abused by those men, physically or sexually. He wondered, as he had over the past year, where Amber was and if she was okay.

"Did anyone ever hurt you?" Surprised at the gentleness in Marcus's voice, Tyler held his breath. Lillie hadn't been forthcoming about what she remembered, and Tyler hadn't wanted to push her. She shook her head, and Tyler could see the relief on Marcus's face.

"Those bas—"

Tyler cut him off before he could finish. First on his list would be to discuss language in front of Lillie. God knows Marcus loved to curse, but he'd have to make a concerted effort to watch his filthy mouth in front of the child.

"Marcus, I'm not sure we need to get into this—"

"They were mean," Lillie interrupted him. "They didn't like me, and I hated them. I like living with Uncle Ty better." She looked over her shoulder at him. "Can I have a snack? We didn't have cookies today."

Making a mental note to stock up on more food for the apartment, he stood, and with Lillie at his heels, went into the kitchen. Now that they'd be living here, he planned to cook most nights; a child shouldn't exist on takeout, and he enjoyed being in the kitchen.

He rummaged around in the cabinets and found a package of chocolate chip cookies. "Go sit, and I'll bring you some and a glass of milk."

Obediently, she climbed up on the chair and watched with avid eyes as he put the cookies on a plate and poured her milk in her plastic princess cup. He sat with her, but Marcus remained in the living room, now busy on his computer.

After she'd munched down one of the cookies and had a sip of milk, he asked, "Why didn't you have a snack? I know you usually do after school." If he couldn't pick her up from school, Lillie would go to Micah and Josh's until her babysitter, Angela, could bring her back home.

"Yeah, but Micah and Josh had to go to the school 'cause they got mad." She ate her second cookie slowly. "Uncle Ty?"

"Yes?" He took a cookie for himself.

"Why would people get mad at two boys getting married?"

He put the cookie down. "Did someone say something at school, or are you just asking me?" His gaze found Marcus, who had stopped working on his laptop and listened with a somber expression on his face.

"Well, some kids were teasing Jacob and Rebecca about not having a mommy and how having two daddies was weird. And the teachers didn't even say anything." Her lower lip stuck out in indignation. "When they said something to me, I called them stupid and told them to shut up."

A flicker of a smile came and went on Marcus's lips, but Tyler didn't join him. "What did they say to you?"

She shrugged and finished her cookie, then hopped off the seat. "They kept asking me where my mommy was and why I lived with you. I wouldn't answer them, and they said maybe I was a weirdo like Jacob and Rebecca and you were gonna marry a boy too."

Hence her questions about marriage and boyfriends. "Would you rather not live here? You can tell me the truth; I promise I won't be mad."

"Nooo, I love my room and my toys and everything. I don't wanna leave. I'll never see my friends again." Her eyes filled with tears, and Tyler rushed to comfort her.

"Okay, don't worry. I want to make sure you're happy, that's all." He gave her a hug and a kiss and to his surprise she left him and went to join Marcus.

"Thank you for letting me stay here. I promise not to break anything or be bad."

"I know."

After Lillie had gone to her room to play, Tyler once again stretched out on the sofa and found himself dozing off watching Marcus work. Tyler was still catching up from last night; between the dancing and the amazing sex, his ribs still gave him a painful twinge every now and then.

Warm lips met his and he responded, the taste of Marcus already familiar on his tongue. Nothing about kissing him was peaceful and serene. The fire Marcus lit up inside him incinerated everything else in its path. He slid his arms around Marcus's neck and slanted their mouths together, hungry and demanding, plunging his tongue past Marcus's lips, where they met and tangled.

Reality forced its way into the fog of lust building in his mind. "Marcus," he said, breaking off their kiss and gasping for air. "We have to stop. We can't do this here."

Marcus kissed his forehead, then leaned against it with his own. "I know. I got carried away seeing you lying there. You can make it up to me tonight."

Tyler squeezed his ass. "It's a date."

Surprisingly, Marcus stretched out next to him; if Tyler didn't know better, he'd think they were cuddling. Except Marcus didn't cuddle.

"I didn't like what happened at that school today."

Shocked that he'd care, Tyler ran his hand down Marcus's back and began to massage him, enjoying Marcus's obvious pleasure, if the rumbling, almost purring noise under his hands was any indication. "Unfortunately, even little kids can have prejudices. They're obviously picking things up at home."

"But the teachers should stop it. Isn't that their job?" Marcus glided his hand across Tyler's stomach and with a somewhat frustrated grunt, Tyler moved his hand to a safer spot farther up his chest.

"I can't have your hands down my pants with Lillie in the next room. What if she came out?" But he kissed Marcus's cheek and neck, hoping it would mollify him. "And to answer your question, yes, they should, but hopefully the kids will stop teasing once they don't get a reaction."

"I think you should complain like Micah and Josh did. They have a responsibility to not let that happen."

Fear sliced through him. By allowing her to go to the preschool, he took a chance at discovery, but luckily Amber had left all Lillie's paperwork, including her birth certificate, and they'd gotten a doctor friend of Micah's who was a pediatrician to give her medical clearance. Tyler told everyone he was her legal guardian, and they accepted it at face value.

None of it was true. He had no rights to Lillie that he knew of. And if the government stepped in, would they give him custody, a single gay man who danced in a nightclub for tips? Doubtful.

"No, leave it alone. Hopefully it was only one day and by tomorrow they'll be on to the next. Besides, Micah and Josh went today, so I'm sure it will be handled." He sat up and gazed at Marcus. "I think we can change the topic and find something to discuss that we can both share, don't you?" He could always distract Marcus with thoughts of sex.

Marcus's beautiful violet-gray eyes fired sparks. "What do you have in mind?" He pulled Tyler to him, his mouth hovering over Tyler.

He moaned at the first swipe of Marcus's tongue against his heated skin. "Why don't you come with me and find out?" With Marcus holding on to his shoulders, keeping him close so Tyler could feel the heaviness of Marcus's erection pressing up against his ass, they walked into the bedroom and closed the door behind them.

Chapter Nineteen

"WHAT'S THE MATTER, boss? You seem preoccupied. Everything cool?"

Darius looked at him over the sheets he was studying. It was their monthly loss-prevention check-up meeting, and normally Marcus barreled through the numbers and had everything at his fingertips. Today, though, he had little patience for it all. Tyler had been out looking at potential space to rent for a dance studio, and Marcus was as excited about it as if he was starting a new business himself.

Over the past month Tyler had begun teaching dance not only at Lillie's preschool but at preschools throughout the city, and the response had been tremendous; so much so that he was making more money than he ever did dancing at Sparks. Parents contacted him for private lessons for their little darlings, and Marcus wanted him to give up the dancing at Sparks and make teaching a business. Today was the first step. He had an appointment to see a space in Chelsea that looked promising, and Marcus was waiting for a call from him.

When he told Darius about it, the man's eyes lit up. "That's cool. My little nieces and nephews love dance; their school has an African dance class that is booked solid every year." He leaned back in his chair and stretched out his legs. "Good for him. I told Ty right from the beginning he was too good for this place."

"Hey, there's no shame in dancing here, but yeah, his talent is wasted dancing for a bunch of horny rich men who only want to make a grab at his ass."

"Especially when that ass belongs to you now, right?" Darius quirked a brow. "You guys have been together like what, a month? And it's working out fine, huh?"

No doubt Darius wanted to shoot the shit like he normally did, and for years Marcus had regaled his friends with stories of his sexcapades. Things change—*he* changed—and what once was the norm was no longer part of his reality.

He met Darius's steady stare. "Yeah, it's fine. Let's finish these numbers, and then you can meet the guys downstairs to check on the stock."

Surprised for a moment, Darius narrowed his eyes. "Well all right, then." They went through the rest of the numbers, matching them up against inventory, and Marcus noted the small changes Sam had suggested already saved him money. Darius shuffled the papers together and slid them back into his folder.

"Okay, boss, I'll see you later." The door closed behind Darius with a loud snick of the lock.

Marcus barely registered his departure; his thoughts remained not with the club that had occupied so much of his life for years, but with the man who shared his home, his bed, and increasingly his heart. Last night he'd gotten home late, dead-tired, and in a piss-poor mood. He might not like Tyler dancing for tips, but the bonus was having him there at the club with him. Now that he'd moved away from that to teaching, their paths didn't cross in the evenings, and Marcus missed him more than he imagined possible.

To his surprise, Tyler had waited up with a small meal he'd prepared for Marcus and sat with him while he ate. After the meal, Tyler undressed him, put him in the shower, and made such slow, incredible love to him, even now Marcus trembled from the memory of Tyler's mouth and hands moving over his body with tender precision. They fell asleep wrapped in each other's arms.

"I need to get out of here," said Marcus to himself. For a place where he'd poured his life and soul into for years, the office walls now closed in on him; he hoped Tyler was finished with his appointment. He wrote him a text message; then, before he hit Send, remembered that after the appointment with the real estate agent, Tyler had a private dance lesson with a client who lived way over on the Upper East Side.

"Shit." He only hesitated a second before texting Julian and Zach in their group chat.

Anyone free for lunch?

Within two beats both Julian and Zach responded with: *When?*

He texted back with their usual spot in the city since—*Sorry, Zach*—he didn't feel like dragging himself into Brooklyn today. He was on his way out the door when his phone rang.

The number that flashed on his screen was unfamiliar, and normally he wouldn't take it, thinking it would be a sales call, but he thought maybe it was Tyler calling from an unfamiliar phone.

"Hello?"

"Is this Marcus Feldman?" a harassed-sounding woman queried.

"Yes. Who is this?"

Few people had access to his personal cell phone, so if the call wasn't from Julian, Zach, and now Tyler, it was likely not good news. A sense of foreboding arose within him.

"This is the nurse at Playtime Academy. Lillie is okay, but is there anyone who can come pick her up? We have no water in the building today, so we are asking all the parents to come pick up their children. We tried calling Mr. Reiss, but he isn't picking up his phone."

Panic set in. Him? Pick up Lillie? A thought sprang to mind.

"Can you send her home with Faith? She's the babysitter for Dr. Steinberg's children."

"I'm sorry, but the children aren't in today. They had doctor appointments. How long before you can come pick her up?"

Fucking hell. What was he supposed to do with a little girl all day? If he had normal parents, he could've called his mother, but that wouldn't have worked anyway as she was still in Paris.

"Uhh…" His mind worked furiously, but he couldn't come up with an excuse not to get Lillie. Then Marcus thought of how frantic Tyler would be if he knew no one would be there for Lillie, and gripped the phone tighter in his sweaty hand. "I'll be there in twenty minutes."

On his way out of the club, he texted Julian and Zach cancelling their plans and the reason why. It didn't take but two minutes before he spotted a cab with its light on, and he flagged it down. He gave the cabbie the address, and they were soon winging their way over to the preschool.

If anyone would have told him a few months ago he'd be picking up a four-year-old girl and spending the day with her instead of working at Sparks, he would've told them they were fucking crazy and laughed in their faces.

Yet when Marcus ran from the cab and finally found the nurse's office only to see Lillie sitting there so forlornly, his heart squeezed in his chest with an unfamiliar emotion.

"Hey, Lillie-bug."

A smile of pure delight broke over her face. "Marcus." She dropped the crayons she'd been coloring with and ran to him, giving him a hug around his legs. "You came? Where's Uncle Ty?"

He froze for a second, then bent to speak to her at eye level. "Your uncle is teaching a dance class, so I came. Let's go." As he waited for Lillie to collect her things, he signed the form the nurse gave him that released Lillie to his care, and almost as an afterthought, he mentioned the teasing incident of a month earlier to the nurse.

"I hope those kids who picked on Jacob and Rebecca were spoken to about intolerance and bullying. The earlier you start the better, don't you think?"

Instead of agreeing with him, she pursed her lips in a disapproving line and folded her arms. To Marcus she looked like an evil version of Mrs. Claus.

"Children have a right to express their opinions, especially about things that aren't normal to them." She narrowed her gaze at him, muddy-brown eyes turning crafty and fox-like. She checked her notes, and Marcus swore he could hear the sneer in her voice. "Exactly how do you fit into Lillie's home life, Mr. Feldman?"

Bitch. Before he met Tyler and learned to temper his anger and cursing in front of Lillie, Marcus would've backed this woman up against the wall and flayed her with every curse word in the book. The uptight old harridan probably hadn't gotten laid in years. But he'd discovered that sometimes putting his needs second wasn't such a bad thing, and Lillie was too innocent to hear the words he itched to say.

"I'm a good friend of the family." He bared his teeth in what he hoped was a semblance of a grin, then felt a tug on his jacket and looked down. "Ready?"

"Yes."

Without saying goodbye to the nurse, he walked out with Lillie into the sharp cold air. There was nothing like winter in the city, and even though Marcus never bothered to celebrate any of the holidays, secretly he enjoyed the decorations and the overall liveliness it brought.

"I'm hungry." Lillie gazed up at him. "We didn't eat our snack or lunch today."

Marcus had no clue what to do with a little kid, so he did what came naturally and texted Zach for help.

What do I do with a four-year-old girl? She's hungry, and I haven't a clue.

Within a minute, Zach answered.

Take her someplace fun. Here's a list.

Marcus could've kissed the phone. He scrolled through what Zach sent him and deciding on a place, hailed a cab and beckoned Lillie.

"Come, let's go have lunch."

She climbed in, and he buckled her seat belt tight. All bundled up in her pink puffy jacket and purple hat, Lillie was a really cute kid.

"Where are we going?"

"It's a surprise."

Her face lit up, blue eyes shining like twin sapphires.

"Oooh, really?" She bounced a little in her seat. "I love surprises."

He listened to her chatter away about her friends and thought how uncomplicated a child's life was at that age. All they needed was someone to make them feel secure and loved. It was only when they grew up that they realized that sometimes those who were supposed to care for them were often the ones who hurt them the most in the end.

Twenty minutes later, the cab drew up in front of the restaurant. He paid the fare and got out, waiting for Lillie to follow. His heart lurched when, as they walked inside the restaurant, she slipped her hand in his. He looked down at her, and she gave him a smile; he squeezed her hand.

"Table for two?" The hostess smiled at him.

He nodded, and they made their way through the front of the restaurant which was decorated like a general store. Even he'd heard of Serendipity's, and when he saw all the kids, he sent a silent thank-you to Zach for, as usual, coming through for him in the clutch.

"What would you like?"

She looked around the restaurant, and her gaze lit on the table next to them. Two children were sharing a hot dog that looked as tall as Lillie and a plate of french fries. A huge glass of some frozen chocolate thing sat between them.

"Can I have that?" She pointed to their plate.

Why the hell not? She could have whatever she wanted as far as Marcus was concerned. Anything to keep her happy and smiling. "Sure." He called the waitress over and ordered. While they waited, he watched Lillie take in the sights around her, enjoying the crowds of midday shoppers.

Two young girls around her age came in with their mother and sat down two tables away, a pile of red shopping bags at their feet. They pawed through the bags until they each pulled out a big doll and began playing with them.

Lillie's eyes grew even rounder. "Oh, those are the new American Girl dolls. Rebecca got one for her birthday last month." The waitress came with their food, but Lillie's attention remained on the two girls playing with their new dolls.

"Come, eat your food before it gets cold." He put some ketchup on the side. "Do you like mustard on your hot dog?"

Distracted, she nodded. "Yeah okay."

No human being could eat this thing in one piece, so Marcus cut the hot dog up into what he hoped were small enough pieces.

Finally, Lillie turned around and began to eat, although she still sneaked looks over to the girls and their dolls.

"What's so special about them?" To Marcus they looked like big dolls, nothing more.

Growing more animated by the minute, Lillie proceeded to regale him with the history of every doll. She did manage to eat some of the food, but neither of them could finish or put much of a dent in the frozen hot chocolate drink.

After he paid the bill they walked outside to hail a cab to go home. As they waited on the sidewalk, Marcus noticed nearly every young girl walking with her family had one of the red bags from that doll store Lillie had talked about. He quickly Googled the address, and although Tyler had told him not to spoil Lillie with too many things, how bad could it be? It was only a doll, after all. And since Lillie loved surprises, he knew exactly what to do.

He put his hand out, and a cab pulled up in front of them. "Come on, let's go."

THREE HOURS AND two hundred and fifty dollars later, Marcus lay sprawled out on the sofa in his apartment, utterly wiped out.

"Never again," he muttered to himself, rubbing his feet. It was a miracle he hadn't gotten killed between women pushing strollers over his toes and the ear-splitting screams of little girls he swore he could still hear ringing in his ears. "No wonder so many mothers drink."

Lillie came over to him, holding on to the doll he'd bought her. She hadn't let go of it since the cashier handed her the bag in the store. "Do you feel better?" She put her hand on his head. "Uncle Ty always feels my head when I say I'm sick."

If Marcus had his way, Tyler would be feeling other parts of Marcus besides his head.

"I'm okay, thanks."

"Can we play dress-up? You don't have to do anything. I want my dolly to wear her new clothes. And I want to try on the nail polish too." With careful concentration, she sat her doll on the sofa next to her and put the bottle of glittery nail polish on her lap.

Too tired to care, Marcus shrugged. "Knock yourself out. As long as I don't have to get up, you can do whatever you want."

"I'll do mine first."

Marcus yawned and stretched. Hopefully she wouldn't get nail polish all over the new doll, but he didn't really care. Taking care of a kid wasn't as bad as he'd thought.

Chapter Twenty

A LL SORTS OF problems ran through Tyler's mind upon discovering Marcus had been conscripted to pick up Lillie from preschool. And a reassuring text that they were having "fun" didn't set his mind at ease as it should have. Fun for Marcus meant something very different than it did for an ordinary person.

He was so nervous that he broke his own rule and took a cab home rather than wait for the eternally slow subway. Raymond nodded and waved hello to him as he hurried past.

"Marcus and Lillie are upstairs."

"Thanks," said Tyler over his shoulder, running to catch the elevator. Now that he was back, he realized how silly he was being. Marcus had lived with Lillie for two months now and while he never spent any time alone with her, he tolerated her as an amusing presence in his life. Hearing voices inside, Tyler inserted his key in the lock, curious and a bit anxious to see how Marcus had spent almost an entire day with a four-year-old girl.

The two of them sat on the sofa, surrounded by dolls. Doll clothing and shopping bags lay strewn about their feet. Lillie caught a glimpse of him, picked up a big doll which he knew she hadn't owned prior to today and ran to him.

"Uncle Ty, look what Marcus got me."

"That's nice, baby-girl."

Tyler barely glanced at her; the sight of Marcus had him transfixed.

"Don't say a word."

Tyler bit his lip, but it was impossible not to break out in laughter. "What happened?" he managed to get out in between bursts of hilarity.

Marcus glowered, his eyes flashing. Beams of late-afternoon sunlight picked up on the sparkling tiara resting in Marcus's sleek black hair. And, if Tyler wasn't mistaken, a suspicious pink sheen of lip-gloss gleamed on Marcus's lips.

"Marcus played dress-up with me. He said it was okay." Lillie looked between the two of them. "Did I do something wrong?" With slow, hesitant steps, she walked over to Marcus. "Are you mad at me?"

And then Tyler watched something extraordinary occur. Marcus picked Lillie up and sat her in his lap. As gentle as Tyler had ever witnessed, Marcus smoothed back her hair from her brow and gave her a kiss on the forehead. "Not a chance, Lillie-bug. Now why don't you gather all your stuff up and go to your room for a bit. I think your uncle Tyler and I need to have a talk."

"Are you gonna fight? Please don't fight and say mean things."

"No, we're not going to fight. I promise." Marcus swatted her on the backside. "Go on now."

Amazed, Tyler watched Lillie pick up all her things, lug them into her bedroom, and shut the door behind her. Tyler imagined she was more than happy to stay behind closed doors and play with whatever else Marcus had bought for her.

They stared at one another across the room until Tyler couldn't take it any longer and walked over to Marcus. "So, Princess, do you mind telling me what happened here? But first let me get my hello kiss."

Tyler leaned over and kissed Marcus, tracing his lips with the tip of his tongue. As always, whenever they kissed or touched, a rich warmth flooded Tyler, soaking up all the coldness he had inside, though after two months with Marcus, those cold unhappy places had become harder than ever to find.

Tyler wasn't about to let Marcus get away without a little (who was he kidding—*a lot*) of teasing, and he licked his lips. "Umm, strawberry." If possible, the scowl on Marcus's face grew even blacker.

"You're a fucking riot, Tyler. What was I supposed to do? She had to get picked up, and there was only me. You never told me you put me down as her emergency contact after you. We went to lunch, and there were all these other kids with stuff from that Girl place."

Vacillating between shock and horror, Tyler stared at Marcus. "You aren't telling me you took her to the American Girl store? That place is a pit of hell for parents."

Marcus pulled the tiara off his head and set it down on the tabletop. "Yeah, well, except for a slight dent in my credit card, I made it out alive and unscathed. It's really no big deal; I was happy to do it, and she's thrilled."

Bemused at Marcus's attitude, Tyler caught sight of Marcus's hand and almost choked. "Marcus? What's on your fingers?"

For a brief second Marcus checked and curled his fingers into his palms as if by hiding them, Tyler could possibly forget what he'd seen.

"Nothing."

Nice try. "Let me see your hands, now." He used the same tone of voice on Marcus he normally reserved for Lillie. "Come on." He gestured with his hand, shooting Marcus a stern look.

After a little grumbling, Marcus reluctantly held out his hands, and Tyler whooped with laughter, doubling over.

The fingernails on Marcus's right hand glittered with pink-sparkle nail polish, while the ones on his left sparkled purple. Except for a bit of smearing at the top, they were surprisingly neat.

"What...how—how did that happen?" Laughter bubbled through Tyler's words.

"She asked," said Marcus, frowning. "How was I supposed to say no to her?" He scratched at one nail. "I didn't want her to cry."

This couldn't be the same Marcus he knew from only a few short months ago. That man would never have spoken to a child, never mind play with one and let her paint his nails. Still, he had to understand Tyler made the parenting decisions and wasn't about to let her fall into the trap of buying her whatever she wanted.

"We've spoken about giving in to her and spoiling her with too much stuff. I don't want her drowning in more toys than she'll ever use."

"She was going on and on about how Rebecca got this doll, and then all these kids in the restaurant had one too. I didn't think it was so wrong, and before I bought it for her I made her promise to donate some of her toys to the children's hospital and the homeless shelter Zach volunteers at."

This was the side no one else ever saw of Marcus; the charitable, giving side. There was so much more to this man than Tyler had ever imagined. Somewhat mollified with the explanation, Tyler gave in grudgingly. "Well, that's better than nothing, I guess."

"I knew you'd see it like that."

But he wasn't about to let Marcus get off that easily. "Care to finish the story? How did you get from buying her an American Girl doll to wearing a tiara and strawberry lip gloss?" He kissed Marcus. "Not that I mind, because you taste delicious, but I'm curious."

"I haven't the faintest clue," said Marcus, rolling onto his side, facing Tyler, his slow, easy smile lighting up his face. "But in case you didn't realize it, she's kind of hard to say no to. Kind of like her uncle." Marcus reached for him, his warm palm cupping the nape of his neck, sliding into his hair.

They kissed again, slow and warm with the burgeoning pleasure that comes with a new relationship where you've been intimate, yet still know there are pieces of your lover you've yet to discover. Tyler pressed his mouth to Marcus's, deepening their kiss.

With a low growl that sent shivers up Tyler's spine, Marcus pulled him close, molding their bodies together, and Tyler could feel every hard bump and ridge of bone and muscle pressing into his flesh. Even through his clothes, Marcus's hardness was impressive, and Tyler wrapped his legs around Marcus's hips, nestling their groins close.

"Let's go to the bedroom." Marcus slipped his strong hands under

Tyler's shirt and kneaded the tension from his back, sending shock-waves through Tyler's body. "I've been thinking of you all day and how much I want you." He continued to nuzzle Tyler, kissing his neck and teasing the shell of his ear with his hot tongue and breath.

Desire rippled through Tyler, the pleasurable ache flowing through him like chocolate, rich and sweet. He moaned, and Marcus chuckled in his ear, low and deep.

"It's going to take all night to do the things I want to you." He stood and tugged Tyler up, lacing their fingers together. "Maybe longer."

"Don't you have to go to work tonight? Angela is coming at six. I need to shower and get down to the club as well." Angela was the overnight sitter they hired when they both worked at the club. Tyler had about as much desire to dance tonight as he did in running naked through Central Park in the snow.

"I called her earlier and told her not to come and that we'll see her on Monday. I'm taking the night off."

Tyler's eyes widened, but he remained silent. He'd been working at the club for three months and couldn't ever remember Marcus taking a night off, especially a Friday night.

"Really?" He kept his voice casual, but inside Tyler couldn't be more thrilled, though he wondered at this sudden change of heart.

"Yeah. I thought we'd all have dinner, and then the two of us could spend the entire night together, by ourselves, instead of me watching other guys ogle your ass."

As they walked into the bedroom, Marcus slipped his hands inside Tyler's jeans, fondling him. Tyler grew harder by the minute, his cock straining painfully against the zipper of his jeans.

"You have nothing to worry about. This ass is yours—I'm all yours."

Marcus pushed him down on the bed. "Fucking right you are. And no one else has a right to touch what's mine." His powerful thighs straddled Tyler's hips, and Tyler, who'd never liked a controlling, dominating man before, wanted Marcus to take him hard. "I don't even like when they watch you, thinking that they have a chance."

He watched Marcus strip off his shirt and toss it on the floor. "Show me how much you want me, then," said Tyler. "Right here." He popped the buttons on his jeans, shimmied out of them, and lay back, stroking his cock; Marcus stood, quickly unzipping his pants, then leaving them in a pile on the floor, along with his black boxers.

"Every time I see you shake that ass in the club I want to fucking kill every man who even looks at you." Marcus flung his leg over Tyler's hip, and their erect cocks slid together, creating the perfect friction; Tyler bucked up, opening himself wide.

Tyler grabbed Marcus's face between his hands. "Fuck me so hard you'll leave a part of yourself in me. You have to know after these months it's only you I want."

The inscrutable expression on Marcus's face unnerved Tyler. Did he reveal too much, too soon?

"I am?" Marcus caressed his face, the pads of his thumbs sliding over his cheeks, running down the length of his jaw.

A heartbreaking vulnerability shone on Marcus's face, and Tyler's heart swelled, beating rapidly. Had no one ever told this man they loved him? Tyler studied Marcus's unsmiling face and for once, let down his own guard and listened with his heart. Instead of the arrogant, self-assured player, Marcus's genuine hesitancy made him so much more desirable to Tyler.

So much easier to love.

"Yeah. Only you."

Sensing that talking alone wouldn't prove to Marcus his feelings, Tyler slipped his hand between their bodies and stroked Marcus, loving his thick, hard cock and his heavy balls. He rubbed his thumb over the wide head of Marcus's cock, spreading the copious early fluid dripping from the head, then brought his finger to his mouth and licked it. "Um, love your taste."

Marcus grinned. "Funny, I was about to say the same thing." He edged down the bed and took Tyler's aching cock into his mouth, swirling his tongue over the head and down the vein of his stiff shaft. Marcus wet his finger, then slipped the tip just inside Tyler's hole, while still keeping both tongue and lips occupied with his dick, which threatened to explode.

Tyler moaned, craving the stretch and thickness of Marcus to fill him up. "Please, come on." He reached out blindly with his hands. "Please."

With one last wet and juicy suckle, Marcus released him. "Since you asked so nicely," said Marcus, and from beneath half-open eyelids, Tyler watched him roll on a condom and slick himself up.

"You want it nice and slow, right, baby?" Only the wide head of his cock pushed inside Tyler, and he writhed underneath Marcus who grinned wickedly back at him, sliding his hands up Tyler's chest to tweak his nipples. "I don't want to rush it; we have all night to make it right." He pushed Tyler's legs up, hooking one over his shoulder, and Tyler nearly lost his mind as Marcus slid deep inside.

Tyler turned greedy and wanting, urging Marcus on. Marcus didn't pound him into the mattress, but instead sank inside his passage torturously slow. He rocked his hips in a steady pace until the rest of the world fell away and Tyler's entire focus rested on the point where their bodies joined; nothing mattered except the feel of Marcus in him and on top of him. Becoming a part of him Tyler never knew existed.

Then the rush of his orgasm swept through him, and he blinked back the threat of inexplicable tears as he spilled hot and sticky between them. Every nerve ending quivered, and Tyler's body clenched tight, then shuddered to completion, so thoroughly shattered his bones rattled under his skin.

"Marcus, oh God, Marcus." In the distance he could hear himself crying out yet strangely felt no shame, only the pure and perfect reality that right here with this man was where he was supposed to be.

In an unexpected show of tenderness, Marcus slid their hands together, lacing their fingers until they held tight. He ran his nose along

Tyler's cheek, driving himself deeper and faster, moaning his pleasure, and though Tyler lay spent, happiness washed over him, warm like a cleansing rain.

"Oh baby, fuck," Marcus choked out, his breath coming in gasps as he rammed into him deliciously rough and hard at last. Tyler tilted his hips, slotting Marcus farther inside, until he could no longer tell where he ended and Marcus began. It was somewhere next to his heart, which had regained its purpose now and began beating for the first time in forever. Marcus pinned him to the bed, their fingers still entwined, and he came, pumping the condom inside Tyler full of liquid heat.

Marcus's heart beat a crazy tattoo against Tyler's chest as they both struggled to regain their breath. Showing no signs of moving, Marcus planted lazy kisses down his neck, and Tyler turned his head to the side, granting him greater access.

With one last kiss, Marcus peeled himself off Tyler and withdrew from Tyler's body. He tossed the condom in the wastebasket and came back directly to bed, wrapping Tyler in his arms.

"Let's take a nap before dinner."

He'd been serious, then. Tyler hadn't fully believed Marcus at first when he said he wasn't going to the club tonight. Getting this night with him and no one else was a gift.

Tyler pulled the covers over both of them. "Sounds like a plan."

Chapter Twenty-One

THE SMELL OF something delicious teased Marcus awake the next morning, but he had no desire or inclination to move from the warmth of his bed. Without opening his eyes, he reached for Tyler, wanting nothing more than to wake up the way he fell asleep in the early morning hours: with his arms around Tyler, holding him close, and his cock resting in the sweet cleft of Tyler's ass.

But instead of touching naked, warm flesh, his arms flailed, touching nothing but cool air and even colder sheets. Having woken up with Tyler tucked in tight to him for over a month now, and after the emotionally draining night, his absence this morning worried Marcus.

Was it too much for Tyler? They'd yet to talk, but it had become more than obvious to Marcus—and never more so than last night—that what was happening between him and Tyler was more than sex and comfort. He'd been with too many men to count, but their one commonality was they were forgotten before they were gone, and replaceable in the dark. None of them had touched any part of him.

But, Marcus thought as he left the bed to go to the bathroom and brush his teeth, he'd never let anyone close enough; aside from his friendships with Julian and Zach, he allowed no one near, and he believed himself happy. Until Tyler arrived at his club and blew apart his neat and solitary life with his challenging honesty and unswerving dedication and responsibility.

Marcus admired and respected Tyler, more so than any other man he'd ever met. Through no choice of his own, he'd been left with a young child, and rather than endlessly bitch about it or turn her care over to a stranger, he put his head down and changed his whole life around to give her the best, putting his dreams aside.

Marcus grimaced at his reflection in the mirror as he shaved, knowing full well he'd never done that for anyone, ever. His motto had always been: pleasure first—his pleasure. He'd lived a life built solely around his own wants and needs, and where did it get him?

As a child, Marcus had promised himself not to grow up to be a man like his father. Now that he'd reached that point in his life, Marcus came to the conclusion that he'd grown up to be no better, only he didn't have a wife and child to let down. The only person he could ever disappoint was himself.

Dressing in a button-down shirt and well-worn jeans, Marcus followed the delicious aroma scenting the air and headed out of the bedroom toward the kitchen. Tyler stood at the breakfast bar, with Lillie on a step stool next to him, instructing her how to make muffins.

"I know Marcus likes banana, so we can take some of these bananas, mash them up, and put them in the batter; what do you think?"

Lillie thought for a moment as if the question was of the utmost importance in her life.

"You should put chocolate in them. Marcus likes chocolate. He kept stealing sips of my big drink yesterday.

He grinned. "I did not, Lillie-bug." He sauntered into the kitchen and kissed the top of her head. "Good morning." Over the top of her head he met Tyler's eyes. "Hi. I woke up, and you weren't there." *And I fucking hated it*, he wanted to add, but refrained for Lillie's sake.

Tyler licked his lips, and Marcus stood transfixed, wishing he could lean over and kiss him until they both couldn't breathe. He blinked and looked away.

Jesus. He had it bad, whatever "it" was. His heart beat a little faster, kick-starting as if he knew the answer but wasn't yet ready to admit it to himself.

"Yeah, I thought it would be nice to have a special breakfast or brunch here in the apartment." He turned back to the stove and slid the tray of muffins inside. "I hope you don't mind, but I called Julian and Zach and invited them over."

Tyler stated that piece of information in such a nonchalant tone, Marcus almost missed what he said as he poured his cup of coffee.

"You called my friends?" He placed the cup on the countertop and sat on the chair. "Why?"

Tyler faced him and took a cup, then poured his own coffee. Lillie wandered away to the sofa and started playing with the doll he'd bought her. She hadn't let it out of her sight; it sat at the table with them when they ate the Chinese food they'd ordered, and when he and Tyler put her to sleep last night, it was tucked into bed with her, under the covers.

"I know you guys are really close, and I felt bad the way I behaved the last time." He took a sip of coffee. "I wouldn't want you to think I was keeping you from seeing them; plus, they most likely think I'm an asshole for running out that time; and then the way we acted at the club that night…"

"Asshole? You? No, that spot's already reserved, since Julian has made it clear to me that I'm the one who needs to change my way of thinking."

Tyler leaned his elbows on the bar, bracing his chin in his hands. "And what's your way of thinking?"

Unsure how much Lillie could hear of their conversation, Marcus leaned forward until he could almost kiss Tyler.

"Self-centered and unwilling to invest in any personal relation-ships."

The edges of Tyler's mouth quirked up in a grin, and his eyes crin-kled with humor. He touched Marcus's face, ghosting those long, sensitive fingers that brought Marcus such pleasure along his jaw until he cupped Marcus's cheek. "Funny; I don't know that man. Want to know what I think?"

Mesmerized by their proximity and the unfamiliar emotions swirl-ing around inside him, Marcus could only nod his assent.

"See, I'd heard a lot about you before I even came to live here. About how kind and generous you were to your friends and even your staff. I brushed it off because I thought you were all flash with no substance; that you were only interested in me to get into my pants."

"I like what's in your pants." Marcus kissed Tyler's palm.

"Don't joke," said Tyler, his eyes snapping fire. "You use sarcastic humor to avoid getting close and revealing your feelings." Tyler brushed the pad of his thumb over Marcus's cheek. "You're so much more than the sum of your parts; you don't need to use sex, or think it's all about sex for me, because it isn't."

His throat constricted, and Marcus couldn't speak if he tried.

"You left your office without hesitation yesterday to pick up Lillie, and that would've been wonderful enough for me. But then you stayed with her and gave her a magical day she won't ever forget. And don't think it was about the toys you bought her, because it wasn't."

"No?"

"Nope." Tyler kissed him, and Marcus wished he was that man Tyler and Lillie thought he was. He wanted to be.

"She told me the best part of the day was playing with you in the apartment and how you didn't care when she put her makeup on you. Other kids at daycare talk about their fathers who are either never home to play, or too tired when they get home."

"I know that type," said Marcus grimly. How many days, weeks, years did he spend as a young child, waiting for a father who never came home, or when he did, could care less if his son wanted to see him?

"Yeah?" Tyler came around the counter to stand next to him. "Want to talk about it?" He ran his hand down Marcus's thigh. "I never even knew who my father was."

"I did, and I guarantee you might have had it better than me."

Tyler's hand halted its caress. "How can you say that? You had a stable, two-parent home where they obviously took care of you. You never had to wonder where your next meal was coming from."

"True. But sometimes living in an emotional wasteland is as bad as a physical one. I often wished I was an orphan—you want to know why?"

Staring at him with confused, sad eyes, Tyler nodded.

"Because then if people adopted me, it meant they really wanted me. Do you know I once came home all excited because we had my favorite flavor of ice cream in the fridge? I scooped out the biggest bowl and was about to sit down and eat it when my mother came in, saw me, and took it away."

"She probably didn't want you ruining your appetite; that's what parents do."

"Fuck that." He kept his voice low. "She told me I couldn't have any because it was my father's and he might want it." The memory tasted like bitter ash in his mouth. "Who tells a child they can't have ice cream and then takes it away from them?"

"Marcus, she probably—"

"There's no probably; I know. My mother never wanted children. All she ever cared about was my father and pleasing him. I was always second place." His eyes stung. Almost thirty-five years old and yet it still mattered. Fuck. This. Shit. This was why he didn't do relationships or even second dates. Everything was going fine; why did—

"Hey, it's okay."

Tyler wrapped his arms around him from behind, and his chin rested on his shoulder, in the crook of his neck. "I can't imagine how that made you feel."

Sympathy made his skin crawl, and he pulled away from Tyler. He needed some space; all this made him feel suffocated and unstable. Time to check out of all this togetherness bullshit.

"I gotta go." He pushed back his chair and virtually ran into the bedroom to put on his socks and sneakers. His hands shook, so he couldn't tie his laces, and he cursed under his breath.

"God damn." He jammed the laces down the side of the sneakers.

"Marcus?"

He closed his eyes and took a deep, cleansing breath before answering. "Yes, Lillie. What?"

"Are you leaving? Where are you going? I thought we were gonna have breakfast." She sniffed. "I helped."

Fuck. A knife's blade of shame swept through Marcus. He'd gone right back to that cold bitter place, forgetting that others might depend on him now. He always was a selfish bastard.

Through the viselike grip in his chest Marcus sucked in one more heartsick breath and then opened his eyes to see not only Lillie standing there but Tyler, his brow furrowed with confusion.

"If you'd rather, I could call Julian and Zach and tell them not to come. And we could clear out for a few hours."

When he didn't answer, Tyler, now pale and defeated-looking, put his hand on Lillie's shoulder. "Come on, honey. Let's go."

A few months ago he would've agreed to that; hell, he would've demanded it. He had waltzed through life, believing himself invincible and capable of taking on the world, alone and unencumbered.

But then yesterday Lillie's little hand slipped into his, placing her trust in him that he would look out for her and keep her safe from harm. And at that moment the path he'd been traveling on changed, forcing him to rethink everything he'd believed in all his life.

It had taken him this many years to figure out who he was and where he'd planned on going. Opening the Pandora's box of his lifelong hurt and struggle now would most certainly destroy the carefully constructed persona he'd built to show the world. But Tyler would expect nothing less; total honesty and truth were his guideposts. If it wasn't so ironic and pathetic, it would be amusing that he, Marcus the consummate loner, who some people called morally bankrupt, had fallen for a man who carried a tractor trailer load full of responsibilities, and put those responsibilities above himself and everyone else.

"Don't go."

For the first time in his life he spoke from the heart and asked a man to stay. Tyler's bent head and slumped shoulders evidenced the extent of the hurt and betrayal Marcus's actions and words had inflicted on him. He kept on walking although Lillie continued to shoot looks at Marcus over her shoulder.

"Ty, please?"

Finally he stopped, straightened up, and turned around. Marcus caught his breath and a fresh wave of sadness washed over him at the lines of hurt etching deep furrows in Tyler's face. To think he'd caused this man pain when all he'd done was offer him comfort, brought him to a new low.

Marcus's entire childhood had been spent attempting to please people who honestly didn't care; he could've stood on his head and recited the alphabet backward without any notice from his father and an indifferent shrug from his mother. That apathy had shaped him into the man he'd become. Ruthless, cold, and self-indulgent. And now he could add cruel as well.

But Marcus no longer wanted to be that man; he hated him in fact. What had it gotten him but a string of anonymous, grasping lovers who cared nothing about what lay beneath his designer clothes and seemingly fast life? The men he'd slept with in the past had used him as much as he did them, but it didn't make it any less wrong of a way to live.

Maybe the greatest happiness wasn't the rush he'd get from sleeping with a different man each night, but instead it was waking up to the sleepy morning smile of the person you'd been dreaming of. Was this his new normal? He'd always hated that word—normal. Who determined the right way to live? Some preconceived notion that had been handed down for centuries but that no longer made any sense?

If that were the case, then Julian and Nick and Zach and Sam, married or planning their lives together would be abnormal, and no one could tell him that their happiness was bad or evil.

"What do you want from me, Marcus? I thought it would be nice to have everyone over here; they could meet Lillie, and we could enjoy a quiet day. I didn't mean to dredge up past hurts, but when the person I care about is obviously in pain, I'm going to do the only thing I know how and that's offer to talk about it." His sweet-sad smile drove a stake into Marcus's heart, shattering the final illusion he'd clung to from the past—that he was better off alone.

He didn't ever want to see Tyler hurting or sad, nor did he want to be the cause of that pain. Now he understood why people put their own feelings aside for the benefit of others, and that their greatest happiness came from others' enjoyment. Knowing he'd hurt Tyler made him reckless and desperate enough to speak from the heart without stopping to think.

"I don't want you to go. Ever. I'm…I'm sorry. It's not easy for me to talk about this, and I promise we will later. But right now I'm sorry for almost wrecking this surprise you and Lillie-bug made for me."

"Why do you call me that?" Lillie stood before him, demanding an answer like a little queen. "Bugs are gross."

"But ladybugs are cute, and they bring good luck." He brushed the hair off her face. "And I'm thinking you and your uncle Ty have made me a very lucky man."

"Can we go back to the kitchen? I'm hungry, and Uncle Ty said the muffins should be cool enough by now, and I want a taste."

"How about a little hug first?" He held out his arms, and she flung herself into his chest. His arms closed around her sturdy little body, but it was Tyler's eyes he sought over her shoulder. Amazed and somewhat shocked, Tyler's eyes gleamed, like he knew a secret but was intent on keeping it to himself for now.

"Okay, let's go and get you something to eat and get ready."

Lillie ran ahead of them to the kitchen, and he caught Tyler by the shoulder before he walked out of reach.

"Thank you."

"For what?"

"For coming after me and forcing me to see what's real."

Tyler met his gaze. "I don't know what's real or not. But it sounds to me as though you're fighting a battle with your past and how it relates to your future. And that's a difficult thing to come to terms with."

Marcus nodded. "And the realization that you've become the one person you've despised the most." He huffed out a self-conscious laugh.

"Don't beat yourself up about it. The people who love you see the real person and know who you are."

Tyler's words hung between them, but Marcus wouldn't, he *couldn't* take that step. And knowing Tyler wouldn't push him, he chose the easy way out.

"The guys will be here soon. Let's get ready for them."

"SHE'S A LITTLE charmer, isn't she?" With his ever-present sketchpad in hand, Julian had been sitting and watching Lillie perform the little dance routine she and the other children at the preschool had learned from Tyler. "And it's obvious she's crazy about you."

Watching Lillie's fierce concentration on her steps, Marcus grinned. "The child has excellent taste, what can I say?"

"Either that or you've bribed her, which is more your style."

Zach sat by Sam on the sofa, and from the tender expression on his face as he too watched Lillie, Marcus knew once his friend and Sam got married, the next step would be to have a child. If ever anyone was made to be a father, it was Zach.

Observing both of his friends with their lovers, Marcus marveled at the changes their relationships had brought to them, though in opposite ways.

Julian's sharp edges had smoothed, and while he always dressed like only moments before he'd stepped off a fashion runway with his models, the overbearing, slightly intense attitude had quieted. Marcus knew it had to do with Julian's good-looking burly husband, Nick, who no longer harbored his dark secrets and was finally free to live life again with a smile in his dark-blue eyes.

Zach too had changed, but in a different way. The awkward and diffident personality faded; he'd become more assertive, voicing his opinions often. He'd filled out some and dressed more like an adult rather than slopping around in faded tee shirts and jeans like an overgrown teenager hiding out from the world in his mother's basement. Zach hadn't lost his inherent sweetness and kind nature, yet he now carried himself with a self-confidence that only heightened his overall appeal. Sam, who Marcus could see wore the smile of a man well satisfied by his lover, had found the way to bring Zach's best qualities to the forefront.

How ironic that he was the one to end up in a relationship with a man who had a child. But Lillie was special. He narrowed his eyes, waiting as she performed a complicated step she'd had trouble with, and clapped as she got it right. When she'd finished and gotten a hug from Tyler, she ran right over to him.

"Did you see me? I got it right."

Marcus gave her a hug. "I sure did, Lillie-bug. I think after you change, you deserve a cookie."

"Two cookies." She smiled up into his face.

If she could bottle that charm, she'd make a million dollars. "Maybe."

She sidled up to Julian, peeking at the open sketchpad on his knee. "Is that me?" She pointed to the drawings.

Julian studied her for a moment. "Yes. Do you like them?" He held out the pad to her, and she took it, cocking her head one way and then the other.

"Yeah. I like them. They're pretty."

"I could make them for you."

Her eyes lit up. "Really?" She tore off, heading to Tyler, who was talking to Zach and Sam.

"Is that something new? I didn't think you were doing a children's clothing line." Marcus poured him another mimosa from the pitcher sitting on the counter. They'd polished off the huge breakfast of bagels, lox, and French toast Tyler had prepared and, groaningly overfull, were now sitting around and catching up.

"I never know when the inspiration will strike, but, why not? And not a full line yet. I can start with dance outfits and see how it takes off."

"Well, if Lillie's any indication, you'll do great."

"Maybe Tyler would let her do the modeling for it; she's adorable and might pick up some money doing odd modeling jobs."

Marcus nodded thoughtfully. "It's a good idea. I'll talk to Tyler about it. He's very careful with her, and I'm in agreement. He doesn't want her thinking she can have everything she wants."

Julian placed the sketchpad on the counter, then sat back and rubbed his chin. "How does it feel being a father?"

Coughing up half of the mimosa he was drinking, Marcus wheezed, gasping for breath. "Father?" he said, sounding more frog than human. "What the hell are you talking about?" He wiped his eyes with the napkin Julian handed him.

"Oh come on, Marc, be serious." Julian waved at Zach, who'd passed by them moments before and now came back out of the kitchen with a cup of coffee, to join them. "Zach, don't you agree?"

With a wry smile, Zach set his mug down on the counter and crossed his arms, smile lines fanning out from his eyes. Gone were the days when despondency swamped Zach, crippling him with indecisiveness. Marcus had finally stopped worrying about him.

"Do you know how many times over the years you've asked me, 'Zach, don't you agree?' and I could kick myself for not asking you first what you were talking about instead of answering 'yes' off the top of my head?"

"Ha. He's got you there, Juli. Zach's always been too smart for you."

Nonplussed, Julian the Jackal wasn't about to give up if he smelled fresh meat.

"Fine. Here's the question. I merely asked Marcus how he felt about being a father."

Wide-eyed but unable to contain the grin breaking out across his face, Zach leaned back against the countertop, his blue eyes sparkling behind his glasses.

"Well, now that's a whole different story. Yeah, I'm with Julian. How does it feel?"

"You two are insane. I knew once you got married and you got engaged," he said pointing to Julian and Zach respectively, "that would be the end of your brains, and you'd insist on making me—"

"Stop it already."

Shocked into silence by Zach's unusually stern voice, Marcus obeyed, more curious than annoyed with Zach.

"You're so intent on proving how much you don't care about Tyler you're going to drive him away. Is that what you want? To be alone again, picking up random men and hooking up instead of facing the truth that being with Tyler is the best thing to ever happen in your life?"

Funny how he'd always thought it would be Julian who'd pin him to the wall, since they so often butted heads. Instead, quiet Zach, possessing an inner core of steel neither he nor Julian imagined, stepped into the fire, knowing Marcus wouldn't dismiss him outright and would listen.

"It's time to grow up, Marcus, and be a man. The man I know you can be, that you *are* if you'd only wake up and take a look at what you have right in front of your face. Admit it to yourself, even if you won't to us, that you're in love with Tyler."

Awareness prickled up his spine. Had Tyler heard Zach? He shot an uneasy glance over his shoulder to see if Tyler had overheard what Zach had said, but lucky for Marcus, he was still in the living room, happily discussing football with Sam.

"Don't worry; he didn't hear Zach," said Julian, no longer laughing, looking more frighteningly serious than Marcus recalled seeing him in a while. "I was afraid to say anything because I knew you'd bite my head off like the last time at brunch when I tried to talk to you about Tyler." He set his glass down on the counter and held Marcus's eyes. "But now that Zach brought it up, I agree with him. It's hard and scary as hell when it happens, but once you accept not only the place that happiness holds in your life but your right to be happy, you wonder how you could ever have lived without it."

"Did you two plan this ambush, waiting for a time when I'd be alone to stalk and harass me about my love life?" Marcus grumbled, but it was halfhearted at best, and Zach stifled a gasp.

"God. Julian you were right. Look at his face." Zach nudged Julian who broke out in a wide smile.

"Well, well, well; let me write this day down." He made a great show of clicking his pen and flipping the pages of his sketchpad. "November 28. The day Marcus Feldman mentioned the words 'love life' instead of 'just fucking around.'"

"Oh, fuck off," said Marcus irritably. "I'm not nauseatingly annoying like you two. Maybe it's gas."

Julian's smile faded from his face. "You know, Marc, for the first time since I've known you, this apartment seems like a home, not a place to change your clothes or screw some random guy you'll never see again. You're only fooling yourself."

And Zach, who had picked up his coffee mug in preparation to return to Sam, left him with one of those comments you see on social media in greeting-card form that people use for inspiration.

"When the thought of living without Tyler scares you more than being with him for the rest of your life, you'll understand. But I think you already know the answer to that question."

Nodding but without adding a word, Julian gathered up his pad and mimosa and followed Zach, leaving Marcus alone to contemplate and wonder when his life had been reduced to an Internet meme.

Chapter Twenty-Two

MONDAY DAWNED COLD and bright and Tyler bundled up Lillie in her puffy purple coat she'd gotten over the weekend for school. Tyler couldn't help but smile, remembering the terrified look on Marcus's face upon entering the children's department of the store; he looked ready to bolt. It took a few shots of scotch, a scorching-hot blowjob, and a shower massage before he calmed down when they'd returned home. And that was before dinner. Next time they'd go by themselves.

"Who's picking me up today? Can I go to Rebecca's house after school?"

"Let's check when we get to school." Tyler took her hand, and they walked down to the subway at the corner. The train came after only a few minutes of waiting and in less than fifteen minutes they were walking down the block from the preschool.

"Look. There's Rebecca and Jacob with their daddy. Can I run up and meet her?"

Tyler nodded but cautioned, "Don't run."

She half skipped, half ran until she caught up with them. They stopped and waited for him to catch up, then Lillie, Rebecca, and Jacob walked ahead of them, while he and Josh Rosen caught up.

He liked the sandy-haired lawyer and found him much less intimidating than his husband, Micah, who reminded Tyler of Marcus.

"How's everything?" he asked.

"Busy as usual. But in a good way." Josh's good humor shone from his eyes. "Have to find ways to pay this tuition."

Being that that was still a sore spot with Tyler, he didn't feel like commenting. "Uh, Lillie wanted to know if she can come over to your house after school."

"Sure, but she doesn't need to ask; she has a standing invitation anytime." Josh pulled out his phone and texted. "I'll let the babysitter know, so you're good to go."

"Thanks, man. I appreciate it. I don't want to wear out her welcome. She loves your kids, and I'm still trying to find a dance studio space that isn't going to bankrupt me every month."

Josh nodded. "I hear you. It took me a while to find office space for my practice. I can ask around and see if any of my clients know of some storefront space."

"Great, thanks."

They headed up the front steps into the school, behind the children, and greeted the teachers as they passed them in the hallway. After saying goodbye to Lillie and telling her she'd be going home with Rebecca and Jacob, Tyler checked his watch and saw he had over an hour before his dance class at a charter school uptown in Washington Heights. He and Josh were walking down the hallway, retracing their steps to the front, when the headmistress of the school, Mrs. Meyers, stopped him.

"Mr. Reiss, may I have a word, please?"

He said goodbye to Josh and followed Mrs. Meyers into her office, where she closed the door behind him. Unsmiling, she sat down behind her desk.

"Is there a problem?" he asked politely. For some reason a cold sweat broke out across his back and his heart began to race.

"Mr. Reiss, I'm not going to beat around the bush here. Exactly what is your legal status regarding Lillie?"

The bottom might have dropped out from under his feet, yet Tyler, schooled in the art of faking his emotions after all the theater and dance training he'd had, held on, gripping his hands tight.

"Lillie is my niece. I'm watching her for my sister."

"And you have the legal right to sign her paperwork and medical records and such?" Mrs. Meyers smiled, but there was no warmth in the depths of her cold gray eyes. "I'll need the power of attorney you received from your sister to make these decisions." Her hawklike gaze pierced him. "You do have one, correct, Mr. Reiss? We took Lillie into the school as a favor to Dr. Steinberg, but we aren't going to flout the law for you."

Love had a habit of changing a person into someone they'd never imagined. Tyler hated liars and strove to always tell the truth, but not here, not when Lillie's whole future rested with him.

"It's with my attorney, but he's on vacation until after the New Year." Amazing how smoothly the lie rolled off his tongue. "I can have it for you next month."

"And there's no way to get it any sooner? Your attorney has no associate or secretary who can forward it to you?"

His threadbare temper snapped a bit. "What's brought this on? Lillie hasn't been any trouble." He cursed himself and bit his tongue.

"We don't like people telling us how to teach, Mr. Reiss. We are here to educate children, not to get involved in social problems."

Thoroughly confused, Tyler rubbed his palms on his thighs, warming himself, his desire to flee at odds with the need to discover what the hell she was talking about. He inhaled deeply, struggling to keep his composure.

"I'm not sure what you're saying."

Her upper lip curled in a sneer. "I suggest you talk to your friend who picked her up from school."

Marcus? Impossible. They'd talked about the need to remain circumspect and not involve themselves in any way that might draw attention to the fact that Tyler had zero legal rights to Lillie. He needed to get out of here right now and go home and talk to Marcus.

He mumbled a paltry excuse that probably made no sense and ran out of the office, his heart pounding so hard and loud he was certain everyone he passed could hear. Once he pushed open the front door and reached outside, he bent his head between his knees, bracing his hands on his thighs, hoping to take in enough air for his suddenly constricted lungs to prevent him from fainting.

"Tyler, what's wrong?"

Josh rushed over to him and took him by the arm to lead him over to the line of parked cars by the street.

He shook his head, waving off Josh's questions for the moment. Even though this day had to come eventually, Tyler thought he'd have more time to prepare and not be completely blindsided.

Staring at Josh's concerned face, Tyler hoped he wasn't making another mistake by talking to someone who, though kind, was a virtual stranger to him.

Beggars can't be choosers, idiot. Time to put aside your pride and do whatever it takes to keep Lillie.

"It's the school. Technically I have no legal rights to Lillie." He quickly sketched the problem. When he finished, Josh's face looked uncharacteristically grim.

"Shit, Tyler. Whatever made you think you could keep this up?"

"I don't know, I don't know." He ran his hand through his hair, wincing painfully as he dragged his fingers through the tangled waves. "I wasn't thinking. I only wanted to keep Lillie with me. I can't have her taken away." Frantic, he pulled out his cell phone. "I have to cancel my lessons for the day and find a lawyer. Then I'm going to hunt Marcus down and ream him out for what he said. I can't believe he was so fucking stupid."

To his surprise, Josh plucked the phone from his nervous fingers and pulled him farther down the block, away from the parents and students still milling about.

"No. First thing you're going to do is calm down. One thing I've learned is to never say things in the heat of anger, because for some reason that's what people never forget."

"But Marcus—"

"You have plenty of time to find out what he said, but right now that isn't the most important thing, is it?" Josh glared at him.

"No, of course not."

"Okay. Now in case you've forgotten, I happen to be an attorney, and I'll be glad to help you out. Let's go back to your apartment, and we can sort through this mess."

Tyler took back his phone and barely paid any attention to what happened after that. They were in a cab, inching down Broadway, and he wanted to scream, cry, and tear his hair out. But first he had to call Marcus and let him know what he'd done.

He pressed the Speed Dial and in a few seconds Marcus's deep voice greeted him.

"Miss me already? I thought you'd had enough of me after last night and this morning."

Normally he'd join in the sexual banter, even revving Marcus up. Even now his body hummed with the pleasurable ache from their lovemaking. But he squelched his desire for Marcus and instead thought about how angry he was and all the damage Marcus had caused.

"I'm in trouble. You said something to someone at the school they took the wrong way, and now they're making me prove I have legal rights to Lillie which we know I don't have."

Dead silence on the other side of the phone.

"Marcus, are you there? Do you realize what you've done? This isn't something you can get out of with a wink and a charming smile. If I can't get this fixed, I stand to lose Lillie to foster care."

A brief pause. "Where are you now?" said Marcus.

"I'm in a cab with Josh, going back to the apartment. Luckily he was with me when this all happened, or I might have gone insane, if I'm not already."

He threw Josh a grateful glance, and Josh squeezed his shoulder. "We'll work something out. Have faith."

"I'll see you soon, then. I'm sorry, Ty."

He ended the call without answering Marcus back, afraid of what he might say.

"HOW FUCKING STUPID could you have been? I told you never to draw any attention to Lillie at school; we even had a conversation about it."

Marcus had been waiting in the apartment when he and Josh arrived and opened the door, looking visibly upset. Marcus's feelings weren't Tyler's main concern at the moment, and he lost no time ripping into him.

"You've ruined everything."

Tyler stormed around the apartment, while Marcus sat with his head in his hands. Josh's gaze ping-ponged between the two of them until he stood before Tyler.

"Enough."

Tyler halted; he'd been close to cursing Marcus out and bolting.

"I understand you're upset, Tyler, but flaying Marcus to pieces isn't going to help the matter. You and he need to present a united front and do what's best for Lillie." Josh put a reassuring hand on his shoulder and gave him a squeeze. "I'm going to go in the bedroom now and make some phone calls to people I know in the court system." He shot Tyler a stern look, and he squirmed under that piercing gaze. "I expect this to be settled when I come out."

Chastised, Tyler watched Josh retreat to the bedroom and close the door behind him.

"Ty, I know you think I was wrong and I'm sorry, but—"

"There is no but, Marcus. Not when it comes to Lillie. I can't lose her. She's all I have." He braced his hands on the kitchen counter, bent at the waist. "If I lose her, I have nothing." Unbearable pain sliced through him as if he'd been cut with a jagged-edged knife. How could he explain to her that she might be taken away? Worse, how could he forgive himself?

And suddenly Marcus was there, his arms around him, holding him close. The steady beat of his heart brought no comfort, though.

"That's not true. You have me." His warmth and strength soaked through Tyler and for a moment he relaxed, pretending everything was perfect and this would last forever. "And I'm sorry I screwed it up for you. I didn't mean to do it."

Tyler nodded against Marcus's broad chest. He was so tired of being strong and holding everything together. All his life he'd had to be the strong one, pretending he could handle things on his own, when in reality he was flying by the seat of his pants. For once he wished he could give up his responsibilities and think of no one but himself. Foolish thought.

"This is my fight; I'll understand if you find it too much. You never meant to be tied down; you've given us more than I ever thought possible."

Marcus tightened his hold and buried his face in the crook of Tyler's neck. Tyler shivered from the kisses trailing along his collarbone and sighed his pleasure. When did it happen? When did he fall in love? He thought he'd been so careful and strong to guard against it, yet here it came, creeping up on him like a thief in the night to steal his heart away.

And in choosing a man like Marcus who didn't believe in relationships, commitment, or love, Tyler knew he was holding on only to let go.

Only a moment more, he promised himself, sinking further into Marcus's embrace and inhaling his warm and spicy scent; then he'd back away.

He turned to face Marcus, noting the strain in his eyes and the tight, hard lines emanating from his lips.

"It was hard for me to learn to trust, and yet you made it so easy. And all I can say is that I'm sorry I drew you in where you never wanted to be."

"So you think now you know what's best for me, I gather?" Marcus quirked a dark brow but didn't relinquish his hold, keeping Tyler within the circle of his arms.

"I know you're not interested in permanence or anything that sounds like a relationship. You made no promises about a future. And at the time I was the same: keeping it light and fun, making sure it would be easy to walk away from."

The violet of Marcus's eyes darkened until they looked like merciless, glittering chips of onyx. "And that's what you're planning to do? Walk away from me?"

"I have to." Tyler broke away from Marcus's disconcerting nearness. How could he be expected to think with Marcus's hands on him? Leaving him was going to be the hardest thing he'd ever done in his life, but Tyler was used to putting himself second.

"I'm thinking of you, don't you see? The last thing you need is to be caught up in my drama. Lillie and I can be gone by tonight, and you can go back to Sparks and forget you met us." Loneliness welled up inside him; he didn't want to leave, but how could he stay? He fled to the living room and dropped onto the sofa.

Marcus remained standing by the kitchen, a dark statue carved from ice. "And is that what you want? For once in your life, Tyler, be totally selfish and think of yourself first. Stop overthinking it and tell me. What do you want to do?"

Before he could stop himself, the words rushed out. "I want to stay with you. I don't want to leave."

With swift steps, Marcus joined him on the sofa. "Tell me why." His voice breathed hot against Tyler's cheek. "Please."

"You're going to make me say it, aren't you?" Warmth burst through Tyler, chasing away the chill of his entire world falling apart.

"Yes." Marcus smiled against his cheek. "Only if you want to, of course."

Everything happens for a reason; good or bad, these experiences shape the future in ways never imagined when the journey begins. He'd had a lifetime of bad; Tyler was ready to accept some good for a change.

"I don't want to leave because I need you." He pressed a clumsy kiss to the corner of Marcus's mouth. "I love you."

Marcus stilled and held Tyler a bit closer. "Do you know that's the first time anyone's ever said that to me?" The joking tone had vanished.

He lay back against the pillows, a frown pulling down the corners of his mouth.

Astonished, Tyler bit back the sarcastic joke he'd been about to make and gazed down at Marcus's serious face. Surely that couldn't be true. Without thinking, he pushed back a few locks of hair that had tumbled over Marcus's brow to hide his eyes.

"Everyone loves you, Marcus. You're the first on the guest list to the best parties; the club is packed every night. And I'm sure your parents love you."

"Forget about my parents." Unable to meet his eyes, Marcus picked at an imaginary spot on his jeans and huffed out a choked laugh. "As for the rest, it's all the superficial shit. I'm the great pretender; haven't you realized it yet? But when the crowds go home and shit gets real, I've always been alone." He looked up then, and Tyler caught a glimpse of that loneliness reflected in his eyes. "Until you came and changed it all."

They both hid from the world in different ways: Marcus with his flash and sarcastic wit, trading sex for companionship, while Tyler pushed people away, allowing mistrust and false pride to control his life, refusing genuine offers of friendship and goodwill.

"I didn't mean to bully you into saying it."

"I think you know by now I don't say things I don't mean." And there was so much more to say between them, but not now when emotions ran high and Lillie's future hung in the balance. "We'll talk later, okay?"

Marcus nodded, and at that moment, Josh chose to reenter the room.

"All safe? I didn't hear any flying objects hit the wall or glass breaking."

"We're good, Josh. Tell us what you know." Marcus sat up, brushing off Josh's attempt at humor.

Tyler knew by now that when it came to important matters, Marcus didn't joke around. He was a man Tyler was glad to have on his side.

Josh sat at Marcus's desk, a pad filled with notes before him, and slid his glasses down over his eyes to read. He'd cancelled all his appointments for the day, and Tyler knew he'd never be able to repay him not only monetarily, but with gratitude for the immediate help he offered, without any questions.

"I spoke to the person who handled our adoption of the twins, and she doesn't believe Lillie will have to go into foster care. You've created a stable environment for her, and the fact that she's now attending school and formed relationships with other children is a plus."

"Go on. There's stuff you aren't telling me though, right?"

"I can get a judge to grant you temporary custody of her, but it doesn't look good that you dance in a club for a living."

"That's bullshit." Marcus struck out, his voice hard as a whip. "What he does should have no bearing on how he is as a parent. He'd die for her."

Touched, Tyler kissed his cheek. "It's okay. I'm not dancing any-more, remember? I agreed that teaching is the direction I want to head in."

Josh nodded with approval. "That's great, Tyler. And yes, Marcus, it may be bullshit, but there are plenty of old-fashioned judges out there who won't like it. So Tyler being a teacher is better for him in the long run." He consulted his notes. "We need to try and get in touch with your sister. It would be so much easier if she would show up and we could get her to give you parental rights."

Once again anger swept through Tyler, this time directed at his sister. "Don't you think I've tried? I wouldn't have the faintest idea where to start looking."

"I do." Marcus had his phone out. "We'll call Sam. He's a private investigator."

Tyler's head whirled. He had barely enough in his bank account to cover the rent he insisted on paying Marcus, plus the expenses in feeding and clothing Lillie.

"I can't—"

"If you're going to finish that sentence with afford it, I'm going to have to kick your ass."

Marcus said this in such an amiable tone of voice, it didn't register with Tyler at first. He did however see Josh's lip twitch, holding back a smile.

"Listen, Marcus…"

"No, you listen." He spoke into the phone, then held it by his side. "I've got more money than I know what to do with, and you and Lillie are my family. So get down from that high horse of yours before you fall and break your neck, and do what's best for her, not what makes you feel like a better man."

Damn. "We're your family?"

Marcus's face softened. "Yeah. And I take care of my family. Please, Ty." He was begging, and Tyler had never heard Marcus beg before. Not outside of the bedroom at least. "Let me do this for you."

They faced off across the room, and every last bit of Tyler's resistance crumbled.

"Give the guy a break, Tyler." Josh whispered in his ear. He startled Tyler, who'd forgotten Josh's presence, he'd been so caught up in Marcus.

"I live with a man like Marcus. It takes a lot out of them to ask permission or to not step in and take control."

"I'm not used to people who want to help and don't expect anything in return."

Josh gave him a wry smile. "I think he already has everything he ever wanted, don't you?"

Tyler walked over to Marcus and slipped his arms around him.

"Okay, then. Do it for us."

Chapter Twenty-Three

"GO OVER IT one more time, please." Sam not only took copious notes but recorded their meeting. Marcus had every confidence that if anyone could find Tyler's sister, it was Sam.

Looking more wiped out than he'd ever seen him, even after a night of dancing, Tyler lay stretched out on the sofa, his head pillowed in Marcus's lap. Without opening his eyes, he spoke as Marcus massaged his head, sliding his fingers through Tyler's silky locks. Josh had left in the afternoon and agreed to have Lillie stay at his house so they could meet with Sam without fear of interruption.

"One morning, about a year after she and Lillie came to live with me, Amber said she was going to do some shopping and she'd be back in a few hours. I know that should've tipped me off, since she didn't have any money."

"Did she say where she was headed? Try and recall."

"I have; don't you think that's all I've been doing?" Frustration edged the anger in Tyler's voice, and Marcus bent down to murmur in his ear.

"He's only trying to help. Don't get all upset."

Tyler exhaled and stared up at the ceiling. "I'm sorry; I don't mean to take it out on you. I've replayed that morning a thousand times. She spoke about some boyfriend named Dante who lived in the Bronx, but other than that, I'm clueless. I didn't know Amber would leave Lillie with me and disappear."

Being the people watcher that he was, Marcus looked to Sam's facial expression for clues as to his inner thoughts, but the man's stony expression gave nothing away. Sam flipped his notebook closed and tapped it with his pen for a moment, staring into space.

"So, can you help us?" Marcus couldn't take the silence any longer. "Or is it hopeless?"

The smile Sam gave them was filled with unexpected charm. "I never say anything is hopeless. I'm going to make a copy of all the papers she left behind."

Tyler sprang up and headed into the bedroom. "I have copies of everything—all of Lillie's health records, her birth certificate and social security card. Amber left behind an expired food-stamps card with her picture, so that should be helpful, right?"

His voice faded as he entered the bedroom, but he reappeared almost immediately. Marcus knew Tyler kept the information in the drawer next to the bed, and it wouldn't take long to find what he needed.

Once again, Sam flashed that disarmingly sweet smile. Marcus wondered if that was how he managed to get all the information he collected from witnesses and other people he questioned in his line of work. A handsome man can get a lot of answers with the right kind of arrows in his quiver. Idly, he watched him go through the papers Tyler brought out.

"These are perfect, Tyler. I'll start looking into it immediately." Sam took the papers and slid them into a manila envelope, which he then put in his briefcase. "Give me your cell phone number. I only have Marcus's."

Sam collected all his notes and rubbed his eyes. It had been a long afternoon. "Hopefully with all the information, we can pinpoint where Amber is, and maybe she'll come back."

"Oh, she'll be back, if I have to drag her here myself," muttered Marcus to himself.

Tyler walked Sam to the door, and Marcus collected their coffee cups to bring to the kitchen when he saw Sam pat Tyler on the shoulder, offering him comfort, and Tyler returning a shadowed smile. Once Sam left, Tyler's smile immediately fled, and Marcus's heart hurt for how he held himself together even as his world shattered around him. His strength, especially when it came to Lillie, was what he loved most about Tyler.

Then Marcus realized his thoughts, and he stood stock-still in the center of his kitchen. He loved Tyler. Loved him in the way the air seemed alive when he opened the front door now, instead of dead and quiet before Ty started living there. Loved him in the way he woke up every morning and reached for Ty to see his smile.

Loved him because he was Tyler.

"What's wrong? Are you sick?"

Blinking and shaking himself out of his reverie, Marcus discovered a concerned Tyler standing before him. He opened his mouth to speak, but no words came out. What could he say? "Oh hey, by the way, I realized that I love you?" He'd sound like a dick, and coming on the heels of Tyler telling him that he loved him, Marcus wanted to make it special. After the trauma of the day, Tyler deserved it.

Touching his forehead, Tyler peered into his face as if he were a child with a fever. "Are you sure you're not coming down with something?"

If he had his way, something of Tyler's would be coming up very shortly.

Marcus caught Tyler's wrist and pressed a kiss to the underside. "I'm fine. I think we should order dinner and relax tonight. You've had a traumatic day and could use a night of nothing but pampering." The pulse under his lips fluttered, and Marcus sucked at Tyler's skin. He pulled Tyler close, molding their bodies to a naturally perfect fit and couldn't help the smile of satisfaction as Tyler wound his arms around him.

"I'm not really hungry," said Tyler, and Marcus stifled a groan of longing as Tyler pressed kisses down the side of his neck, giving payback by sucking the skin along the throbbing vein. Taking Marcus' by surprise, Tyler hooked one leg around Marcus's waist and hoisted himself up, locking his ankles behind Marcus's back, all the while continuing to kiss his neck and jaw.

"It pays to have a bendy boyfriend," said Marcus, chuckling, and he cupped Tyler's ass and carried him to the bedroom, still clinging to his waist.

"Where are you taking me?" Tyler slid down Marcus's torso, allowing Marcus to feel every hard, muscled inch of him. Anticipation curled in the pit of Marcus's stomach at the prospect of an uninterrupted night of lovemaking. Because tonight, for the first time, only love would be between them.

"I said you deserve some pampering. Get undressed, and I'm going to run you a bath. A bubble bath."

Tyler's eyes gleamed. "The tub is big enough for two, you know. I expect you to scrub my back." He pulled off his shirt and stepped out of his jeans, passing in front of Marcus naked and aroused. "If you're good, I'll make it worth your while."

Marcus pulled off his own clothes and joined Tyler in the bathroom. He gazed appreciatively at Tyler's taut, muscled ass as he bent over to turn on the taps to the bathtub. Unable to resist touching that smooth expanse of naked skin, he ran his palms down Tyler's back and over the globes of Tyler's ass, then slid his finger up and down the shadowed cleft, teasing for a second at the tight little hole.

"Umm." Tyler sighed and rubbed back and forth on the digit. "Feels amazing."

Pressing a kiss to the back of Tyler's neck, Marcus reached down and turned off the flow of water. He picked up a small bottle and poured it in the water, then pressed a button on the side of the tub, turning on the jets. Instantly the water foamed, creating clouds of bubbles and scenting the air with a cool, lemony fragrance.

"Go on in while I get the washcloths."

Tyler slid down under the foam and moaned, leaning his head back on the tiles, his shoulders glistening from the soapy water. A dreamy smile rested on his lips, and his eyes fluttered shut. Marcus made certain to remain as quiet as possible and leaned over to kiss Tyler on the lips.

"Mmm." Tyler sighed, and wound his arms around Marcus's neck. "Come in."

"I have every intention of doing so. Multiple times tonight."

A tiny grin flickered over Tyler's lips, but he didn't open his eyes. Marcus stared for a moment at Tyler, wondering when the world had changed and having Tyler here was worth any sacrifice he might have to make. And that giving himself was really no hardship at all.

He entered the tub and dunked the washcloth underneath the bubbles, then squeezed out the excess and proceeded to knead and massage Tyler's chest, shoulders and abdomen, staying clear of Tyler's cock which rose up slick and reddened from the heated water. Tyler's eyes remained closed.

"Turn around and let me wash your back."

Tyler finally opened his eyes, and they simply stared at one another for a moment. The clouds of steamy heat and fragrance enveloped them in a sensual haze. Tyler got to his knees and turned around so his back faced Marcus, sidling close so his ass hugged up against Marcus's erection. He hummed his approval as Marcus swirled the washcloth down his back. The strong muscles flexed and rippled under his hands.

Unable to resist any longer, Marcus dropped the washcloth and reached forward to grasp Tyler's erection. Tyler turned his head as if to speak, but Marcus grabbed his jaw and ruthlessly took his mouth in a brutal kiss, plunging his tongue deep.

Tyler's cock jerked and swelled as Marcus pumped him. Their kiss grew desperate, lips wet, tongues searching, and Tyler thrust hard into Marcus's hand, both of them heedless to the water slopping over the side of the tub. A harsh cry split the tranquil atmosphere of the misty room, and Tyler came, shuddering from his release, spilling into Marcus's hand.

Marcus slid his other arm around Tyler, holding him tight until his trembling ceased. Over the past year he'd laughed as his friends fell in love, mocking their obvious happiness. He scorned Julian's devotion to Nick and, though mindful of Zach's sensitive nature, still teased him where Sam was concerned. Love to him meant suffocation, boredom, and losing one's sense of self.

Now, with his lips buried in Tyler's damp hair, and Tyler's heavy, wet body molded to his own, Marcus wondered how he'd lived without it all these years. Had he been sleepwalking through life, waiting for this moment to wake him? And if he hadn't taken this step and opened himself up, he thought, kissing Tyler's shoulder, he'd have spent the rest of his life half-alive.

The water had cooled and the bubbles faded, however neither of them made a move to get out of the tub. Tyler leaned back, resting his head on Marcus's shoulder. Marcus continued to kiss along Tyler's neck up to his ear.

"Ty?" Marcus ran his nose down the curve of Tyler's cheekbone.

"Hmm?"

"I love you."

"I think I must have water in my ear. Can you repeat that?"

"Don't be an ass."

Tyler's eyes twinkled with laughter, and Marcus's lips twitched in a failed attempt to contain his smile. "You're going to make me work for it, aren't you?"

"Every minute of every day."

"Forever?" Marcus nuzzled Tyler's neck, soaking in his warmth.

"I think that could be arranged."

Without speaking, they both rose from the tub and dried themselves off, then headed to the bedroom. They lay down together in their bed; it wasn't just his bed any longer. Tyler had become a part of his life and his heart as if they occupied the same skin.

There was no fumbling between them as they came together, no hesitancy or second-guessing; only a sureness that this was right and meant to be. And when Marcus slid into Tyler's body, fitting inside as sweetly tight as in a handmade suit, it took every ounce of control not to let the tears fall, knowing at last, he'd risen to the height of the mountain and stood on its peak, having conquered the last demon holding him back. After all the wasted years, he'd discovered on his own what everyone else had told him, yet he refused to accept until now. Until Tyler. His heart had woken up and come to life.

Love was inescapable, indefinable, and sometimes ill-advised. It took you by the throat and shook you until your brain rattled, yet just as gently, cradled you in its loving arms.

Tyler held him tight as they rocked together with increasing fervor, their passion for each other escalating with every thrust and whispered word. He brushed the dark spill of hair off Tyler's face and stared into his eyes.

"What?" Tyler reached up to touch his cheek, but Marcus shook his head. It was all too real, too fresh to speak, so Marcus showed him the best way he knew how with his body, driving Tyler into the mattress, loving him.

Tyler sobbed out a choked cry, his body convulsing beneath Marcus, who lost himself in the rawness of his own orgasm splintering through him. Shaking and breathless, he collapsed on Tyler, his heart banging against his breastbone.

They lay together, and Marcus, after withdrawing from Tyler and disposing of the condom, came back to bed, sliding flush up against Tyler's sweat-dampened body. And though he was exhausted, the scrape of Tyler's hairy legs, the smell of his skin, flared the desire always simmering in Marcus's blood.

With a fierceness that surprised even himself, Marcus cupped Tyler's jaw, turning his face so their eyes met. "I promise, if I personally have to search every fucking person in New York City myself, we will find your sister."

"I love you, Marcus. Not for what you do for me, but because of who you are when it's only us."

"I like the only-us part. That's because I'm greedy and want you to myself. Preferably naked and under me." He turned serious. "I meant it, though. I never thought I'd want this, but I do. I love you." He tugged Tyler to him, tangling their legs together. "When imagining a life without you meant no life at all for me, I knew I was doomed."

"Doomed, huh?" Tyler settled in next to him, a comforting weight against his shoulder. "You say the sweetest things."

He rolled on top of Tyler. "Talk is cheap, baby. And actions speak louder than words." He kissed Tyler's cheek. "Get some rest now, 'cause I'm planning on keeping you busy later on tonight."

Chapter Twenty-Four

A MONTH HAD passed, and though Tyler tried to keep his spirits up for Lillie's sake, it became harder than ever to pretend. Even Marcus and his friends spoiling Lillie for both Christmas and Chanukah with a ridiculous number of toys failed to get a rise out of him to tell them to stop. As he figured it, they'd have to leave quickly once the judge ruled him incapable of taking care of her, so he'd allow her to collect as many good memories as possible.

He didn't share his worry with Marcus; not when things were going so well between them that sometimes he woke in the middle of the night to make sure he wasn't dreaming and that life had, for the moment, given him all that was perfect. He'd stare at Marcus's sleeping face and wish they could grow old together.

He'd yet to secure a space for his dance studio and continued on with teaching at various schools throughout the city. Lucky for him, he kept busy every day, the running back and forth preventing him from dwelling too long on the search for Amber. That didn't stop every phone call from ratcheting up his nerves, thinking it was Sam with some news. They'd had many leads, a few promising, but when they thought finally they'd found Amber, it fizzled out like a worn-down sparkler.

To his credit, Marcus had been an unrelenting bulldog in the search for Amber. He spoke with Sam every day, and Tyler suspected he did a little digging on his own as well. But with the deadline looming for him to provide the school with the necessary paperwork, Tyler knew they were running out of time.

Meanwhile, he had his students. Watching the various parents and babysitters pick up the boys and girls after class was over, Tyler couldn't help but smile. Teaching them new routines and dancing for them gave him the release, however fleeting, to forget for a little while what awaited him.

The last little boy had been picked up by his mother only a few minutes ago, and he sat for a moment in the studio, busy with the next day's schedule. At this rate, he might have to hire an assistant and made a note to go to some of the dance schools in the city to see if any of the more advanced students would be willing to work for him on a part-time basis. He needed to find a suitable space fast, yet if he was leaving… Tyler shook his head in dismay.

"Finished for the day?"

Marcus lounged in the doorway, and as always Tyler marveled that this beautiful man loved him. His heart squeezed in his chest at the thought of leaving him, now that he'd finally found someone to love. Instead of his usual clean cut, business attire, Marcus hadn't shaved this morning; the dusting of stubble gave him a rakish appearance, and a swell of longing grew within Tyler. Although they'd made love only this morning, the ache of his desire for Marcus hadn't waned. He doubted it ever would.

"What are you doing here? I thought you'd be at the club?"

Without answering, Marcus advanced to where he sat at the small desk and stood over him, looking down with a frown.

"You look upset. What's wrong?"

Unable to answer, Tyler merely shook his head and went back to his tablet, pretending to work on the schedule. To his surprise, Marcus took the tablet out of his hands and pulled him into his arms.

"Hey. It's going to be all right." Marcus slid a hand beneath his shirt, and Tyler dropped his head to Marcus's shoulder, relishing the warmth of his touch. If only forgetting the problems that loomed in front of him everywhere he turned were that easy.

"How can you say that?" He inhaled Marcus's scent as if imprinting it in his memory to carry it with him after he'd gone. "This isn't something you can throw money at to make it go away. If the judge says I can't have Lillie, we have to leave."

Marcus drew back to gaze at him. "Is that your plan?" His face hardened, and Tyler watched a muscle twitch along his jawline. "You're planning on running away—taking the coward's way out?"

Stung by Marcus's unusually harsh rebuke, Tyler lashed back. "What am I supposed to do? Wait until they take her away? Look at me." He pushed Marcus away. "I'm a single gay man with no steady income, living off another man's good graces. What kind of role model am I?" A sense of helplessness such as he'd never felt before swept over him.

Never one to shy away from telling others how he felt, Marcus stared him down. "So instead of fighting for her, you're going to do what? Live on the run and drag her along? You can't do that to her, Ty. She's got a life here now." Marcus hesitated. "I thought we had one as well. Or at least we were building one."

Shit. Tyler scrubbed his face with his hands. A bossy and stubborn Marcus he could deal with, but when he let down his guard and showed his vulnerable side, something Tyler knew he rarely did, he fell in love with Marcus all over again.

"We do; I don't want to leave."

"Then we fight. Get yourself a studio and sign a lease. That'll show the court you're capable of caring for her. They aren't going to take her away from her blood relative to put her in with strangers." Marcus took him in his arms again, and Tyler sank into his strength. "Josh's contact at Children's Services said they want to keep families together."

"I wish I could be as trusting in the system as you. All my life they've failed us."

Marcus hugged him tight. "We're in this together now, and failure is not a word I accept." For a few moments, with Marcus's arms around him, the problems in his world faded and he could pretend.

Marcus's phone buzzed in his pocket, and Tyler laughed. "And here I thought you were exceptionally happy to see me."

The words died on his lips at the look of excitement on Marcus's face. "What is it?"

"It's a text from Sam. He says he's talking to someone right now who may have information about Amber."

Adrenaline spiked through Tyler, and his heart began to pound. "Where? Where are they?"

Marcus scrolled through his phone. "Some place in Brooklyn… Canarsie, he says." Marcus's brow wrinkled. "Where the hell is that?"

Tyler chuckled. "Farther into Brooklyn than I'm sure you've ever been. Almost on the border of Queens." He gathered up his stuff. "Let's go. Lillie is with Angela, and they're home. Since I wasn't sure if I'd have any appointments to look about renting studio space, I asked Angela if she could give Lillie dinner tonight, so we're covered." His brow creased. "It's going to be a fortune to take a cab out there."

"Fuck it. I've told you to stop worrying about money." Marcus yanked him close again and nuzzled his neck. "See what I do for you? I'll go to the ends of the earth."

Marcus meant the comment in a lighthearted manner, however the utter willingness he'd shown to jump into his life pulled Tyler in conflicting directions. From when he first left home to come to New York and try to make it as a professional dancer, Tyler had refused to sell himself to advance his career. That automatically put him at a disadvantage, knowing that sex in exchange for coveted roles was how the game was played.

When Lillie came into his life, changing his priorities, his focus shifted to earning enough money to give her the necessities. He never allowed the anger he'd felt at his sister's betrayal to bubble over to where Lillie would see. No matter what, Amber was her mother. He simply soldiered on, doing whatever he could to make a living for them.

Being with Marcus meant giving up the piece of himself he'd always held back, even from himself. Somehow Marcus had circumvented all the roadblocks he'd set up to keep people out; with his refusal to accept the word no, Marcus reached inside and pulled out the part Tyler had hidden from the world since he was a child—his ability to trust and depend on someone. When everyone in your life has always failed you, it made it almost impossible to believe a person would give you their heart, expecting nothing but to be loved in return.

Now that there might be a chance of actually finding his sister, another worry descended over Tyler, one he hadn't thought about before this moment, and he was certain Marcus hadn't either.

"Marcus?" He hated to break the intimacy of the moment, yet Tyler had to ask the question that had been tugging at his heart.

"Hmm?"

"What if she wants Lillie back? I'll have to give her up, won't I?"

Marcus sighed and pulled him close, his arm resting comfortably around Tyler's shoulders—a perfect fit. They walked out of the dance studio and down the steps of the school to the street before he answered.

"Let's get there first and see what Sam's dug up." His voice grim and his normally laughing eyes dark with some unreadable emotion, Marcus held up his hand to hail a cab. "No use speculating. It's one of my least favorite things to do."

A cab pulled up, and they got inside, Tyler sliding in after Marcus, barely hearing the address to where they were going. The only thought occupying his mind was whether or not Lillie would still be his by tonight.

"ARE YOU CERTAIN?"

Tyler spoke through frozen lips, the unspeakable sorrow crushing him from all sides. A cold, sleety rain had begun, pelting the windows with melted ice. The street lights glowed, and the blacktop of the road glistened as the cars swooshed by on the avenue. They sat at a booth in the back of a small, dimly lit coffee shop. The tired waitress had taken their order and now leaned on the counter, checking her cell phone. Every once in a while she'd roll her shoulders, or shift her feet encased in thick, rubber-soled walking shoes.

The sympathetic look Sam gave him set Tyler's teeth on edge. Only Marcus's hand, holding his tight to the point of pain, grounded him to reality.

At Sam's nod, something crumbled inside him, and he broke apart. Marcus took him in his arms, Tyler's tears wetting his chest.

How could his little sister be dead and he not know it? They used to be so close those days long ago when he'd protect her from the bullies at school or hold her hand when she cried after their mother left them. Now she was gone too; the last vestige of his past wiped clean, as if he'd never existed before this moment.

"How did it happen and when?" Tucked up tight against Marcus's chest, Tyler took comfort in the rumble of his voice.

Sam consulted his notes, his sympathetic voice giving Tyler little comfort. "She'd left work late; she was a waitress at a bar in a little strip mall nearby and had taken an extra shift. It was raining hard, and maybe she didn't see the driver or he was texting. All we know is that he hit her head-on as she crossed the street."

"I was never notified though," said Tyler, wiping his eyes with the napkin Marcus handed to him. "How do you know it's her? Maybe it's a mistake."

Sam took a sip of his coffee and made a face. "I wouldn't have called you all the way out here if I didn't check all the facts. I showed her picture to the people she worked with. Amber didn't use her real name; she went by the name Tiffany Snow. And the place she worked at"—Sam paused for a moment to rub his eyes—"it wasn't the type of place that cared much if you gave a fake name or not."

"Why?" Tyler couldn't help whisper into Marcus's chest. "Why would she choose to live like this instead of with us, with her child?"

Marcus's arms tightened around him. "I don't know. Sam? Any ideas?" His hands smoothed circles up and down Tyler's back. Tyler would never have been able to handle this by himself. Sam may be kind, but it was Marcus who gave him the strength he needed not to fall apart. A strength he'd never thought he needed.

Sam's hesitation spoke volumes, and Tyler swiveled around in Marcus's arms to face him and pin Sam down to answer the questions gnawing at him.

"She was in trouble, wasn't she? Tell me, please." He could care less if he begged; it was his sister.

Sam sighed, his gaze flickering between Marcus and Tyler. "She was a prostitute, Tyler. Whatever money she made working at the bar as a waitress and, um, hooking, she gave to the guy she lived with."

Fury raged through Tyler. "Where is he?" He half rose from his seat. "I'll fucking murder him." He shook off Marcus's hand. "You're not going to stop me. Tell me, Sam."

"Tyler, he's gone. The people I spoke with who were even willing to talk to me all said he left as soon as she died. Those types always melt away at the first sign of trouble. And he wasn't only her pimp."

Sam's sad hazel eyes sent a chill through Tyler. What more did his poor doomed sister have to bear?

"He was her drug dealer. He got her hooked on meth, and she used her prostitution to supplement her drug habit. I'm so sorry, Tyler."

Tyler barely heard Sam; the cacophony of rage and sorrow boiled over in his head until he wanted to scream his pain out loud. Instead, he began to shake uncontrollably, and Marcus once again came to his rescue and took him in his arms to offer him solace.

"I was able to get the little belongings she left; the bartender felt sorry for her and kept them. It seemed she did talk about a brother and a child but wouldn't give any names, so he had no way of finding you."

Drained and numb, Tyler merely nodded. Dead. Amber was dead, and he had nobody, only Lillie. Oh God.

"What's going to happen to Lillie now that her mother's dead?"

Sam reached over to the chair next to him, hefted a small box Tyler hadn't noticed before, and placed it on the table.

"You might want to take a look at what's here. Amber might not have been in the best frame of mind, but she kept a kind of journal." He pulled out a small notebook and handed it to Tyler. "The rest is only a few pieces of costume jewelry you might want to save for Lillie and a couple of romance books."

Tyler peered into the box, noticing several romance books stacked up the side. "Since she was a teenager she loved reading them; she was always dreaming of her prince coming to take her away. Amber was all about a happy ending."

In real life, there would be no happily ever after with her Prince Charming.

A small smile teased Sam's lips. "Zach is like that too; he refuses to see any movie where the people or the dog dies."

Flipping through the pages of the notebook, his name in Amber's sloping handwriting caught his eye.

I know I did the right thing by leaving Lillie with Tyler. He's so good with her, and I know he'll be the best parent. Better than I could ever be. And she loves him so much. I hope he forgives me for leaving her with him, but that's where I want her to be.

His eyesight blurred, and he shut the notebook before his tears wet the pages. Still clutching the notebook, he raised his gaze to meet Sam's.

"So that's it, then. Where—" he said, swallowing past the lump in his throat. "Where is she buried? I want to give her a proper burial."

"I'll check with the city, but I know most unclaimed deaths get buried on Hart Island." Sam made a note in his book. "I'm really sorry about this Tyler, but I thought you'd want to hear it from a friend and come out here to see where Amber lived, rather than do it in your apartment with Lillie right there."

None of it mattered; one place was the same as another to hear about death. "It's fine, and I appreciate everything you've done, Sam. I'm not the type to kill the messenger." He pressed a napkin to his eyes, soaking up what remaining tears he had left to cry. "My only hope is that she didn't suffer too much, and that I grant her last wish of being able to raise Lillie."

Marcus, who'd been on his phone while Tyler had been reading Amber's journal, gave him a grim-face smile. "I texted Josh and gave him a brief summary of what happened and Amber's journal. He seems to think that will go a long way to you keeping Lillie and even adopting her if you want."

The obvious choice would be for him to adopt Lillie; he was sure he'd be able to find a dance studio and make the dream of teaching dance to children a reality. Not that he had to give up his personal dreams of dancing professionally, but Tyler knew at his age, serious careers in dance were already in full swing. And the thought of leaving Lillie to go on tour held little enjoyment for him.

Then there was Marcus. His solid strength was Tyler's reality now. The man he'd originally shunned and dismissed as a slut without any morals had instead proven to be a dedicated and caring lover, and though Marcus might deny it, a family man who'd defend the people he loved to the death. Tyler had yet to pierce the facade of what made Marcus the man he grew up to be, and though they still struggled some days with who held the power between them, he relished the time they'd share together peeling away his layers.

This man, the two of them plus Lillie, was the life he chose to keep and fight for. But he needed to know how Marcus felt about having Lillie permanently in his life.

"Sam, thank you." He mustered a smile, and Sam nodded. "I know it's not easy to give this kind of news to anyone."

Sam slipped his notebook in his pocket and pulled on his jacket. "I'll be in touch about, well, what we talked about. I should have something definite for you by the weekend."

"Tell Zach hi, and we'll see you all on Sunday for brunch." Marcus glanced up from texting on his phone. "We're coming to Brooklyn, right?"

"Yeah."

Sam left, and then it was the two of them in that sad little booth in the corner. The rain streamed down the windows, and he watched Sam hurry across the street to his car, dodging puddles. After he drove away, Tyler collapsed against the back of the cracked faux-leather banquette. Never had he felt such bone-sapping weariness.

"Ty, c'mere."

With a grateful smile, he slid into Marcus's open arms. He stayed that way for several minutes, soaking in Marcus's warmth and familiar scent.

"I'm sorry about Amber, but it's better that you know now and can start planning for the next step."

Practically, Tyler knew Marcus's business-like attitude was correct: Amber was dead, and dwelling on the whys and hows of her life didn't help present circumstances. And yet he still resented Marcus's blasé attitude.

"Can you give me at least a minute to mourn her, or does that interfere with your plans?"

Marcus stiffened. "Um, what's going on? You seem to be angry with me, and I'm not sure why. I'm only trying to help."

Studying Marcus's confused face, Tyler's resentment dissipated. It wasn't Marcus's fault Amber ran away and made horrendous choices. At any time she could've contacted him, and he would've given up everything to bring her back home; he knew Marcus would've helped him, without him even needing to ask.

So why was he angry at him? Perhaps it was that Marcus's life seemed so easy; there'd been no struggle to accomplish anything. Whatever Marcus had ever wanted had been given to him, no questions asked.

"I-I know. And I appreciate it. I'm still not used to having someone who thinks enough about me to care. I've always been alone."

The tight lines on Marcus's face softened; his lip curved upward in a small smile. "But that's no longer true, right? I thought we moved past the *myself* part and on to the *us* part."

Returning Marcus's smile, Tyler nodded. "We have. It still takes me a moment to remember that sometimes."

They paid the bill and walked outside. The rain had stopped, and the early evening air blew fresh and cool. Cars swept by on the busy avenue, and evening commuters hurried past them, eager to get home after their workday and start their dinner and nighttime routines. Curious now as to his earlier thoughts, Tyler waited to ask his question until Marcus had finished calling for a car to bring them home.

"You never speak about your childhood. I'm assuming your parents are both gone, and I know how tough it must be."

Marcus barked out a laugh and turned wide, amused eyes on him. "Never assume. As far as I know, my parents are both alive; I visit my mother once every two or three months and my father not at all. It suits our purposes to keep it that way."

A black sedan pulled up, and Marcus indicated they should get inside. Once settled, Tyler continued to press Marcus with questions.

"Surely your parents had money and could give you everything you wanted."

Before he could go on, Marcus placed a warning hand on his arm, his face an unreadable mask.

"I'd like to end this conversation."

"But—"

"Please. Leave it alone." The evident strain on Marcus's face shocked Tyler into silence. Marcus didn't beg; he rarely became emotional about things. He was one of the most practical men Tyler had ever met, which was why he was so successful. Living with Marcus, Tyler had seen a dark side to his personality, one Marcus thought he kept well-hidden from everyone else. And he did; Tyler was certain even Marcus's closest friends had no idea what lived inside his mind.

When you live with someone and love them, they creep into your blood and soul, leaving irrevocable imprints on your heart. Living with a man like Marcus also meant Tyler knew when to back off. This was not a battle he chose to fight now, not when his and Lillie's future hung in the balance.

"Okay. I didn't mean to pry. I'll call Josh when we get home to go over everything."

Visibly relieved, Marcus kissed him. "Thank you."

Now Tyler knew the key to Marcus rested with his parents.

Chapter Twenty-Five

"**I** THINK THIS space is fantastic, Ty. It has everything you need, and it's close to the club, which is an extra perk for me."

Standing next to Tyler in the new studio he'd only moments ago signed a lease for, Marcus surveyed the room with satisfaction and a business eye.

"You could also take this corner in the front and set up a juice bar or café to keep the parents or babysitters here when you're teaching their little darlings." He grinned. "Why lose the money when they're only going to go sit for an hour in an overpriced coffee shop anyway?"

Still nervous despite all of Marcus's accolades for the space, Tyler gave him a brief, shaky smile and ran a hand through his hair, mussing it up, which made him even more attractive than Marcus thought possible. He paced the length of the storefront, talking to the real estate agent, while Marcus remained up front.

And though they'd only rolled out of bed less than two hours ago, a sharp pang of desire rose within Marcus, and he wanted Tyler again. There was something to be said for hot and heavy sex early in the morning. Or late at night.

Knowing Tyler was his had quashed his desire for any other man. He'd hired a replacement dancer for Tyler; a tall, sinuously striking man with art-worthy tattoos across his back. In the pre-Tyler days, Marcus would've had no qualms about sleeping with him, and the dancer had made more than one offer about being available for a "private show," if Marcus was interested in seeing all the dance moves he reserved for special customers.

It never occurred to him to say yes.

To his surprise, in the months he and Tyler had been living together, Marcus hadn't once thought of another man, nor did he miss the insanity of the nightlife he'd once immersed himself in so completely. Where variety had once been his mainstay, the only spice in his life now came from Tyler, and Marcus found that infinitely more appealing. He sometimes wondered how he'd kept up the pace he had. Spending less of his time at Sparks, he'd delegated more and more of the day-to-day responsibility of the club to trusted employees and promoted Darius to overall manager. All so that he could spend more time at home with Tyler and Lillie.

"So you think it's good, right? You think I'm doing the right thing?"

Tyler stood before him, biting the swell of his full bottom lip, his expression both nervous and hopeful. Starting one's own business was never easy, and a business based only on referrals could be doomed to fail almost before it started. But Tyler hadn't done this on a whim, and when he presented Marcus with his business plan, it was obvious he'd done his homework.

"I know you are. You've got this, babe." He kissed him, knowing how much Tyler needed the reassurance. Cupping Tyler's face in his hands, Marcus studied his face. "I'm so proud of you. And I'm thrilled you let me invest in it with you."

Tyler chewed his bottom lip, a sure sign, Marcus had come to learn, that he was worried.

"Stop damaging the merchandise." Marcus kissed him again. "I need that lip for later tonight."

"Are you guys all set, then?" Their real estate agent, Barbara, had gathered all the necessary paperwork and stood before them with a fond smile on her face. "I can't wait to see the studio open, Tyler. With all the cuts in arts education in the schools, I think you're going to do great."

"That's what I told him, Barb." Marcus squeezed Tyler's shoulder. "See? Have faith. I'm going to take him to get liquored up now in celebration."

"Good idea." She gave them each a hug. "Have one for me too. I'll be in touch when all the paperwork is filed and you can take possession, but I'm thinking within the month."

"Thanks for everything. I know I was a nervous wreck." Tyler bent to kiss her cheek. "I appreciate all your hard work in finding this. It's perfect."

After she left, Tyler stood in the center of the studio and spun in dizzying circles, a smile on his face, arms spread wide. Bemused, Marcus watched him, understanding the need to express joy often couldn't be spoken.

Finally Tyler stopped spinning and came to rest with the smile still on his face. "I can't believe it. After all these years I finally have something concrete to call my own. And all because of you." He jogged across the space to wrap his arms around Marcus and hug him close. "Thank you for believing in me more than I ever did myself."

Hugging him back, Marcus felt the pounding of Tyler's heart against his chest. "I've always known what you could accomplish. You're a fighter. And just like you fought to get to this point and own your own business, you'll fight before the judge next week and get to keep Lillie."

"I couldn't have done any of this without you, though."

"Of course you could've." Marcus took Tyler by his shoulders and pushed him back to stare into his eyes. "Maybe I helped by being the catalyst, but you were never destined to remain a dancer for me. I watched you on the dance floor, and I could tell you were special. You had bigger dreams than that."

"Lots of people have dreams. But you've changed so much from the first time I met you. I thought you were this selfish, self-absorbed, arrogant—"

"All right, I get the picture." Marcus punched Tyler lightly on the shoulder, then pulled on his jacket. "Let's go. I told the guys not to start without us since we might have some news for them."

Tyler stopped dead. "You didn't really say that, did you? They're going to speculate like crazy."

Unable to keep from laughing out loud, Marcus held the door open for Tyler. "Yeah I know. And I'm going to let them squirm for a while. Play up with me, okay?"

Tyler nudged his shoulder. "You're evil. It's one of the many reasons I love you."

"Tonight you'll show me all the other reasons." With his arm around Tyler's shoulders, Marcus walked down the block. "One by one and slowly."

The restaurant was located only a ten-minute walk from the studio, but Marcus made certain to arrive a bit late. With everyone so busy lately, it seemed like they never had a chance to get together much anymore as a group, and while he understood the dynamics of the group had changed since Julian married Nick and Zach had fallen in love with Sam, he still missed his friends.

Steph had the day off, so an unfamiliar waitress led them to their usual table. As Marcus had hoped, the guys were already there. Julian's eyes lit up when he caught sight of him and Tyler.

"Ah, there they are. We were about to send out a search party. You're never this late." Julian's gaze found Tyler, and his face softened. "I'm sorry about your sister, Tyler. If there's anything we can do, let us know."

Marcus squeezed Tyler's shoulder, then let him go to shrug off his jacket and sit down. A faint smile of gratitude was about as much as Tyler could muster when it came to Amber. For several nights after they found out about her death, Marcus had found Tyler sitting by Lillie's bed in the dark, watching her sleep, and it broke his heart.

"Thanks, Julian. I've gotten over the initial shock, and now all I feel is kind of numb."

Zach nodded. "I totally understand. It's exactly how I felt when I heard my father died."

Tyler settled next to him, and Marcus slid his arm around Tyler's shoulders, his fingers playing along Tyler's neck. He caught Julian watching him with a gleam in his eyes and a self-satisfied smirk.

"Tyler," said Julian, bracing his elbows on the table and giving him a frank stare. "I've decided to start a children's dance line. Your little niece inspired me, and I'd love to use her as the model for the print campaign. What do you think?"

Tyler stiffened beneath his hands. "Seriously? I'm not sure. I'd hate for her to get caught up in that world at such a young age."

Julian nodded. "I understand. But I'll personally make sure she's always safe and never feels overwhelmed." He pulled out his sketchpad and flipped the pages until he reached the desired page. "Look. I think you'll like the name."

He turned it around to face them, and Marcus gaped at the picture of Lillie in a ladybug ballerina outfit, dancing in a field of flowers.

"Lillie-bug Designs?"

Julian smile grew broader as everyone at the table clamored to see the sketches, and he passed the pad around.

"I heard Marcus call her 'Lillie-bug' and thought it was cute. And ladybugs are supposed to bring good luck." He slanted a look at Tyler. "What do you think, Tyler? Do you think Lillie will like the outfits?"

Tyler snorted. "Are you kidding? She'll love them." He took the sketchpad out of Marcus's hands. "I'm still not sure about getting her involved in the modeling aspect."

"I think Lillie would be perfect," said Marcus, holding the sketches. "After all, Julian got the idea from her. She'll need an agent, and you'll need a lawyer to deal with the contracts."

"Always thinking with your business head." Tyler patted his arm. "I'll think about it."

"And you'll make some extra money that you'll need, especially now."

"What do you mean, 'especially now'?" asked Zach. "What's happened?"

Marcus waved over the waiter. "Bring a bottle of champagne, please. Tyler and I have an announcement." He sat back and let his friends pepper him with questions, knowing that they expected him to announce they were getting engaged or married. Marcus had yet to understand the rush to get married; no one could convince him marriage was necessary. Look at his parents; they were the prime example that marriage wasn't right for everyone.

He waited until the champagne was poured and everyone at the table shut up and gave him their undivided attention. With his glass raised, he stood and faced Tyler.

"To Tyler. Congratulations on signing the lease on your new dance studio. I know Up On Your Toes and you will be a massive success."

Julian sighed, his disappointment obvious. "I knew you were setting us up." He raised his glass. "Congratulations, Tyler. I second Marcus; I think you're headed for great things."

Nick, Zach, and Sam all joined in, and Marcus sat back with a satisfied smile, watching Tyler easily accept all the accolades that were his due. He'd come so far from the defensive, secretive man Marcus had met months ago; gone was the dark, mistrustful glare and the refusal to accept help.

It was odd for him to be this close with another person, to have become intimate enough to see the changes time had brought to their personality. And yet, there could have been no other way; it was meant to be—fated, for lack of a better word, although Marcus would sooner slit his wrists than admit that to anyone out loud. From the first, Tyler had fascinated him, his body and his extraordinary looks being the catalyst for the attraction. But neither a beautiful face nor body had managed to hold his attention before. And as the old saying went, all cats are gray in the dark. For the Marcus he once was, one man was the same as all the others.

Not Tyler. After their first time together he'd become like a fever in Marcus's blood, consuming him from within. Tyler's willingness to give himself up completely, unafraid for Marcus to see his true self, was a revelation. Even now, Marcus wasn't sure who he was inside—he'd spent many years perfecting a Teflon exterior where nothing stuck so that nothing could penetrate and hurt him.

But Marcus knew he'd changed. From Tyler he'd learned that love wasn't a weakness of the mind or a loss of personal identity or control. He did what he did for Tyler and Lillie simply because their happiness made him happy. Unlike his mother, who craved the scraps of attention his father threw her way, never expecting and therefore never receiving anything in return, he knew his and Tyler's relationship was one of equality, built on a foundation of trust, desire, and love.

Damn, he'd turned into Zach.

And as if he'd somehow been foolish enough to speak out loud, Zach nudged him on the other side. "I'm happy for you. Tyler seems like a wonderful guy."

Still somewhat prickly and unwilling to share the depths of his and Tyler's relationship, even with Zach, Marcus shrugged off Zach's good wishes.

"It's not like we're running to get married or engaged or anything. I'll leave that for you lovebirds."

But Zach, who next to Tyler knew him best, wasn't so easily put off.

"You can run from it, Marcus, but you can't hide. Not from me at least. I've known you too long. There's nothing wrong with admitting out loud how you feel about Tyler."

Tyler had gone to the restroom, and Julian slipped into his vacated seat on the other side, trapping him in between.

"I know we've all kidded you about it, Marc, but the truth is I'm seeing what being in a relationship has done for you. For the first time since I've met you, you're calm. Tyler's given you peace within yourself, hasn't he?"

"You two should get your own afternoon reality talk show," Marcus grumbled but allowed himself a small grin.

"Give us a little something; come on," said Julian, elbowing him in the side. "God knows we've waited long enough."

He ignored them, preferring instead to watch Tyler walk back to their table with his unique, sinuous grace. Julian stood, but not before whispering in his ear.

"You don't need to say anything. The look in your eyes says it all."

Julian returned to his seat next to Nick, and Marcus had no typical sarcastic comeback—it was hard to argue with the truth. A heavy hand dropped on his shoulder, and a cold voice he'd hoped not to hear again in his lifetime returned to suck the joy from his afternoon.

"Marcus, I need to speak with you."

Gazing up into his father's cold gray eyes, Marcus called up the hardened exterior of years past and raised a brow.

"Well if it isn't dear old dad. Sorry, but I'm busy here. Call my club and make an appointment, but I must warn you I'm booked up, so it may take several weeks to get back to you."

Tyler craned his head to get a glimpse, then leaned over to murmur in his ear. "Are you sure you don't want to talk to him? He looks pretty upset."

Glancing back over his shoulder, Marcus did think his father seemed off-kilter. Still perfectly dressed, yet blurry, as if someone smudged his sharp lines and edges. Not his problem.

"He's upset that he's forced to acknowledge his gay son in public." Speaking to his father directly, he couldn't keep the sneering disdain from his voice. "We have nothing to say; you can run back to whatever young girl you have waiting for you. And say hello to Mother, when and if you see her."

He picked up his glass of champagne and drained it, then beckoned for the bottle. Now he needed to get drunk.

"Your mother's in the hospital, Marcus."

Chapter Twenty-Six

"STOP PUSHING ME. You don't understand."

Marcus stomped around the apartment, and Tyler sensed he was one step away from throwing something against the wall. Or at him. Tyler leaned against the kitchen counter and used his most reasonable voice in an attempt to soothe Marcus and coax him down from his anger. Thankfully, Lillie was on a playdate with Rebecca and Jacob and wouldn't be home until dinnertime.

"You're right. I don't understand. Your father wanted to talk, and instead of agreeing, you lashed out at him and ignored him. Even when he told you your mother was sick."

"That fucker can't walk into my life after ignoring me since I was a child and think I'm going to follow his orders like a puppy dog."

"But—"

"No, no buts, Tyler. I'm not going to see her. I'm sure he's exaggerating; it's what he does to get his way. He doesn't give a shit about her or me. He's doing it to save face."

Marcus stormed over and grabbed him by the shoulders. "He wouldn't even acknowledge you, did you notice? Imagine living like that every day of your life."

That explained so much about Marcus. All this hurt he internalized and kept bottled up for years now spilled over like an angry, raging river.

"Is that how it was for you? Your father ignored you?"

Tyler hadn't heard a laugh so bitter in years.

"Ignored me would have been good. He didn't know I existed. And lucky for my mother, she had Zach's house to ship me off to so she could concentrate on making everything perfect and right for her husband, without the pesky interference of her child."

Marcus let go of him and stalked to the bar, poured himself a double shot of something, and drank it down. He wiped his mouth on his sleeve and poured another shot. "God forbid she should put her child's needs ahead of her husband's."

"Your mom didn't spend time with you? Don't bite my head off," he added hurriedly when he saw Marcus open his mouth as if to snap at him. "I'm simply trying to understand."

Marcus had collapsed on the sofa and was staring off into space. Tyler joined him, close enough to touch, but he kept his hands off. "I'm not only here when the times are good, like me celebrating signing a lease. Or the sex. I can get that anywhere."

"The fuck you say," Marcus growled at him, and Tyler couldn't help but laugh.

"You know what I mean. Sex is easy to get. Love, not so much. And I told you in the beginning this relationship is a two-way street, so if we're going to have any chance of making this work, you have to trust me to help you. I'm in it for the long haul."

Marcus stared into his glass. "How'd you get so smart?"

He took the glass out of Marcus's hand and set it down on the table. "I knew you'd have to love me for my brains as well as my body."

"Not gonna lie," Marcus said, nibbling on his neck and causing him to sigh with pleasure. "That ass of yours caused me many a cold shower."

Reining in his burgeoning desire, Tyler pulled away from Marcus's questing lips and hands. If he didn't stop now, they'd end up naked on the sofa, and while he was all in favor of an afternoon quickie, Tyler understood what Marcus was up to. With great restraint, not to mention a balls-deep ache, he edged over to the opposite end of the sofa, breathing heavily.

"I know what you're trying to do, and you can forget it."

Marcus lay down fully on the sofa, hugging a pillow. "Come on, Ty. Lillie will be home soon, and I want you now. I don't want to wait until tonight after she's asleep."

"This is going nowhere until we settle the issue of you seeing your mother."

Stubborn ox that he was, Marcus set his jaw in a mutinous angle and glared at him with hostility.

"I'm sure it's nothing serious, and right now I need all my concentration to be on you and Lillie, not my mother. She's probably rundown from living on the edge, always waiting for him, wondering where he is. If it were really serious, he would've told me, mainly to guilt me into seeing her. We have the preliminary hearing in Lillie's case coming up in two days. I'll deal with it after that."

Tyler relented. "Okay, you have a point. But I'm not going to forget."

Marcus yanked him close and began unbuttoning his shirt. "Oh, me either. I promise." He dipped his head and kissed a path down Tyler's abdomen, pausing only to pop the tab of his jeans and lower the zipper with his teeth.

MORE NERVOUS THAN he'd ever been, Tyler wondered if he had time to run to the bathroom and throw up. Everything depended on him today. Marcus may stand staunchly by his side, as he knew he would, and Julian, Zach, and Sam had also shown up to support him, for which he was grateful, but in the end, Tyler knew everything rested on his shoulders.

He adjusted his tie for about the thousandth time, and Julian, who'd sent him over his outfit, to *"make sure you look your best,"* as the accompanying note read, slapped his hand away and fixed it himself.

"Stop pulling at it. You look perfect; like a runway model. Leave yourself alone." Standing back and facing him with a critical eye, Julian nodded. "You've got this in the bag."

"Don't be an ass, Juli," Marcus snapped, and Tyler could tell his nerves rested on a hair trigger. "Tyler's not going to get granted custody because he's good-looking." Marcus too had dressed in a rich charcoal-gray suit so dark it looked almost black. His pristine white shirt had thin black and purple vertical lines, and his tie was a solid swath of heavy violet silk. Used to only seeing Marcus in his solid-black club outfits, once again Tyler wondered what someone with the looks and money Marcus possessed saw in him.

"I'll ignore your rude and obnoxious behavior because I understand how tense you are," said Julian mildly, tweaking Marcus's tie. "You're in a fragile state right now, so I can't tell you to go to hell."

Tyler watched the unusual dynamic between the two friends and wished he had something similar to their easy friendship in his life. People he could count on no matter what. He'd never had a close male friend growing up; the guys in his small town were jocks for the most part and ignored him. The majority of his time was spent trying to find hidden-away places so he could practice his dance. Amber had always had boyfriends, and now, in hindsight, he wished he'd paid more attention to her life.

When Marcus put his arms around him in the next moment to hold him close, Tyler smiled into the curve of his neck, inhaling his warm scent—the scent he now couldn't fall asleep without—and realized he did have that, right here in his arms.

"Thank you."

"What's wrong? Your face…you looked so sad for a moment. Like everything was lost."

"No." He kissed Marcus's cheek. "I think I've finally found everything I need, right here."

Zach gave him a slow nod and a smile. Tyler knew Zach would understand without him having to explain.

Family Court was the single most intimidating place Tyler had ever set foot in; lawyers rushed by with files piled under their arms, families stood about looking as bewildered as he felt, bickering couples obviously in the throes of nasty custody disputes spat angry, hateful words at each other. The institutional gray hallways, flanked with anonymous doorways marked Courtroom *A*, *B*, or *C*, leading to who knows where, had his heart beating so fast, his vision blurred. What if at the end of the hearing the judge decided he wasn't the best guardian for Lillie, and that a two-parent family with a mother and a father were the better choice?

He couldn't imagine life without her anymore.

Josh beckoned him. "Come. It's time to go in."

Marcus came in with him, and Tyler hadn't noticed he'd taken his hand until Marcus squeezed it tight.

"Breathe. You're her uncle, her only living relative. Why wouldn't they pick you?"

Because life never turns out the way it should. Good things didn't happen to people like him; aside from Marcus, nothing in his life had ever worked out the way it should have or how he'd planned.

He stood behind the long pitted wooden table with Josh and all their documentation spread out before them; Lillie's birth certificate and his, all her medical records, her school reports from her teachers indicating her positive interactions with the other children.

In addition, Micah Steinberg wrote a letter detailing how close his children and Lillie had become, as well as in his professional medical opinion, what a well-adjusted, happy child Lillie was, and the stable home life she now had with Tyler and Marcus.

Tyler's heart fell at the sight of the judge as he stepped up to the bench. An elderly, gray-haired man, Judge Ira Fleischman radiated conservative disapproval to Tyler. He placed his bifocals on his nose and read through the various reports filed by the state-appointed caseworker, occasionally peering over the top of the sheaf of papers to gaze at Tyler with a frown.

"He hates me; I can tell," said Tyler with a sinking heart. "Look how he's staring at me."

"You're acting crazy; stop it," said Marcus from behind him in the front row of seats.

"Tell me what this is about. We have the case of a four-year-old girl here, I believe?" The judge pinned the social worker with a dark, unreadable gaze.

Vera Ingersoll, the social worker who'd worked tirelessly with him, cleared her throat and began to speak.

"Your Honor. Lillie Reiss is a four-year-old female whose mother is deceased. We have no record of her paternity."

"The mother didn't name the father on the birth certificate?" The judge rifled through the papers on his desk, picked up one and perused it. "Yes, I see. Continue."

"The child and her mother came to New York City approximately two years ago and began living with the child's maternal uncle, Mr. Tyler Reiss. Upon the mother abandoning the child, Mr. Reiss assumed full care of her, and she's been living with him ever since. She attends preschool in Manhattan, and when Mr. Reiss is at work, she has a full-time babysitter."

The judge shifted his attention to Tyler, and Tyler lifted his chin and met the intimidating stare full on. He wasn't going to go down without fighting.

"Mr. Reiss. Tell me a little about yourself."

He glanced over at Josh, who gave him a subtle nod.

"Um, Your Honor, I'm thirty-three years old and have lived in New York City for over five years. I trained to be a professional dancer and recently signed a lease to open my own children's dance studio here in the city." He licked his dry lips and swallowed. "I teach dance to children at different schools throughout the city right now."

"I see." The judge made some notes and continued to read through the paperwork.

Tyler relaxed; perhaps this would be easier than he'd suspected.

"Were you planning on telling me about your career as a male stripper, or did you intend to hide that from the court, hoping we wouldn't discover it?" Leaning back in his chair, the judge frowned.

Tyler winced and heard Marcus's muttered "Fuck" behind him. Gathering his wits, he willed his shaking voice to settle before speaking.

"Your Honor. I was not a male stripper. I worked as a dancer in a club. I did what any parent would do—the best I could to take care of my child." He stopped for a moment and took a drink from the glass of water sitting before him.

"Every day mothers and fathers sacrifice themselves, working long hours at jobs they simply endure in the hopes of giving their children a better life than they had; every generation wants something better for their children than the one that came before. I did what I did because the money was good; I'm not going to lie and tell you I didn't make money from the tips. But it was all legal, and I have the owner of the club here with me who can testify that I was paid on the books and never did anything against the law."

"That was a very impassioned speech, Mr. Reiss."

"Your Honor, I love Lillie. She's all I have left of my sister and of my family, and I'll do whatever I have to do to keep her. My partner and I have created a stable home for her where she's loved and cared for. She's our number-one priority, as if she was our own daughter."

"And is your partner here today?"

Tyler turned around and pointed to Marcus. "Yes, Your Honor, Mr. Marcus Feldman. He is the owner of the nightclub where I used to dance."

"Step forward, please, Mr. Feldman, and join Mr. Reiss and his attorney at the table."

Pale yet with a determined tilt to his jaw, Marcus walked over and stood next to him.

"How long have you and Mr. Reiss known each other?"

"We've known each other about five months now, and we've been together for around three months."

"And you own a nightclub?" The judge didn't look up as he spoke but rather jotted notes down on the pad before him.

"I do. Until recently I was the owner and manager, but since Lillie and Tyler moved in, I've handed over the day-to-day management of the club to others, so I can have more time at home with them."

"And you think you're equipped to take care of a four-year-old child? What experience do you have with children, Mr. Feldman?"

Marcus stiffened, and Tyler held his breath, hoping Marcus would hold back any cutting words he might have and save them for when they were outside the earshot of the judge.

"I may not have experience with children, but I know what not to do. I know not to put myself first, that their needs take precedence over mine. I know not to ignore them when they ask questions that might at first not make sense but if you spend time listening, can give you insight to what is happening in their world."

Tyler could hardly believe the words coming directly from Marcus's heart. What an extraordinary shift in his behavior from the shallow, glittery personality he'd once maintained. Or perhaps it was always there, lurking, seeking the right time to show what a truly wonderful person Marcus was.

"Lillie has taught me what it means to love and be loved. And no matter what happens here today, I'll make sure to be a part of her life. But you can't take her away from Tyler; she needs him—they need each other. If you do, she'll lose not only the one person she loves more than anything, but she'll lose her family and her memories."

Stunned by Marcus's heartfelt words, Tyler could only whisper, "Thank you." There was little more he could add to what Marcus had so beautifully stated. To hear how much he loved Lillie was as if all the discordant notes that played in his head settled into a beautifully played symphony.

Seemingly impervious to Marcus's plea, the judge continued on. "I've read the letter from Dr. Steinberg and more importantly, your sister's journal." Judge Fleischman took off his glasses, and suddenly he didn't look so intimidating; he seemed almost grandfatherly. "I'm very sorry for your loss, Mr. Reiss. Your sister may not have made the wisest choices in her short life, but for the most important thing, the care of her child, after listening to those who've spoken up in your behalf today, I'd say she made the best choice of all."

It took a few moments for the judge's words to sink in and make sense to Tyler. Somewhat stunned, he turned to Josh whose grin lit up his face.

"Is he saying what I think?"

"Yes, Mr. Reiss, I am. As of now, I'm granting you temporary custody of your niece with an outcome toward full guardianship."

No longer stern and foreboding, the judge's warm brown eyes twinkled. "I have a granddaughter her age. I believe you'll have your hands full, but from what I've witnessed today, I have no doubt you can handle it."

After receiving congratulations from Josh and the social worker, Marcus grabbed him.

"I knew you'd do it. You stood up and spoke your mind. I'm so proud of you." He hugged him close.

Tyler spoke into Marcus's shoulder. "Everything I have, every dream, is from taking a chance and trusting you. And love. Always love."

The shift in the air, that recognition of a moment to be frozen in time—Tyler held on to Marcus, letting the love they shared wash over him. If he had known this love and this man would be waiting for him, it wouldn't have made this moment half as sweet. Without love, Tyler wasn't sure the struggle was worth it.

Everything happens for a reason: the missed elevator or that wrong turn taking you miles out of your way, only to have you end up right where you were meant to be. Even though they may be standing in a grimy little courtroom, Tyler's heart knew as long as he was with Marcus, he was home.

"Let's go home and tell Lillie her forever starts today."

Marcus smiled into his eyes. "Yeah. I like the sound of that."

After saying goodbye to Josh and giving both him and the social worker their thanks, Tyler and Marcus met the guys in the waiting area. Nick had arrived in his firefighter jacket, stopping by on his way back from teaching a training class.

"So, what happened?" Julian rushed up to them.

Tyler couldn't hold back the smile. "I won."

The cheers got them kicked out of the waiting area, with the court officers not amused nor interested in anything they had to say. Out on the street, everyone hugged him, and they decided to meet tonight at their apartment for a little impromptu celebration. It wasn't until they were in the cab going home that the nerves finally got to him and he began to shake.

And just as he'd been from the very beginning, Marcus was right there. "It's okay. Let it go. I understand."

And so he wept for his poor, dead sister and his little niece who'd never know her mother. After several moments he wiped his eyes and pulled himself together.

"Thank you. I know this was never your plan to be saddled with a child, so I am letting you know you don't have to feel obligated to me or Lillie. What you said in the courtroom was beautiful, but,"—he shrugged helplessly, afraid to hold on to Marcus too tight and yet fearful to let go—"I'll understand."

Marcus cupped the nape of his neck, drawing their mouths close.

"What part of forever don't you understand?"

Chapter Twenty-Seven

T HE PARTY WAS in full swing by the time Marcus came home from spending some much-needed time at Sparks. Marcus gladly put aside the daily running of the club to help Tyler, however there were some things only he as the owner was able to sign off on.

He and Tyler had spent the early part of the afternoon with Lillie, explaining to her that she never had to worry about someone else coming to take her away; her uncle Tyler and he were always going to be around to take care of her.

And because she was an intelligent child, so aware of her surroundings, Lillie listened to Tyler with wise eyes and had only one question.

"Are you and Marcus going to stay together forever?"

Tyler smoothed her dark curls. "I'm hoping so, honey. But no matter what, we both will love you always, okay?"

Holding tight to the doll Marcus bought her, Lillie nodded. "I don't wanna hafta leave."

Marcus took her on his lap. "And so you won't. I see you, Uncle Tyler, and me together until you're an old lady."

She giggled. "As old as you?"

He tickled her. "Waaay, way older."

That proclamation was enough to satisfy her, and when he left, Tyler was busy creating a card to mail out to the list of clients he'd been compiling, announcing his new dance studio.

When he opened his door in the early evening, he was greeted not only by Tyler, Lillie, and his friends, but Josh and Micah had come with their children and another couple. Marcus recognized his former neighbor and Micah's best friend, Alex, who married the guy Marcus vaguely recalled flirting with years ago. Sparks was in its infancy then. A lifetime had passed since he thought of the handsome man who lived a floor above him in that walk-up; once he started making money from Sparks, Marcus moved from that depressing building to the luxury of this apartment and never looked back. With a pang, he also remembered his old dog, Jameson. Maybe Lillie would like a dog.

To his surprise, Zach's mother was there with an older man, who, Zach informed him, she'd recently begun seeing "for coffee." Lillie sat in all her glory on Cheryl's lap asking if Cheryl could braid her hair, and Cheryl happily complied, insisting she was always free to babysit this "adorable child, since she didn't have any grandchildren of her own yet."

"That's great. I'm glad she's finally putting her past behind her and moving on." He handed Zach a beer and was about to leave the kitchen, but stopped at the touch of Zach's hand on his arm.

"Don't you think it's time you did the same?"

He checked himself, then froze, giving Zach a death glare.

"What the hell are you talking about?"

"Don't play dumb with me. You know what I mean. Your father said your mother was sick. Have you gone to see her?"

If it were anyone but Zach, Marcus would tell them to mind their own fucking business, thank you very much, and ignore them. Not with Zach.

"You know I haven't. And I don't plan to, either."

"Why not? Marcus, come on. I know you never got along well with them, but she's still your mother." Always the sensitive soul, Zach probably imagined that now, because he was in a relationship himself, Marcus was full of hearts and flowers like he was. Total bullshit. Zach gave him an encouraging smile that faded when he saw it wasn't reciprocated.

"I know what you're trying to do, and while you mean well, you don't know anything about it." Years of neglect couldn't be erased with a simple "I'm sorry." And frankly he didn't care any longer. For the first time in his life he was happy, and no one, not even his closest friend, could guilt him into doing something he didn't want to do.

"I feel sorry for you, Marcus. I thought you'd changed and had grown up. But it seems you're still as self-centered as ever." Zach's somber expression sent inexplicable waves of guilt through Marcus. "If you don't give a damn, then why not go see her? It won't take more than ten minutes." Zach left, joining Sam on the loveseat, easily falling into a conversation about Internet games.

Later that night, after the party was over and everyone had left, Marcus sat on the edge of the bed, half-undressed and staring off into space.

"Wow, she did not want to go to sleep—" Tyler stopped short at the doorway to the bedroom. "What's wrong? You look weird."

At his continued silence, Tyler shot him a strange look but said nothing further. He pulled off his shirt, took off his pants, and went into the bathroom. The water ran and within minutes, Tyler returned, showered and bare-chested, though he'd donned a pair of sweatpants. Tyler joined him on the bed, where he'd remained sitting in the same position as before.

"Now, do you want to talk?"

"Do you think I've changed since I met you?" Marcus tossed his shirt onto the top of the dresser to bring to the dry cleaners. "Or am I still selfish and self-centered?"

Tyler scrambled to the center of the bed and sat cross-legged, his long legs folding easily beneath him. Being a dancer, Tyler manipulated his body in ways Marcus could only dream about.

"Pervert," said Tyler with a laugh, his blue eyes clever with knowledge.

Unashamed at being called out, Marcus stretched on the bed, facing Tyler. "But am I? Selfish, I mean?"

"What's brought this on?" Tyler nudged him with his foot. "Did someone say something?"

"Zach." No reason to hide it.

"Zach?" Tyler's brows shot up in surprise. "That doesn't sound like him."

"He's mad because he thinks I should see my mother. Let bygones be bygones, no matter how I feel. Because she's my mother." The rancor curdled in his chest, but it was easier to hold on to the guilt than take that next step.

"Seeing her doesn't absolve her of what she did to you, nor does it mean that you have to let go of your anger. But what if she dies and you lose that chance to say whatever is in your heart? You can never get that back." Tyler inched closer and kissed him. "And for the record, I don't think you're selfish at all."

No longer interested in talking about his mother with Tyler's warm body next to his, Marcus slid his hands up Tyler's chest, tweaked his sensitive nipples the way he'd come to learn Tyler enjoyed, then dragged his nails back down his abdomen to the top of his sweatpants. Tyler sighed his pleasure and shifted closer.

Spurred on by the increased cadence of Tyler's breathing and very interesting swelling beneath his sweatpants, Marcus pulled down the pants to reveal Tyler's cock already hard and reddened. As he watched, a tiny drop of fluid dripped from the slit, and he lapped it up. God, he could drink him down like a fine wine every night.

He nuzzled, licked, then took Tyler's balls into his mouth one at a time, carefully keeping away from his cock which thrust itself up as proud as a flagpole on the Fourth of July.

"I love you, Marcus."

"Love you too," he mumbled, his face buried in Tyler's groin. If there was any better scent in the world, Marcus had yet to come across it, and he nibbled and sucked his way past the slant of Tyler's hip, across his belly, to his swollen cock.

Shifting on his knees, Marcus bent and licked around the thick base of Tyler's cock, moving upward, delicate as a cat with a bowl of cream.

With the flat of his tongue he traced the veins, then swirled around the head, finally heeding Tyler's moans and soft cries of enjoyment and fully engulfing the entire shaft in his mouth, reveling in the sharp and salty taste of Tyler's precome spurting into his mouth.

Marcus had no problem taking Tyler's thrusts deep, and he swallowed him down, taking everything Tyler gave to him. Even in lovemaking now, Marcus found equal pleasure in giving as well as receiving, knowing the love Tyler gave him was a gift he would never abuse or take for granted.

Tyler's cock softened, and Marcus let it slip from his mouth, then kissed his way back up Tyler's body as he feasted on his warm skin. When he reached Tyler's face, he stared at him for a moment, drinking in his strong profile, dark brows winging upward and hair lying across his brow in a riot of waves, before leaning down and rubbing their noses together, then kissing him.

Tyler opened his mouth, and Marcus slid his tongue inside where they met and teased together. God, he tasted sweet, like hope and love wrapped up in the gift of forever. A wave of longing swept over him so strong, Marcus took control of that kiss, nipping at the swell of Tyler's bottom lip, sucking at his tongue; showing Tyler with his body and his heart how much he needed him.

And as he always did, Tyler understood and let Marcus take from him, arching into his touch, urging him on, giving him his trust in return.

"Let me."

Tyler nuzzled against his cheek, and Marcus, panting and trembling, knew what Tyler wanted.

He nodded, and Tyler scooted to the table to get the bottle of lube. Tyler prepped him, sliding slick, cool fingers inside, but Marcus didn't want it slow and pretty, and shoved himself hard on Tyler's fingers.

Tyler's eyes bore into his. "Are you ready for me?"

"Now." Marcus opened himself wide. Tyler guided himself in, pushing his thickness inside Marcus. They were the way it was meant to be. Skin to skin. Heart to heart.

Once he was fully seated, to Marcus's surprise, Tyler framed his face between his hands and kissed him sweetly, his soft lips traveling slow and gentle across Marcus's own, like a benediction to his soul.

"I love you, Marcus. I only want you to be happy."

Tyler flexed his hips, sinking deep inside with each thrust and push until they rocked even faster, holding on tight to one another.

The beat of their hearts, their breaths sighing in the stillness of the evening air, it all played like the music Tyler danced to, swelling until the final crescendo of their bodies shook them, and they cried out in tandem from their shattering, mutual release.

With his heart still banging madly, Marcus lay under Tyler, whose hot breath stuttered past his ear.

"I think I saw the face of God," said Tyler.

"Thank you." Marcus couldn't help chuckling.

Tyler smacked his hip, and Marcus retaliated by giving Tyler's ass a firm squeeze, then pinching it.

"Jesus, Marcus."

"I'm Jewish." Marcus squeezed again, and Tyler shook with laughter, his face buried in Marcus's shoulder. "Try again."

Tyler pulled out, and Marcus trembled, his body more sensitive than ever; it was, he realized, the first time in his life he'd had sex without protection. Guilty, he glanced over at Tyler.

"I didn't ask how you felt about it. I'm sorry; I got caught up."

Tyler's sweet smile reassured him. "Don't apologize. I wanted it as well. I've been tested, and I assume you've been too."

"Yeah, of course. I don't want you to think I don't care about your opinion, or your health."

"I don't. But you see? You've answered your own question from before—you're not selfish. You're concerned and caring about my feelings."

His head spinning, Marcus merely nodded and followed Tyler into the bathroom where they showered together in silence. He didn't speak until they were lying together again.

"I think you're right."

Tracing his fingers over Marcus's skin, Tyler stiffened in his arms. "About what?"

A bit bemused after all their discussions, Marcus laced their fingers together and kissed his hand.

"I'm going to see my mother tomorrow."

He caught the edge of Tyler's smile in the dark.

"What changed your mind, if you don't mind me asking?"

He rolled onto his side, taking Tyler with him, hugging him close. "You did. You changed *me*. In every way possible. When I told the judge today that I put Lillie's needs above my own, I meant it, and tonight it occurred to me that I wouldn't be setting a very good example for her if I went against everything I said in court."

With his free hand, Tyler stroked his back. "I'm proud of you."

"You're the first person to ever say that to me. And I'm not saying that to get your sympathy. I say it because up until now I haven't been the type of person who deserved it."

"You're too hard on yourself."

Marcus shook his head. "No. You don't know who I was and what I did in my life before I met you. And I have no regrets for the past. But when I saw myself becoming like my father, that's when I realized I needed to change."

"You could never be like that. I saw what you're like with the guys in the club and your friends. You care about people. It's why I fell in love with you; despite trying to affect that I-don't-give-a-shit attitude, your actions show me the exact opposite."

Tyler yawned and lay flat against the pillow. He'd already begun to sink into drowsiness, and Marcus couldn't blame him. It had been a hell of a day.

Still, he reached out a hand and instinctively Tyler took it and tried to reassure him in a sleep-softened voice. "You'll feel better about everything in the morning."

After a few moments, Marcus heard Tyler's easy breathing and knew he'd fallen asleep. He, on the other hand, stared at the ceiling, watching the shadows of the night creep along the walls until dawn.

Chapter Twenty-Eight

"**W**ILL YOU AT least tell me what hospital your mother's in? I'm not planning on checking up on you. It's a normal question."

Marcus sipped his coffee and quirked a brow at Tyler, who glared at him across the counter. He enjoyed riling Tyler up if for no reason than he looked hot when he got angry. His eyes sparked blue fire and his cheeks flushed, giving him that look like he'd been fucked well and good. Guess he hadn't lost his shallowness completely.

"I'm not certain when I'm going, so there's no point in telling you." He finished his coffee, and Lillie came out of the bedroom with a sleepy smile.

"I'm thirsty."

"Go brush your teeth first, and then Tyler will give you breakfast. What are you doing today?"

Preschool was on winter break, and they'd been splitting up babysitting duties. Today was Tyler's day.

"Jacob and Rebecca's babysitter was gonna take us to learn ice skating. Can I go? Please?"

Like he could refuse that face. No wonder advertisers put little kids in commercials. They could sell cow shit to a farmer.

Tyler had his head stuck in the cabinets, pulling out the pancake mix and the bag of chocolate chips. "Yes, honey. I spoke with Josh about it yesterday. I'm going to drop you off there after breakfast." He waved the bag. "Now go brush, and we'll make pancakes, and then you have to clean your room before you go anywhere."

"It's not dirty."

Marcus choked on the remainder of his coffee. "Lillie-bug, you have every doll out on the floor. There's no place to walk."

Staring at him like he'd sprouted two heads, she spoke as if he was slow on the uptake. "Well, yeah. We were having a party."

"Well, the party's over, so they get put away, or you don't go ice skating." He placed his cup in the sink and gave Tyler a kiss. "I'll speak to you later." He bent to kiss a pouting Lillie. "Be good."

He was out the door before Tyler could stop him. In his mind there was no need to make a big deal out of this visit. He'd stop by, make a few minutes of usual, awkward conversation, and then leave to spend much-needed time at the club. The elevator came, and he absently greeted the other people inside. Although he trusted Darius implicitly and the reports he received showed the nightly take as high as ever, the businessman in Marcus didn't like other people running his brand. People expected to see Marcus Feldman when they went to Sparks.

He hailed a cab and gave the driver the address of the hospital, then settled in for the rush-hour traffic. If he was being honest with himself, not something he often was, he didn't miss the long nights. What he did miss were the people and the friendship that could only come from working together every night.

Perhaps, he mused, a better compromise was to go into the club but not stay until closing. If he was at Sparks from ten to midnight or one a.m., he still had plenty of time at home with Ty and enough time at the club to make the rounds, check in with everyone, and keep his finger on the pulse of his business. Being in a relationship didn't mean giving up everything he'd worked so hard to achieve, and he didn't believe Ty would want him to give it all up either.

Satisfied that he'd solved one problem in his life this morning, Marcus stared out of the window as the cab turned onto the Brooklyn Bridge. The waters of the East River crested gray and choppy this morning; not many boats were out in the harbor, save for the Staten Island ferry in the far distance. When the weather got warmer they could take Lillie and Micah's kids for a ride. Kids loved that stuff.

Alone with his thoughts for the first time since Tyler had been granted custody, Marcus experienced a prickle of fear. What the hell had he been thinking to help Tyler raise a child?

He'd started out simply wanting Tyler in his bed for the night. Nothing more than a physical itch. But like a chemical release in his bloodstream, the need for Tyler increased instead of waning; he was drawn to him, to his eyes and his heart. The need for Tyler became a necessity, a broken circle somehow reconnected, making him whole.

Tyler reminded Marcus that there was good within himself; and Marcus rediscovered the soft side he'd buried beneath the persona he'd perfected. Maybe Julian and Zach weren't so wrong about having one person to love who loved you back.

But a child had never been part of the equation.

It was one thing to spend the day and sit around with them to watch them play. But the day-to-day stuff? He didn't know shit about being a parent, and he certainly didn't have role models in his own family to turn to. How could he take care of another human being and be responsible for their existence, when he'd done such a piss-poor job on himself? He scrubbed his face.

"I'm fucked."

The cab bounced through the streets of Brooklyn, getting closer to the hospital, and Marcus's nerves wound exponentially tighter. In his head he practiced the speech to his mother, wishing her well, hoping she'd get better soon; then, when a decent enough amount of time had passed, he'd get the hell out of there and head for Sparks. It was the beginning of the month, and the new uniforms had come in along with the monthly liquor shipment. Time to get back into the game.

The cab stopped in front of the mammoth hospital, and Marcus paid and scrambled out. He realized he didn't even know what building she was in, and sighing with frustration, headed to the information booth.

The friendly woman behind the desk punched in a few numbers

and with a surprised look said, "Um, she's in the ICU. You said she's your mother?"

He knew what she was thinking—how could a son not know his mother was in the intensive care unit? And his father hadn't mentioned she was that ill. Marcus thanked her and headed to the bank of elevators, tapping his feet with nervous energy as he waited. Of course they all came at the same time, but he finally punched in the button and was rattling upward, sharing his space with a family carrying an entire party store's worth of pink balloons sporting "Congratulations" and "It's a Girl."

Luckily his ride was short, and he pushed his way out to freedom. The nurse's station sat opposite the elevator, and he approached a woman who looked terrifyingly competent.

"I'm here to see Mrs. Feldman?"

Her thin eyebrows arched in surprise. "Are you a relative?"

"I'm her son."

Those brows almost disappeared into her hairline. "Oh. We didn't know she had any children. Your father hasn't been here since she was brought in."

"I'd like to see her, please," he said, between gritted teeth.

"Are you aware how ill she is?" The nurse came around from behind the counter to walk with him down the hall. "She's had several severe strokes since she was brought in, each one weakening her further. The last one left her completely incapacitated. Right now we have her on a ventilator, since she's unable to breathe on her own."

Horrified, Marcus stopped walking. "You mean she's brain-dead?" Where the fuck was his father? He knew all this and still wasn't here? "He didn't tell me anything."

But you never asked.

"Technically no. But I'm not certain she'll be able to survive another episode. You can speak to the doctor if you'd like for me to page him."

Marcus nodded, dumbly. "Thank you."

They turned a corner and stood before a long glass window, behind which he saw a small figure lying in bed, hooked up to machines. A nurse sat at the bank of monitors, checking charts. The beeping and hissing from all the different machines already drove him crazy, and he'd been there less than a minute.

"Can I go inside?"

The nurse nodded. "Because she's critical, we're allowing family in. If you speak to your father, you might want to tell him to come." She hesitated. "We've left several messages."

Fucking bastard. "I'll do my best."

She squeezed his arm, and he stiffened. The last thing he wanted right now was a stranger's sympathy. He entered the room and sat by his mother's bed, watching the machine breathe for her. What he really wanted was for this day to start over, with him back in bed with Tyler. He ran his hand through his hair; he couldn't stop shaking. Never in his life had he felt so fucking useless. He wanted Tyler; he'd know what to do.

He checked his watch and saw it was already ten thirty. Tyler would be on his way to drop Lillie off for ice skating, then on to his classes. It wasn't right for Marcus to bother him; he would deal with this by himself, like he had for all these years.

One thing he had to do was tell his father to get his sorry ass down here. He pulled out his cell phone, and the nurse immediately shook her head.

"I'm sorry sir, you're not allowed to use them inside here; you'll have to step out of the room."

He glanced over at the bed as if he expected his mother to say something, but she remained still and waxy pale.

"I'm sorry, I wasn't thinking."

With the phone still clutched in his hand, he exited the room and stood against the wall. Hesitating for only a minute, he pushed the button to get connected to his father's office. Of course, the secretary answered.

"Mr. Feldman's office. How may I help you?"

"This is his son. I need to speak with him."

Without a break for thought, the secretary answered. "I'm sorry, sir, but he's not in the office. Can I take a message?"

"Yes." Marcus inhaled and made sure to speak as clearly as possible. "Tell that bastard his wife is dying and to get his selfish fucking ass to the hospital. Got that?"

"Y-yes sir. I'll make sure he gets the message."

"You do that." And he clicked off.

His hands shook like an addict reaching for the next blessing of heroin as he paced the hall. Maybe there was something to be said for the sweet oblivion of drugs. He finally managed to slip his phone back into his pants pocket, when he felt a presence behind him.

"Mr. Feldman, I'm Dr. White."

A man of medium height, around his age, stood before him.

"Are you my mother's doctor?"

"I'm the resident. Her neurologist is still on rounds, but the nurse wanted me to talk to you." Dr. White's dark eyes searched his. "Your mother is very ill. Are there any other relatives you need to call?"

"No." His voice came out hoarse, and he cleared his throat. "No. I called my father, but he's not answering. I left a message to come as soon as possible."

"Good." Dr. White nodded with approval. "Your father signed a DNR. I'm not sure if you were aware. From what we can see, your mother is in a very weakened state. I hope he makes it here in time. I'm sorry, but I've always thought it best not to give hope where there is none."

He walked away, and Marcus stared after him. No wonder Micah left his practice to work with seniors. Hopefully he had a better bedside manner than this doctor had. None of which helped him at the moment. Before he returned to his mother's bedside, he texted Micah and told him about his mother's condition, and then he relented and texted Tyler and told him.

You don't have to come. I'm fine. I only wanted to tell you because I was thinking about you. I'll see you tonight.

Any misgivings he might have had earlier about being with Tyler dwindled to nothing as he sat by his dying mother, watching her fade away as the day passed. He didn't want to end up like this at the end of his life, alone with a child who barely knew him and no other family around.

In his heart he promised Lillie and himself he wouldn't make the mistakes his mother had by putting her child's needs second. And he swore to never become his father, a man so selfish and narcissistic he cared for nothing but his own pleasure. He'd been well on his way toward it before Tyler entered his life.

As for his mother, he couldn't understand why she never loved him enough, but he forgave her because it no longer mattered. He'd found Tyler, who taught him that love didn't have to be a prison and caring about someone else didn't mean there wasn't enough love to go around. Love was infinite, a bottomless vessel to dip into, knowing it would forever be replenished.

The loud alarm going off shook him out of his thoughts, and he was asked to leave the room, but he didn't venture far. Marcus knew the time had come.

The nurse beckoned him from the doorway. "If you'd like to say goodbye now…" Her sympathetic gaze surprisingly comforted him. She had picked the right profession.

Standing over his mother's bed, Marcus gazed down at her, the pain of loss unexpectedly acute. It hurt him that she had wasted her life on a man who never cared. And he took her hand and squeezed it, hoping somehow she'd know that in the end, he'd been there. "I'm sorry."

He turned away to find Tyler standing at the door, red-faced and windblown. "I came as soon as I got your text. I'm so sorry, Marcus."

The hot rush of tears burned his cheeks, and Tyler's arms closed around him. He found himself able to breathe for the first time in hours.

"Thanks for coming. At least I was here, so she didn't have to die alone."

"I'm sure she could sense it. And I'm glad you made your peace." Tyler kissed his cheek, and Marcus clung to him, willing his warmth to take away the ice inside him. They sat down on chairs outside the room, waiting to speak to the doctors for the final time.

The nurses offered their condolences, and he accepted them, still feeling like a fraud. He wasn't a good son; he'd never been hungry, cold, or imperiled like Tyler and his sister.

"I was wrong to hold a grudge for so long; I held on to my anger like a child and almost lost myself whoring around."

"That's the guilt talking," said Tyler, massaging his back. "You've carried around a truckload of pain since childhood, and now when you're finally happy, she's gone, so you think you don't deserve it." Tyler kissed his neck. "You're wrong."

"We never tried to work through it. I never gave her a chance." Not that she had made much of an effort, but he chose not to remember that now. He hugged Tyler. "I'm glad you came. I was wrong not to tell you before."

Over Tyler's shoulder he saw his father striding down the hallway, with a grim, determined look. He detached from Tyler and braced himself. "Don't look now, but here comes my darling daddy." He stood and leaned against the wall.

"I came as soon as the hospital called."

"And as usual, too late." There was no way to gild the disgust he had for this man. "Even in death you let her down."

"What about you? You left and ignored her."

"Don't push your sorry-ass guilt off on me. I know you were fucking around on her all these years. Why she loved you I'll never understand. You never gave a damn about her or me or anyone except yourself. Well now you can do whatever you want and not have to think up your bullshit excuses. And I never need to think about your sorry ass again." Marcus took Tyler by the hand and brushed past his father. "I'd say have a nice life, but I don't lie."

"You're as miserable a son as ever. You even had to drag your dirty lifestyle in here."

With a snarl, Marcus turned and backed his father up against the wall.

"Don't you ever talk about Tyler again. Don't look at him or think about him. Got it? You aren't good enough to clean the fucking dog shit off his shoes." For the first time he saw fear in his father's eyes, and Marcus derived a perverse kind of pleasure from it.

"As far as I'm concerned, I have no father."

Without waiting to hear if there'd be a reply, he took Tyler's hand and walked swiftly down the hallway back toward the elevator.

"Marcus?"

"I know, I know. You're going to say I shouldn't have lost my temper."

Tyler grabbed him around the waist. "Nope. I wanted to tell you I think you were amazing." He kissed him hard and pushed the button for the elevator. The doors rumbled open, and he followed Tyler inside. True strength often hid, coming out only in times of crisis. Perhaps he was stronger than he knew, but if so it was due to having Tyler by his side.

Tyler left him alone, content to sit next to him in the cab on the way home and hold his hand or massage the nape of his neck. He didn't deserve a man as good as Tyler, but he was selfish and had no intention of ever letting go.

The cab pulled up in front of their building, and they walked inside, past the doorman and the concierge to the elevators, smiling faintly at people as he passed them in the hallway. It seemed impossible only a mere hour ago he'd been surrounded by death and sorrow, yet here everything remained untouched.

I'm sorry we never talked or made time for each other, Mother. I'm only now beginning to figure it out and know we were both wrong. Better late than never, right?

He stood silent, thinking of all that had happened in the past months. How did the world stay the same, yet his whole life upend itself so completely he wouldn't recognize the person he was a year ago?

The answer, of course, was Tyler.

The elevator door opened, and he pulled Tyler inside and pressed him up against the wall. There were no other occupants, which fit perfectly with his plan. The doors closed, and he smiled.

"Have I told you lately how much I love you?" He kissed Tyler, then pushed the emergency stop button and sank to his knees.

"Marcus, what are you doing?"

Ignoring Tyler's halfhearted protest, Marcus pulled down the loose sweats he wore, leaving them to puddle around his ankles.

"If you don't know by now, I've been horribly neglectful." He nudged Tyler's erection through his boxers, inhaling his wonderfully familiar smell; it was the scent wrapped up in his sheets, all over his skin, and embedded in the scars on his heart. "I'm showing you how much you mean to me."

"You don't need to do that here. We don't need to risk getting caught."

"I'm willing to take the risk, as long as it's with you."

A sparkle entered Tyler's eyes. "Well, if you put it that way, I'd be stupid to refuse." He leaned back and sighed, waving his hand. "Carry on, then."

Life was one big risk as far as Marcus was concerned, and they were all holding on for the ride.

Epilogue

June

LATE SPRING WAS the perfect season in New York City; not too warm but with the cold of the winter long forgotten. It was the final day of his ballet class, and Tyler's students had completed their recital, performing in front of their parents, grandparents, and babysitters.

He handed out the cupcakes Marcus had thoughtfully sent over from Sprinkles and began saying goodbye, as most of these children would be away for the summer. Through his work with the public schools, Tyler would offer low or no-cost dance lessons throughout the summer to children who didn't leave the city.

The kids looked so cute in their costumes, and he was gratified to see almost as many boys in the class as girls. Since the studio opened, Tyler had been busier than he'd ever imagined; setting up classes and choreographing routines took up so much time, but rather than coming home exhausted every night, he felt exhilarated with his accomplishments. He'd even managed to hire a young instructor who'd been able to help with some of the beginning students when he needed to leave and give his classes in the public schools.

He'd handed out a cupcake and said goodbye to the last little girl when he noticed one of the mothers striding toward him with a determined look in her eye.

Uh-oh. Tyler had been lucky so far in dealing with the parents, but there was always one mother or father who thought their little darling didn't get enough time doing a solo or should be the main attraction. He bit the inside of his cheek and gave the woman a smile.

"Mrs. Graff, how nice to see you. Wyatt does so well in the class; I'm thrilled you signed him up again in September."

With her impeccably tailored black suit, hair beautifully styled, and fresh skin so poreless Tyler wondered if she owned her own personal airbrush machine, Liz Graff looked the epitome of a New York City power woman. Scary as hell.

"Tyler, I can call you Tyler, correct?" Without waiting for a reply, most likely because no one dared get in her path, she continued, "I want to talk to you."

"Ye-es?" He wiped his suddenly sweaty hands on a napkin.

"I've watched you teach these children for weeks now and did a little checking on you."

His ire raised, Tyler managed to keep a pleasant tone of voice only because he knew he'd come out on the losing end if he yelled at her. "Checked up on me? For what reason?"

"Because you're too good to be a simple children's dance teacher. And I was correct." She gave him a smug smile. "You were professional-ly trained for the stage, weren't you?"

Reeling from the shock that this woman had looked into his background, Tyler gave her a curt nod.

"And I bet you gave it all up to take care of that little niece of yours, am I right?"

"What is this about? I hate to be rude, but I have a lot of cleaning up to do."

"I don't believe in beating around the bush. I want you to come audition for a play my husband is producing Off-Broadway. You'd be perfect for one of the roles."

"I'm sorry?" This woman was nuts.

"My husband is…" She named a very well-known producer, and his heart began to pound. "He is putting on a production of *Rapunzel,* and I want you to play the prince who rescues her." She ran a critical eye over him. "You're handsome, and you dance like a dream. You'd be perfect, and I already told my husband."

"Wait." This was crazy. Things like this didn't happen to people like him. "I can't just walk in and get the part."

Liz burst out laughing. "Honey, it's his show and my money. I can do and get whatever and whoever I want, and I want you." She handed him her card. "Come by the theater tomorrow and meet my husband. He'll probably want you to dance for him."

Without waiting for him to answer, she turned on her stilettos and swept little Wyatt into her arms, telling him how wonderfully he'd danced. Mother and son exited the studio, leaving him dumbfounded.

"What's wrong with you?"

Austin, his junior dance instructor, gave him a curious stare. Big blue eyes peered out from under a pouf of curly black hair. Tyler had been reluctant to hire him at first; he'd sensed a bit of an entitled attitude, especially once he'd discovered Austin's father was a high-powered partner in one of the city's most prestigious law firms. The last thing he needed was a sulky princess.

But Austin had proved a surprise in both his dedicated work ethic and his obvious enjoyment working with the children. And they loved him.

"Nothing, except Wyatt's mother offered me a chance to dance in her husband's production of *Rapunzel.*"

He proffered her business card, and Austin squealed with excitement.

"Shut up. That's fabulous." He bit his full lower lip. "You're doing it right? You'd be crazy not to."

"Do what? What trouble are you involving my man in, Austin?"

Dressed in drainpipe tight black jeans and a gray Henley that made his violet eyes glitter like chips of amethyst, Marcus leaned against the door with his usual languid grace. That devilish smile Tyler loved teased his lips.

Austin had admitted to Tyler that Marcus scared him a little, and when Tyler mentioned it to Marcus, he laughed louder than Tyler recalled ever hearing.

"Good. I want him a little scared. That'd make him think twice about ever making a pass at you again."

Tyler had thought it funny when Austin had cornered him and tried to kiss him late one afternoon when classes were over, but Marcus was not as amused when he'd come by to meet him for dinner. In very graphic and painful detail, Marcus let Austin know what would happen to him if Marcus ever found his hands on Tyler's body again.

"Not me; I swear." Austin put his hands up and moved out of striking distance. "I don't tell Tyler what to do. I gotta go do something." Nearly tripping over his platform sneakers, Austin ran out the door.

Laughing at Austin's abrupt departure, Marcus kissed Tyler's cheek. "That boy should cut down on those sugary coffee shakes he's always drinking. They make him jumpy."

Tyler nudged him, then continued to clean up the table full of discarded paper plates.

"You make him jumpy, and you enjoy it way too much."

"Forget about him. What were you talking about when I came in? What does he say you have to do?"

Tyler showed him Liz Graff's card and explained what she said to him.

"That's great. I'm so proud of you." Marcus grabbed him and hugged him tight. "It's always been your dream, babe, to dance on stage."

Fingering the paper plates, Tyler couldn't meet Marcus's eyes. "I don't know if I can do it anymore. What if I'm not good enough?" Those last words were spoken more to himself than to Marcus.

"That's bullshit."

Surprised at the vehemence of Marcus's response, Tyler stared at him in confusion. "What is?"

Marcus backed him up against the table. "From the moment I saw you on the dance floor, I knew you were special. You have that indefinable something that separates the mediocre from a star. Now it's time others see it."

Marcus framed his face in the palms of his hands. "I want everyone to watch you, want you, and lust after you, knowing that they can't have you because you're mine."

Marcus's hungry kiss inflamed Tyler's own desire, and he responded with equal intensity, stabbing his tongue to meet Marcus's. He splayed his hands across Marcus's broad back, feeling the strength in the flexing muscles, yet he alone knew how tender Marcus could be, whether he was carrying Lillie to bed if she fell asleep next to them on the sofa, or while he pushed himself inside Tyler, caressing his body and driving him wild with desire with deliberate, featherlight touches.

"That's very possessive of you," said Tyler when they'd finally pulled apart. "I didn't know you were like that."

Not answering, Marcus helped him finish cleaning up the studio. It wasn't until they were ready to leave that Marcus spoke again. "Does it bother you? Every time I see you walk toward me, all I can think of is, 'Damn, that is mine.'"

And Tyler, who never thought he'd enjoy being thought of as a possession, understood that Marcus didn't want to control or own him. They were true partners in their life, whether in the bedroom or out. People perceived Marcus as the dominant between them, and frankly, he didn't give a damn; the Marcus he knew loved being stroked and kissed until he'd come without even touching himself. He spooned in bed and whispered nonsense, dirty pillow talk. That Marcus belonged to Tyler alone and remained behind closed doors.

"Not at all. You think I should do this, then?"

His face serious once again, Marcus nodded. "I know you should; you have to. Remember what you told me before my mother died, when I refused to see her in the hospital? You told me the worse thing to live with in life is regrets."

Tyler remembered, and though Marcus still had dark moments over his failure to reconcile with his mother before she died, he was happy he'd gone to see her.

"You're right. I've regretted enough in my life; my failure to recognize Amber's problems will always haunt me."

"As long as you don't regret me, I'm good."

This vulnerability was the rare side of Marcus that Tyler knew few, if anyone, ever witnessed. And the fact he still needed that reassurance broke Tyler's heart; Marcus's hurt hadn't healed, and Tyler had no idea how to take away his pain, except by loving him.

"That would be regretting the best part of myself. I'd be foolish to do that, don't you think?"

Strangely quiet after all the activity of the afternoon, the air in the studio now hummed with life. Marcus took his face between his hands and placed a kiss on his lips.

"That's the nicest thing anyone's ever said to me. I've never thought of being part of a couple. It's always only been me."

Tyler wrapped his arms around Marcus. "You're not a 'me' anymore. You'll never be alone again. You're an 'us'—a 'we.'"

Marcus looked at him and shook his head, giving him a funny smile, and took his hand.

"What is it?" It was time to go; they had to go uptown to pick up Lillie. It would be a nice surprise if the two of them showed up. They'd been going to a family therapist to help her deal with her mother's death as well as all the changes in her life. And, Tyler discovered, it was good for them as a family unit.

"I remember a teacher telling us in school that 'me' turned upside down is 'we.' And I never understood what the hell she was talking about until now."

Tyler waited, as it was apparent a battle waged inside Marcus's head.

"From the moment I met you, you turned me upside down and made me change the way I looked at the world and at myself. You showed me I could love other people without losing who I was. You were my change, the best part of me. You turned me into a 'we.'"

Marcus kissed him then, and Tyler marveled how two lost people had managed to find each other in a city this big. Everything happens for a reason, and though Amber's death would always remain a pain in his heart, it had unwittingly led him to his greatest joy.

The peace Tyler always found in Marcus's arms wrapped around him as he laid his head against Marcus's chest, listening to the steady thumping of his heart.

"When Lillie came into my life I discovered what it meant to love unconditionally. And I knew she had to come first; I didn't think I'd ever fall in love. But,"—he swallowed back all the emotions that threatened to overcome him—"you made me wake up inside and reach for that brass ring to find my own dreams. Dreams I didn't know I had. Dreams I hid, even from myself."

Marcus pulled him closer. "You make that phone call, Ty. Become the star you deserve to be. That I already know you are."

Nothing could have prepared him for the surprise of Marcus, whose unconditional love and support gave Tyler the inner strength to believe anything was possible.

"You became the ultimate dream I never dared to believe possible. My first and only dream that became a reality when you told me that you loved me." He could no longer separate love and Marcus; they'd become inexorably tied together. One didn't exist without the other in Tyler's life.

Tyler locked the door to the studio, and together they walked down the street, sunlight gilding their path.

Marcus took his hand, and Tyler knew his healing was finally complete.

"You'll always be first in my heart, Tyler."

The End

About the Author

Felice Stevens has always been a romantic at heart. She believes that while life is tough, there is always a happy ending just around the corner. She started reading traditional historical romances when she was a teenager, then life and law school got in the way. It wasn't until she picked up a copy of Bertrice Small and became swept away to Queen Elizabeth's court that her interest in romance novels became renewed.

But somewhere along the way, her tastes shifted. While she still enjoys a juicy Historical romance, she began experimenting with newer, more cutting edge genres and discovered the world of Male/Male romance. And once she picked up her first, she became so enamored of the authors, the character-driven stories and the overwhelming emotion of the books, she knew she wanted to write her own.

Felice lives in New York City with her husband and two children and hopefully soon a cat of her own. Her day begins with a lot of caffeine and ends with a glass or two of red wine. She practices law but day-dreams of a time when she can sit by a beach somewhere and write beautiful stories of men falling in love. Although there is bound to be angst along the way, a Happily Ever After is always guaranteed.

Website: www.felicestevens.com

Facebook: facebook.com/felice.stevens.1

Twitter: twitter.com/FeliceStevens1

Goodreads:
goodreads.com/author/show/8432880.Felice_Stevens

Other titles by Felice Stevens

Through Hell and Back Series:

A Walk Through Fire

After the Fire

Embrace the Fire

The Memories Series:

Memories of the Heart

One Step Further

The Greatest Gift

The Breakfast Club Series:

Beyond the Surface

Betting on Forever

Other:

Rescued

Made in the USA
San Bernardino, CA
02 March 2016